# *Bait*

*To Stephanie,*

*all the best!*

**By Leslie Jones**

*Night Hush*
*Bait*

# *Bait*

## Duty & Honor Book Two

# LESLIE JONES

**WITNESS**
**IMPULSE**

*An Imprint of HarperCollinsPublishers*

EPub Edition APRIL 2015 ISBN: 9780062363169

Print Edition ISBN: 9780062363176

10 9 8 7 6 5 4 3 2 1

*To my husband, Kim, and our wonderful son, Scott.*
*Thank you for believing in me.*

# Acknowledgments

I AM SO grateful to my wonderful husband and our amazing son. They are the sun shining through the gloom to light my way home. Thank you for supporting me unswervingly from the very beginning. Many thanks to my critique partners and beta readers—because of you, my books are tighter, stronger, and more interesting. To my wonderful agent and fabulous editor, I simply could not have done this without you. Thank you for your encouragement, support, and knowledge. And lastly, I would like to extend my deepest gratitude to the men and women of our military forces, who keep us safe and warm in our beds both domestically and around the world.

# Prologue

SOMETHING HAD GONE awry. Christina could feel it in the air, in the looks Yuri gave her. She fought the impulse to clear her throat, gluing her palms to the desk and forcing her body to relax as Yuri searched her for weapons. Wires. Anything that didn't belong. His hands slid under her shirt, across her ribs, and up to the base of her breasts.

"We came to terms yesterday, Yuri. What the hell's changed?" *Be aggressive*, she chanted to herself. Impatient. "Bobby's overseeing the shipment. I don't have time to waste on shit like this. But you said you wanted me here, so I'm here."

The warehouse swallowed her voice. It wasn't more than fifteen hundred square feet, but it was packed with merchandise of all kinds. Yuri's two bodyguards lounged nearby. She looked up at the ceiling as though striving for patience. In actuality, she searched the shadows for more armed men.

"Patience, Chris."

She narrowed her eyes, but her heart sank. The way he said her name . . . he knew. Somehow he knew she was here undercover.

How? The CIA had crafted solid covers for all of them. How had he made her?

"I want your merchandise," she said, going for the bluff. Why the hell was Bobby so far from her? She needed him by her side, ready to back her play. "But there are other suppliers. Ones who won't try to hit me up for more cash at the nth hour."

Fedyenka came up through the central pathway and sauntered to the desk. His sagging, florid face looked yellow in the artificial lighting. A cockatoo rode on one heavy shoulder, wings half spread for balance. She recognized the parrot from their visit to the warehouse the previous day. It leaned forward to grab the chunk of papaya in Fedyenka's thick fingers, then settled back and tore into the sweet treat. Bobby followed more slowly, flanked by the elder Osinov's bodyguard, Stas Noskov, and another thug. Christina evened out her breathing. *Don't let on you know.*

Did Bobby know they'd been made? Did he have a plan? She watched him, ready to follow his lead.

Bobby stabbed a finger at Fedyenka. "We made a deal. You can't go back on it. That's unprofessional, and I'll make sure everyone knows it."

Bobby Roberts had no sense of teamwork.

She cringed inwardly. Whoever had decided he should be in charge of this operation should be shot.

"I'm a simple man," Fedyenka said. His double chin bobbed as he spoke. "Ten percent across the board. Delivery as promised."

Bobby blustered. "A ten percent increase cuts our profit by half. What the fuck?"

Fedyenka's voice grew hard. "Take it or leave it."

"Fuck you. Let's go, Chris." Bobby turned, and she prepared to follow him. Did he, too, sense danger in the air, or was he bluffing, hoping the Osinovs would back down?

A pistol appeared in Yuri's hand. "I don't believe you're going anywhere just yet."

The four goons also drew weapons. Fedyenka folded his arms across his massive chest.

"It's a funny thing," Fedyenka said. "We're cautious businessmen. So we asked around about you. Guess what we found? Nobody knows you. Bobby Hansen and Chris Barlow from Chicago. Specialized importers for specialized customers."

"We're still building our clientele," she said. Damn it! Their cover stories had been carefully crafted. What had gone wrong?

Bobby edged away from the desk. Stas Noskov swung his Ruger to cover him.

"No." Stas had a thick, guttural accent and virtually no English. Bobby understood well enough, though, and halted. Christina felt a wash of relief. Stas loved violence the way some men loved football. He'd've shot Bobby, simply for the pleasure of watching him bleed.

Yuri laughed. "Bet you can't guess what we did find—."

"Bobby Roberts of US Customs," his older brother snapped, cutting him off. Fedyenka jerked his chin at Stas, who stepped to Bobby's side and pressed the barrel of the Ruger to the base of his neck as he twisted his arm up behind his back. "And brand-new operative Christina Madison, joining us from the United States Central Intelligence Agency."

"I'm told this is her very first field assignment," Yuri added. "Good job, Chris. Christina."

Fedyenka rolled his eyes toward Yuri. "Do you think I give two fucks about her experience? She's about to become a corpse."

She'd known this was a possibility. Undercover work was the most dangerous assignment a field officer could have. She'd asked—no, begged—her boss for this chance. For what? To prove what? Her eagerness was going to get Bobby and her both killed. She forced her body into stillness, though she couldn't control her shivers.

Stas turned his dead fish eyes toward her and twitched the gun barrel, tacitly ordering her to join Bobby. Instead, she edged toward Yuri.

"Come here," Stas growled, glaring at her.

In the half-second Stas took his attention from Bobby, the customs agent shoved him as hard as he could and raced down the central pathway, past the first rows of cages, disappearing into the dimness of the warehouse. Christina's heart stuttered.

He'd left her.

Did he know of another way out?

At the same time as those two thoughts flashed through her mind, all four guards began firing at Bobby. The rounds pinged off the metal cages or bit deep into the wood of the crates.

Fedyenka ducked down behind the desk, cursing at his men. "Be careful of the merchandise!"

The shooting stopped. The noise level skyrocketed as the inhabitants of the cages began to shriek in protest.

Yuri hadn't moved. For a precious few seconds, Christina and he looked at one another. The pistol in his hand trembled.

She launched herself at him. He stumbled back, waving the pistol at her, but his finger wasn't on the trigger. She slammed one palm against his left shoulder, yanking on his right sleeve to force him around. Sliding an arm under his neck, she clamped the other onto the barrel of the pistol, immobilizing it.

"Let him go! Fucking let my brother go right fucking now," Fedyenka screamed.

Heart thundering, she pulled Yuri back the way Bobby had run. He must have found another way out. Surely, he would be waiting for her outside?

Christina pressed close to Yuri, pulling him back and forth slightly to create a moving target. It would take an expert marksman and a steady hand to shoot her without harming Yuri.

"Put down your weapons," she called. "Tell them to drop them. Or I'll strangle Yuri."

"And you'll die." Malevolence glittered in Fedyenka's eyes. "Slowly. Painfully. Stas enjoys his work."

"But your brother will be dead. Is that what you want?" She tightened her hold on Yuri's neck.

Fedyenka waved his arms at the guards. "Shoot her!"

The Osinovs' men raised their weapons, looking for a clear shot. She dragged her captive past the first row of cages. The racket had eased somewhat.

Stas sighted down his barrel. One look in his eyes told her he didn't care whether or not he hit Yuri, as long as he nailed her. Her only chance was to get out of the warehouse and run. She backed up as quickly as she dared.

"Shoot the bitch now!"

Stas was the first to pull the trigger. A river of fire flashed across her upper arm. The shock of it robbed her of breath. She lost her hold on Yuri as she stumbled. He yanked himself free, turning to her with clenched fist raised. She didn't hesitate as she ducked inside his guard, driving the heel of her palm up under his chin. His head rocked back. Two more strikes to his face, and she was able to snatch the pistol and reverse it, pointing it at him. He flinched. Three more shots rang out. Yuri jerked as a round caught him in the thigh.

"What the fuck!" he roared. "You shot me."

Fedyenka grabbed Stas by the sleeve and yanked him around so they were face-to-face. "Yuri dies, you die, asshole."

Stas shrugged. "She moved."

"Shoot the bitch, or I shoot you."

Christina grabbed Yuri's sleeve and dragged him with her to the back of the warehouse. The guards followed but did not fire. The door appeared in front of her like a miracle. She wasted no time pushing it open, blinking a little in the harsh sunlight.

Bobby wasn't there. Dammit! He really had run and left her behind to die. She didn't want to believe it, but the evidence was there in his absence.

Rather than waste time cursing, she released Yuri. No clever quip or pithy saying popped into her head, so she simply aimed the pistol at him until she was twenty feet away, then turned and ran for her life.

THE HOTEL ROOM had been stripped clean; not a shred of their equipment remained. Jack and Nanette, two US Customs cops, the third and fourth members of the team, had followed Bobby and Christina from the Osinovs' import/export business to the warehouse. Jack and Nanette's job was to scope out the security in the holding area, then report back to their Interpol liaison, Shay Boyle. He was supposed to connect them with the local police, who would then go in and arrest the lot of them.

But that was before everything had gone to shit.

Shay Boyle had vanished. Bobby had vanished. Had Jack and Nanette seen the firefight? If so, they would have made their way back here. Or had already. Her arm bled freely and burned like nothing she'd ever experienced. Blood soaked through the arm of the jacket she'd liberated from an unsuspecting woman drinking tea at an outside café. She stripped it off and took one of the hotel's towels, pressing it to the wound to try to stanch the bleeding. The bullet had plowed through about two inches of skin but, fortunately, had not lodged in her flesh. After a few minutes, she tore apart another threadbare towel, using a small hole and her fingers. Folding one half, she used the other to tie an awkward bandage around her arm. She cleaned the blood off as best she could, feeling the beginnings of fatigue and dizziness from blood loss.

As she waited for Jack or Nanette, or even Bobby, to show up, she paced the room like a caged fox. Twelve steps to the window. Quick peeps through the thin cotton curtains. Twelve steps to the bathroom door. Back again to the window. The events of the past two days whirled around and around in her head. Where had they gone wrong? Other than Bobby being a blustering pain in the ass, everything had gone as designed. Each of them knew their function. Each of them was a dedicated law enforcement professional. Except her—the CIA was an intelligence-gathering agency, not a law enforcement one. Still, there had been no reason to suspect anything.

A black SUV pulled up to the front door of the hotel and idled there. If she hadn't already been at the window, she would have missed it. As it was, she had to strain to see it. Through the open passenger window, she saw Fedyenka drumming restless fingers. The driver's door opened, and Stas Noskov went inside the hotel.

*Shit.* How had the Osinovs known where they'd set up their

headquarters? Had they captured one of the others? Had they somehow followed her? No, if they'd followed her, they'd've come in to grab her fifteen minutes ago. She needed to disappear, and fast.

Plan A in an emergency said to meet back here, then head to the airport as a group for extraction. If the hotel had been compromised, they were to head straight to the airstrip, making sure they weren't followed. The pilot would wait exactly one hour for any stragglers before he took off. After that, she was on her own to make her way to the CIA office in Kuwait City, 560 kilometers away.

It was time. No one was coming back here.

Unlike a lot of hotels in Baghdad, this nameless, faceless tourist lodging rose only three stories, each level jutting farther and farther out over the street. Its sand-colored walls had no personality; it was merely old and decrepit. Perfect for their needs. The narrow lane at the rear of the hotel dead-ended at an orchard of orange trees. That's where she needed to be.

The small window in the bathroom was her only option. With some luck, she could escape through it before one of the thugs came around back. Shoving Yuri's handgun into the small of her back, she opened the bathroom window, her heart sinking. From the second story, the ground seemed very far away. Still, there were ways.

The window was smaller than she'd have liked. Still, she stepped onto the toilet and hooked her hands over the sill. Wriggling and squirming, feeling her hair and clothing catching on the rough wooden sill, she cried out as her bullet wound collided with the latch. She didn't need to look to know it had started bleeding again.

As she forced her hips through the too-tight space, she felt something jamming into her back. Yuri's pistol had snagged against the frame. She tried reaching back to pry it loose, but there was no room. She twisted, feeling dread rise inside her. An anxious glance up and down the narrow street assured her Fedyenka's men hadn't made it around the building yet.

Christina inched back until she felt the handgun loosen, then propelled herself forward. Before she could fall, she grabbed on to the external air-conditioning unit, praying it would hold her weight. She eased the rest of her body through the opening. When her legs dangled beneath her and the metal unit started to groan, she grabbed a handful of cables running from the roof to various windows, bringing in electricity, phone, and air-conditioning. Hand over hand, she lowered herself as far as she could, then swung her legs up and onto the service entrance sign above the back door. Maneuvering onto the sign was tricky. She swallowed a yelp as a sharp piece of metal sliced her palm. Blood smeared the metal struts anchoring the sign to the building, making them slippery as she climbed down. When she hit the last strut, she spared a look down. Still ten feet to go.

Of the dozen or so people on the street, only a few had stopped to watch her, no doubt wondering what the crazy American was doing. Hopefully, they would have moved on by the time the inevitable "Have you seen this woman?" started.

*Remember your training.* She'd done much more difficult drops during her time at Camp Peary, including climbing thirty-five feet into the air, crawling on a two-inch rope to the center and dropping into the water. The principle was the same. Legs together, arms crossed, chin tucked.

She took a deep breath, and let go.

The impact with the hard-packed earth jarred her teeth, and she swallowed a scream even as she let herself roll backward, reaching with her arms to slap the ground. She was up in an instant, running flat out for the orange grove, praying she made it before anyone saw her.

The towel had already soaked through, and blood trailed rivulets down to her fingers. She tucked her arm close to her side, hoping they would not be able to follow a blood trail. Using the tree trunks as shields, she rushed through the grove until she reached an embankment on the other side. She waited just inside the tree line, scanning in all directions for movement. Nothing.

Scrambling up the embankment meant using both arms. She was dizzy and sweating when she reached the top, stepping into an empty plot with a single scraggly palm squatting like a reverse oasis within the city confines. To her left and right, a collection of haphazard houses and apartments lined a cramped, crooked street. The residential area was virtually deserted this time of day, but a toddler and a shabby dog were chasing a baseball around the street.

Just as she stepped into the street, the black SUV turned the corner. Stas must have jammed his foot to the floor, because the vehicle jumped and roared toward her.

She ran.

Ahead of her on the left, she saw a simple mosque with a cupola. Every stride jarred her arm, but she set the pain aside, determined to reach the mosque before the SUV reached her. She burst through the doors moments ahead of the truck.

Not stopping, she dashed down the wide hallway. Two men in ankle-length robes and long sleeves grabbed at her, shouting in Arabic, faces contorted in fury. She had no trouble understanding the gist as she dodged around them. Women were not permitted in the mosque, and were certainly not welcome without a hijab.

She burst into the main prayer hall, shocking the dozen or so men kneeling for noon prayers. Outraged mutterings began at once. Several stood. Christina regretted her offense to the Muslims, but she knew what would happen to her if the Osinovs caught up with her.

At the end of the prayer hall a door stood ajar, propped open with a folding chair. She shoved it open and ran into a courtyard. Shit. It was enclosed, and there was no gate.

Without missing a stride, she jumped at the wall, digging in with her toe to push herself higher as she reached for the top. From there, she swung a leg up, using hands and feet to pull herself to the top. She rolled over, hung by her hands on the opposite side, and dropped lightly to the ground.

A taxicab idled nearby as a well-dressed man exited the car. She dove inside, yanked the door closed, and yelled, "Go-go-go!"

The startled driver frowned at her.

"I have money." She dug into her pocket and came up with a fistful of crumpled bills. She threw them into the front seat. "Drive. Please!"

The amount got the driver moving. It seemed to take forever for him to put the car into gear and maneuver back onto the street. Christina peered anxiously through the rear window. It was clear.

"Where go, miss?" the driver asked.

"Gamal Airport, please. I'm in a hurry." She dug out a few more bills. "This tip is for you if you get me there quickly." If he broke every rule of the road and ignored land speed records, she might make it to the runway in time.

The driver glanced into the rearview mirror. "Yes, miss."

Christina settled back with a sigh. The driver hadn't even blinked at the bloodstains on her jacket or hand. It was a sight glimpsed much too often in Baghdad. The cab jerked as the driver put pedal to the metal and got them the hell out of there.

It took about fifteen minutes through midday traffic to arrive. As they entered the airport proper, she said, "Down the left road, please. To the private planes."

"Yes, miss." His tone turned respectful.

Gamal catered to small planes for short hops, but a section of the airport was dedicated to the private jets of the wealthy. Before they reached that guarded area, however, she ordered him to pull over and get out. He complied, puzzled. His confusion gave way to alarm as Christina climbed out of the car and brought her pistol up. His hands shot into the air, and he began to babble in Arabic.

"Relax. I'm not going to hurt you." She had to say it several times before he stopped talking. Pointing back the way they'd come, she added, "As long as you turn around and start walking back to the gates."

He bobbed his head several times. She didn't know if he actually understood her words, but he recognized an opportunity to come out of the situation unhurt. He started walking, looking over his shoulder several times until Christina made a shooing motion with the pistol. He began to run.

The CIA kept an airstrip for missions such as this one, but its location was classified. It was nestled far off the beaten path. She buckled herself into the car, and drove to the other side of the exclusive area. With any luck, her teammates would be waiting in the plane.

She slowed as she approached the airstrip, scanning constantly for anything out of the ordinary. The area was flat and open, making her feel exposed and vulnerable. Nothing stirred.

The office building near the runway was nothing more than a squat redbrick building with a blue door and windows on three sides. A storage shed abutted the fourth side. The generator in the rear provided electricity to the office. A tan Chevrolet Optra sat nearly perpendicular to the building. Thank God! Someone had made it here.

The plane, a single-propeller Cessna 206, sat on the tarmac, waiting silently.

Too silently. Where was the pilot? He should be prepping for takeoff by now, if not actually in the air flying the team to Incirlik, Turkey.

He might be inside the office. She slapped her head for her paranoia. Surely they were simply waiting for her out of the heat.

Why had they left her behind?

The question she'd suppressed thrust itself to the forefront of her mind. *No*, she thought. Not now. After we're safe.

Then she would demand answers, especially of Bobby.

She drove up and parked the taxi near the Chevrolet. No one came to the office door, but she sensed movement behind the curtain.

Pulling the handle, she started to open the car door. From behind, she heard the rev of engines and craned her neck around, her heart sinking into her stomach. Two black SUVs accelerated down the road, spraying dust and dirt, closing with the building at alarming speed. One of the Osinov thugs leaned out the window holding an SKS semiautomatic assault rifle. Shots pinged off her roof. One came through the back window and lodged in the passenger seat. She didn't waste time swearing, or wondering how they'd known where to come. She simply rolled out of the car and ran for the building.

A rock exploded near her feet, and another bullet whined past her ear. She wasn't going to make it. Changing directions, she dove for the Chevrolet, scrambling on all fours to get behind the engine block.

Did gas tanks explode?

The front door flew open, and Jack popped out to return fire, the sharp cracks music to her ears. Yanking the pistol from the small of her back, she risked a quick look around the fender, ducking back as she saw one of the gunmen aiming in her direction. She pressed her back against the front tire as a barrage of rounds seemed to explode all around her.

Nanette pushed open the front window and snapped off six rounds. It barely slowed the SUVs. One slammed to a stop on the other side of the taxi, angled in toward the building. The other left the dirt road and slewed around in the rocks and scrub brush until it came to a shuddering stop on the left edge of the building. Which left her completely exposed.

She had no choice. She launched herself off the ground and sprinted away from the second SUV, bending as she ran to get what cover she could from the taxi as she tried for the right edge of the building. If she could just make it around the corner . . .

Yuri and Stas piled out of the car, trying to cut her off. To capture, not kill. She had tweaked his pride and he wanted his pound of flesh? She didn't spend any more time wondering. Lengthening her stride, she dodged Stas's meaty paws.

Yuri tackled her from the side, riding her down until her face met the dirt. She crabbed sideways, trying to pull free of his hold.

He twisted her legs, flipping her onto her back, and yanked her hard. She slid helplessly across the rocks. Ferocity and frenzy in his eyes, he straddled her, wrapping his hands around her throat and squeezing.

Christina tried to drag panicked breaths past his ever-tightening fingers. Black spots appeared in front of her eyes. She brought both hands up to grab his wrists, only then realizing that she still held his pistol. His expression didn't change, his fingers didn't loosen. Didn't he see it? Didn't he care?

For an endless moment they stared at one another. She pulled the trigger.

The noise deafened her. Yuri's face went slack in vague surprise as he released her. He fell sideways off her, writhing in agony, both hands pressed over the wound as blood pooled around his fingers. Uttering tiny choked gasps as blood bubbled from his lungs to his lips, he locked eyes with her, fear and a mute appeal in his. Despite herself, she stayed at his side as she watched the light fade from his eyes.

A bellow of pure rage brought her back to reality. Fedyenka stood by the hood of the other SUV, his face purple with fury as he shrieked obscenities. He grabbed an assault rifle from one of his men, raising it toward her. Knowing she couldn't outrun the barrage of projectiles about to come her way, she still tried to dive for cover.

The unmistakable sound of a .50 caliber machine gun and the shouts of his men distracted Fedyenka long enough for her to scramble to the front of the taxi. Two armored vehicles raced up the dirt road, heading directly into the firefight. Christina almost laughed aloud. The heavy machine guns, mounted on British Special Air Service long-range patrol vehicles, effectively trapped the smugglers between the customs cops and this new, deadly threat. The hail of gunfire forced the men to back toward their SUVs. One jumped in and started the engine with a roar.

She didn't know how, but the cavalry had just ridden over the horizon.

Fedyenka glared death at her. "You're dead, bitch. You just died, right here, right now."

The wail of sirens shut him up. A half a dozen police cars followed the patrol vehicles up the dirt road. He turned and sprinted for his vehicle.

"Police. Damned fucking cops." Stas Noskov glared at her, as though it were her doing, before diving into the back of the SUV with Fedyenka. The SUV roared down the runway, the police cars in hot pursuit.

Whoever manned the heavy machine gun had no trouble recognizing friend from foe. The firefight was short and brutal, ending with the other SUV disabled and Fedyenka's men exiting with hands in the air. As the police cars screeched to a halt and the Iraqi Police Service swarmed the area, Christina set Yuri's pistol on the ground and walked toward the Special Air Service's armored vehicles.

A man dressed in desert camouflage jumped from the front passenger seat and met her halfway, his assault rifle nestled in his hands. He might have been a movie hero of old, striding across the desert like the savior that he was. "You're bleeding. How bad is it?"

She shook her head, although in truth she knew she needed stitches on her bullet wound. And some painkillers.

The man pulled off his helmet. "Are you Nanette Easley?" Concern wrinkled his brow as he looked her over from head to foot. Not waiting for an answer, he turned to the British soldier who'd come up to stand beside him. "Havanaugh, tell them to bring the ambulance up. We have injured."

"Aye, Major." The man saluted and left.

Christina finally got her vocal cords working. "Thank you. I don't know where you came from, but thank you. You saved lives here today."

The major smiled and held out his hand. "Major Trevor Carswell, 22nd British Special Air Service, Counter-Terrorism, at your service."

She put her hand in his. "Christina Madison."

His brows lifted slightly. "Not Nanette, then."

The door to the office opened, and Jack and Nanette emerged, followed by Bobby. Nanette ran to her, throwing her arms around Christina and hugging her tightly. Bobby ignored her entirely and addressed Trevor.

"I'm Special Agent Roberts with US Customs and Border Protection. I'm in charge here."

Trevor shook his hand, then glanced at Nanette. "Thanks for the call. We were getting bored out there."

Nanette gave a shaky laugh. "When we got here and our pilot had disappeared, I knew we were in trouble. I'm just glad you were in range for a rescue."

"My pleasure. Glad we could help out." He nodded politely, then surprised Christina by taking her arm—her uninjured arm. "Let's get you to the medics."

She followed him to the ambulance. "Were you on patrol?"

"Yes and no. We were doing a training exercise with an Iraqi special forces unit. Routine enough. Not as exciting as rescuing you lot."

He stayed with her as the medic forced her to lie on the stretcher and started an IV for a blood transfusion. "You'll need to go to hospital, I'm afraid. I'm guessing about twelve sutures."

Christina nodded, feeling the adrenaline drain from her body. It left her tired, dizzy, and in pain. Trevor said something to the medic, who started a second IV line. Within seconds, Christina felt herself fading.

"Sleep now," she heard him say. "You're safe."

# Chapter One

*11 months later*

REPORTS OF THE assassination attempt on Princess Véronique de Savoie barely made a blip on the news outside of Concordia. The tiny country rivaled Liechtenstein in size and importance. As in, very damned little. Most would be hard-pressed to find it on a map.

Inside the CIA, however, the assassination attempt caused a ripple of reaction, starting in the Office of the Director of National Intelligence, bypassing normal channels, and landing directly on case officer Jay Spicer's desk.

"You want me to do what?" asked Christina Madison, eyes wide as she stared at her boss.

Jay Spicer looked back at her. "Have you been in front of a mirror lately?"

"Sure I have." Every now and then, someone would comment

on her eerie resemblance to the princess of Concordia. Princess Véronique made headlines inside her own country on a regular basis, though rarely outside of it. Concordian cameras and reporters followed her as she labored on various humanitarian projects. She'd been part of a BBC documentary last year on modern royalty in Europe, which Christina had watched out of curiosity. The princess remained gracious in the face of newshounds and paparazzi, even when elbow-deep in dirt planting a new strain of bacteria-resistant corn in Ethiopia or bringing clean well water to rural Bolivians.

Occasionally a European visitor to the Washington, D.C., area would ask if she were, indeed, the princess. Christina would laugh it off with a simple, "Don't I wish." Truth be told, she much preferred her anonymous work bringing down money laundering and smuggling operations. Having cameras shoved in her face and every word and action dissected struck her as repugnant.

For the most part, though, Véronique remained one of the royal unknowns.

Christina grabbed a handful of Skittles from the crystal ashtray on Jay's desk. Red and yellow only. He'd already eaten the green and orange.

"Her face is well known inside Concordia. Resembling someone and taking her place are two different—"

"This comes from the top," her boss interrupted. "From the director himself. The British government specifically asked for your help."

Her head began to whirl. The mandatory photographs of the president and CIA director frowned down at her from behind his head. Boring pictures. Boring white walls. The only interesting thing in the whole office was the life-sized cardboard cutout of Captain America planted to the right of the door. "The British? Not the Concordians? I don't understand, sir."

Jay leaned forward in his chair and tugged at an earlobe, his ADHD making it impossible for him to sit still. At fifty, he still managed to retain the air of an errant schoolboy. He smirked, cracking his knuckles. Christina crossed her legs, not fooled by his antics. Jay Spicer was a shrewd, brilliant case officer. He counted on his façade to cause people to underestimate him. He would clarify the situation in his own time.

"Princess Véronique is engaged to a landed baron in the UK."

"He has enough clout to tap the CIA for help?"

"Sort of." Jay pushed a folder across his cluttered mahogany desk. The beige file sported the banded red and large stamps indicating that it contained classified information.

Christina uncrossed her legs in order to lean forward and snag the folder. She flipped it open. The top page contained a request from . . . Trevor Carswell?

Jay rocked back, the chair squeaking. He grinned, tapping his fingers. "Julian Brumley, the eighth Baron of Daversporth, is a member of the House of Lords. He has enough political and personal clout to assign an elite member of the Special Air Service to head the investigation into the attempt on his fiancée's life. And that lucky son of a bitch is SAS Major Trevor Willoughby Carswell."

Her astonishment and comprehension must have shown on her face, because Jay's expression became downright smug. "You know Trevor's worked with me a couple of times before, so he knows damned well what I look like," she said. His middle name was Willoughby? Who knew? "There are plenty of highly qualified investigators in Great Britain. It can't be coincidence that the fiancé chose Trevor."

"Nope. They're cousins. Second cousins, I think. He'll be heading the investigation. You'll replace the princess."

Her head started to ache as she sorted through the implications. "So I'm being tapped for this job because a fluke of genetics shaped my face the same way as hers? Nothing to do with my abilities?"

He leaned forward on his desk, leg jiggling under the table. "You can say no, Madison. But this is an international request, asking specifically for you. The director himself will be monitoring this assignment. You'll never get another chance like this. You've been hounding me for a big assignment. Well, this is it. Do you really want to step away from it?"

"Of course not." Christina's mouth flattened. Her career was hanging by a thread as it was. The intelligence community had an elephantine memory, and the failed mission in Baghdad had shredded her reputation. Maybe if she could figure out what she'd done wrong . . .

"Well?"

"Naturally, I'm happy to help the Concordian government." What other answer was there? And, truthfully, this represented a huge opportunity for her to redeem herself. This would be high-profile all the way. "You know I'll put a hundred percent into it, sir."

"That's what I figured. And you'll have a bodyguard."

Uh-oh.

"Trevor?" She and Trevor shared a history. She trusted him. He had saved her life.

"No. But you know him. He was one of the Delta Force soldiers you worked with in Azakistan."

And just like that, Christina knew. Of all the people she never wanted to see again, he topped the list. Therefore, it had to be him. She barely kept herself from sticking her fingers into her ears and singing, "Lalalalala."

"Gabriel Morgan."

GABE MORGAN GAPED at Jace, his commanding officer. "You want me to do what?"

His gaze glanced off the multipaned windows on two sides of the main troop area; past the American and North Carolina flags; the mess of desks, chairs and sofas; to his own overflowing inbox and the dead fern on the edge of the desk. He flipped the throwing knife in his hand and flicked it toward the human silhouette tacked to a wooden target hanging thirty feet away, on the other side of the room. Thomas 'Mace' Beckett, his nose buried in the latest John Grisham book, barely glanced up as the blade passed within inches of his head.

He hefted the second throwing knife, pointed its tip toward Jace Reed, then carefully, gently, set it on his scarred and pitted desk. He placed his palms flat against its surface, elbows locked, spine stiff as he leaned forward. He glared into Jace's eyes.

"You can say no." Unintimidated, Jace tapped a manila folder against the gray metal desk, standard Army issue, functional and ugly. "You know. If you think you can't handle it, I can assign you something easier, like walking General McCutcheon's wife's Pomeranian."

Gabe blanched. It wasn't an idle threat. He'd long ago filed both the Pomeranian and the wife under To Be Avoided At All

Costs. He didn't know which was the bigger yappy terror. "Good God. Shoot me now."

Jace snickered.

"I don't understand why we're being tapped instead of the SAS," Gabe said. "If Trevor Carswell is heading the investigation, why isn't his team protecting her?"

Jace glanced around. Gabe followed his gaze. Sandman and Tag were pushing 'em out, egging each other on. The pushup contest had been going on for a while. Ken Acolatse cleaned his Sig Sauer. Gavin had his earbuds in, head and feet tapping in time to God-knows-what kind of music. Alex tacked yet another *Call of Duty* poster to the wall. Kid was obsessed.

"They'll be guarding the real target," Jace said. "He's only got the one team, though, and he can't get authorization for another. He asked for my help, and, lucky you, I'm assigning you the job. It'll be a cakewalk."

Gabe felt a shudder work its way down his spine. "Assign someone else. Jace, Jesus. Nothing's ever a cakewalk when those people are involved." His fists clenched. He wouldn't resort to begging.

Sympathy flickered in Jace's eyes. "I could do that," he said quietly, all humor gone. "We work with other agencies regularly, though. I need you to be able to handle it. Or I need to know you can't."

"You realize that if I do this, I'll be useless for undercover work," he said, even knowing the excuse wouldn't hold water. It wasn't the assignment. He'd done executive protection work before. An executive protector—bodyguard—could do any number of other jobs. There would be nothing to connect him with Delta Force, which relied on strict anonymity in its work. That's not what set his teeth on edge.

It was the who.

Christina Freaking Madison.

"You know better. Even if you're undercover and recognized, that won't ID you as one of the good guys. Maybe the opposite, if you can convince our assassin you're a douchebag." He grinned. "Not a huge stretch."

Gabe ignored him. It had been, what? Six months? Yeah, about that long ago. His team had been in Azakistan, helping foil a plot by a twisted bastard who tried to release a deadly cocktail of poisonous gases into crowds of families on a US airbase. Christina Madison had gotten photographs of the terrorists for them, but she was also an annoying, brash, inexperienced junior officer of the CIA, an organization he loathed. Sure, she was attractive, with a tight little body that revved his motor, but she would also no doubt be a pain in his ass. And certainly not someone he could trust to watch his six.

"Yo. Sleeping beauty." Jace snapped his fingers in front of Gabe's face. "Where'd you go?"

Gabe straightened abruptly, scooping up the knife and flicking it toward the target with barely a glance. It penetrated deep into the wood. "Nowhere. So you want me to pretend to guard a pretend princess? But in fact, she's going to be bait, to draw out the person or persons who tried to kill the real princess? That about it?"

"In a nutshell. You got a problem, Morgan? Let's hear it."

"You know what my problem is." Gabe pushed a hand through his shaggy hair. "You know who she is, boss. She's unreliable. Her team almost got killed in Iraq."

Jace nodded. "And she's CIA, which means you're already prejudiced against her. I get it. Between your mother and the Peru fiasco, you've got some heavy baggage."

Baggage? Hell, yeah, he had baggage. All it took was one CIA motherfucker to ruin a mission. Or a family.

"If it makes you feel any better, her job really is just to be bait. You'll be in charge of security and laying the trap. She's the cheese. You reel in the rats."

Gabe grimaced. "She's a hothead. I don't need to be trying to corral her while I'm laying the trap."

"Her boss assured me of her complete cooperation," Jace said dryly. "Apparently, her ass is on the line. If she messes this up, she's done. And she knows it."

Gabe stalked to the human-shaped target and yanked both knives out of the silhouette's throat. He rammed them back into the special sheaths in his boots.

"Fuck."

CHRISTINA DROVE UP the Capital Beltway toward Silver Spring, cataloguing the things she would need to do before flying to Concordia's capital city of Parvenière the next day: put a hold on her mail, ask her neighbor to water her plants, clean out the refrigerator. She needed to get her leather jacket back from Frank the Fink, but that wasn't going to happen before she flew. The jerk. He'd been anything but frank with her. As soon as he'd heard the rumors about her within the Company, he'd treated her like a plague victim.

Unbidden, her mind slid from unremarkable Frank to six feet one inch of hard muscle and overlong, dirty blond hair. To sculpted cheekbones and a strong jaw that he usually kept covered with two days' worth of stubble. To cynical eyes and lips that tipped up at one corner, as though the world around him both amused and bored him.

The Friday afternoon rush hour and her preoccupation with Gabe Morgan almost caused her to miss the gray panel van. By the time she noticed it, it had followed her from the Beltway onto Georgia Avenue. When she reached Woodside Park on Spring Street, she felt certain she was being followed.

The question was, by whom? Truthfully, Christina couldn't generate much inward alarm. The CIA trained constantly in surveillance and countersurveillance. It wouldn't be the first time a class of newbies in the Surveillance Detection Training Program had been assigned to track the movements of CIA field officers. It provided good practice for both groups. And she could be off the mark entirely; this could be merely a delivery truck.

She turned left onto Ballard Street, past the Methodist church with the blooming cherry tree. Sure enough, the van, which had been lagging five car lengths behind her, appeared moments later. She flicked a glance in the rearview mirror. Amateurs. A tiny smile tugged at her mouth. The trainees were obvious and anxious.

Small houses and mature trees lined the streets. She eased left around a Volkswagen Rabbit and immediately swerved to avoid an elderly couple coming through the gate of a yard enclosed by a brown picket fence. As she passed the No Outlet sign, she chuckled aloud. She could navigate these streets blindfolded. The trainees couldn't.

Third Avenue dead-ended at a yellow house. Without hesitation, she left the pavement for the dirt track, winding her way past the huge logs and tangled undergrowth. In moments, she pulled out onto Second Street. Easing past another elderly couple strolling on the street instead of the sidewalk, she made it to the end of the road and turned left before the van caught sight of her.

She ducked in and out of several more residential areas, switching streets and doubling back. When she felt she'd lost the van, she turned onto a dead-end street and backed into an open carport, turning off the ignition quickly. Yes, they would see a black Corolla if they made it this far. Black Corollas were ubiquitous in the D.C. area. They would only be able to see her front license plate if they were dumb enough to drive into the dead end. She ducked down, pulling a small telescoping mirror from her glove box. Angling it over the dash, she waited.

Her mind wandered back to Gabe Morgan, and how he would react when he found out he would be forced not only to work with her again, but to protect her. The first time they'd met, he'd done everything but tell her outright that she had no place in Azakistan, where she had been sent to recruit an asset. The rumors about her very first mission had washed through the Delta Force detachment on al-Zadr Air Force Base almost before she'd walked through the doors of their Tactical Operations Center. The stories shouldn't still hurt a year after the incident, but they did.

Thirty minutes later, she stretched stiff muscles and started the car again, mirth tugging at her lips. She'd lost the gray van. Score one for field officers, zero for recruits. She'd report the incident per standard operating procedure, then pop down to the surveillance center and have a chat and a laugh with her old instructor. Yawning, she drove out of the maze of houses and headed home, keeping a sharp eye out for other suspicious vehicles. Once she turned onto her own street, she relaxed.

The part of her mind not involved in countersurveillance considered the problem of Gabe Morgan. Convincing him that she would be an asset on this mission would be difficult. She didn't kid herself that she would be in charge. Delta Force teams took orders from JSOC—the Joint Special Operations Command—not from the CIA.

The gray van hurtled out of nowhere, sliding sideways across the pavement and rocking to a halt only feet away from the hood of her car. Reacting on instinct, Christina twisted the wheel hard to the left as she slammed on the brake. The rear of her car protested the abrupt change in direction as it skidded. Her defensive driving training coming to the fore, she did not wait to find out what the van's occupants had in mind. She rammed the accelerator, rocketing sideways and forward, missing being T-boned by millimeters as the van leapt forward to block her path again. It whipped around to follow her as she slipped past, giving her a good look at the driver. Well into his forties, he was too old to be a recruit. He had round, wide features and dark hair. The other remained in shadow. What the hell was going on? This was no surveillance exercise.

Barely a breath ahead of them, she mashed the accelerator into the floor. In moments, both cars shot along the street at breakneck speeds. A sharp turn in the road ahead of her gave Christina a slight edge. She slewed around the corner, trying to take them out of her neighborhood. No way would she endanger civilians.

She dodged around the fast-moving UPS truck in front of her and flashed her brake lights twice before decelerating sharply. As expected, the truck driver stood on his brakes, shouting curses she understood only too clearly through her rearview mirror.

"Sorry, dude," she muttered. "Not your lucky day."

The gray van, unable to slow fast enough, tried to swerve around the truck, only to hit a curve. It shot off the road, across a driveway, and hit a brick-encased mailbox. Through a squeal of brakes and mangled metal, the gray van came to a shuddering halt.

Christina pulled over, reversed along the shoulder, and parked in front of the truck, which had also stopped. The UPS driver, a paunchy, sweaty middle-aged man, jumped out of the truck and started toward her. He glowered.

"This accident was your fault," he said, "and I'm going to make sure the police know it."

She ignored him, her whole attention on the van, her shaking hand gripping the semiautomatic pistol under her shirt. "Hands where I can see them," she yelled. "Get out slowly, hands in the air."

The truck driver gaped at her. "Are you some sort of cop?"

She spared him an irritated glance. "Sir, get back in your truck."

The van's engine revved. It jumped backward, crunching over broken brick, and wrestled itself back onto the road. Christina drew her weapon. The van paused a moment, then roared away.

The balding truck driver's eyes bugged out. "What's going on? Who were those guys?"

She turned to sprint to her car. The van disappeared around a corner up ahead.

"Where are you going?"

"I'm going after them. Wait here for the police." Who would never come, because Christina wasn't going to call them. She was too anxious to find out who those men were, and what they wanted. She dashed to her car.

"But who's going to fill out the police report?" the truck driver wailed as she banged her car door shut.

Those few seconds had cost her. When she turned the corner, the van was nowhere in sight. She searched the area, crossing and recrossing roads until she finally had to admit defeat. Slamming her palms against the steering wheel, she let loose a stream of expletives that would have even Gabe Morgan's ears turning red.

# Chapter Two

PRINCESS VÉRONIQUE WAS elegant, charming, and refined. All of the things Christina wasn't. She could be described as dogged. Intuitive. Maybe even gutsy. But elegant?

"I'm not sure how Jay expects me to pull this off," she muttered. And yet, hadn't she been blending in most of her life? Flitting from personality to personality as easily as a bird shed feathers? It was part of why she'd been recruited to the CIA.

Concordia was a small country, nestled just to the south of Belgium and west of Luxembourg. The flight to its capital city had been long, but peaceful enough. She'd spent the time studying the materials Jay had given her on Princess Véronique and her household staff, the details of the attempt on her life, and the layout of the castle in which she lived. Fourteen hours later, she'd been met by Trevor and his team and smuggled into the princess's apartments inside the royal *palais*.

The palace itself had been designed to impress. Inside, the ceilings soared fifty feet, enough to accommodate the double staircase. The first floor consisted of offices and living space for household staff. The west flight of stairs led to the winter residence of the Comtesse and Comte de Defois-Angonne, Princess Véronique's aunt and her husband. The apartments for the crown princess were located in the east wing.

"Don't worry," the princess said, her musical French accent lilting across the room. She set her wineglass on the sideboard, crossed the length of an enormous reproduction of Peter Paul Rubens's *The Apotheosis of Henri IV*, and joined Christina near the windows. "I have every confidence in your abilities."

"That makes one of us." Christina blew out a breath. "Being in front of the cameras is not exactly my forte."

"What does this mean?"

"It means I'm used to operating behind the scenes. In the shadows. Where no one sees me." Thinking she'd be a natural at it because of her chameleon-like abilities, she'd taken an acting class in high school. It had been a disaster. She couldn't remember her lines or stay in character while she unconsciously tried to blend. Acting meant pretending to be Lady Macbeth or Juliet. Blending was different. When she blended, she fed off the personalities around her and became just like them.

"Don't be so hard on yourself," Trevor said. He stretched, lacing his fingers over his head. His long torso dwarfed the fragile-looking chair, a gilt frame with white cushions sporting elaborate embroidery. "I know you can do this, Christina."

Christina frowned unhappily, looking up at the massive crystal chandelier as she watched Princess Véronique stroll closer to the high windows, framed by burgundy draperies and topped by elaborate pelmets. The windows overlooked a man-made lake, complete with black swans. "You're about the only one. Jay would have kept me at a desk forever if not for you contacting the CIA."

The princess glided back to the sofa and seated herself, crossing one elegant leg over the other. "People see what they wish to see." She glanced at the man sitting across from her. "M'sieur Carswell, do you not agree?"

"Call me Trevor, please, Your Royal Highness. And yes, that's been my experience. Also, we're going to limit your public appearances, Christina."

"You," Christina said, "are going straight to a safe house."

The princess clicked her tongue. "After our princess lessons, *non*?"

Trevor made a sound of assent. "You'll have round-the-clock guards, Your Highness. I'm sorry, but you'll be all but under house arrest."

"I understand." The princess inclined her head in acquiescence.

Christina surveyed the sitting room. It was opulent and formal. Delicate settees, spindly-legged chairs, tapestries, and huge formal portraits on the walls. The sitting room was larger than her entire apartment. She shook her head. It was a different lifestyle, that was for sure. "Your home is beautiful."

Princess Véronique glanced around, as though seeing it for the first time. "Yes, I suppose so. I find myself wishing for something simpler."

"Why don't you redecorate? It's your home, right?" she asked.

Véronique's smile was small. "We are not a wealthy country, Christina. The expense cannot be spared merely for my whims."

"But . . ." She shut her mouth. She wasn't here for that.

Now that she'd arrived in Parvenière, her encounter with the gray van seemed surreal. Jay Spicer had promised to call her if the local police found the van or the men, but he wasn't optimistic. The license plate had been stolen from a hapless teenager's aging

Buick. The sketch artist had done a reasonable job, but Christina had gotten barely a glimpse of the men. No matches had come up on any database.

Now she needed to give her full focus to this mission.

To ensure the secrecy of their plan, the princess's living quarters had been declared off limits to all but the most discreet servants and cleaning staff. Véronique sent her chef on vacation and replaced her with an Italian woman. Trevor had explained the dangers of having Princess Véronique and Lord Brumley in close proximity; Julian had conceded only when Trevor pointed out that Véronique might be in danger simply by being at his side.

The princess had insisted that her private secretary, the longest serving and most trusted member of her household, be brought in on the charade in order to help Christina. She now sat unobtrusively off to the side, in a narrow red velvet chair with an oval back.

"Christina, we've rearranged your schedule to include only those appearances where we can control the environment," Trevor went on. "Also where you won't run into anyone who knows the princess well. At least, that's what we're trying to do. There's one exception to that; and, I'm sorry, but this appearance will be in two weeks' time."

"What is it?" Christina swallowed the dismayed noise that wanted to crawl from her throat. It didn't matter that she'd been a field agent for only a year. She could do this. She *would* do this.

The princess tapped a long, manicured nail against the arm of the davenport. "It is the sixtieth wedding anniversary of my grandaunt and -uncle, the Viscount and Viscountess of Nabourg.

Because my father will be in Somalia on a humanitarian mission and my mother will address the Chamber of Representatives on the plight of our most rural farmers, it was decided that I should represent the royal family. To be truthful, it seems that every member of my family must be elsewhere. What is the American idiom? I drew the shorter straw."

Trevor chuckled. "Amazing how that happens."

"Won't they recognize me?" Christina stumbled over the words, more alarmed than she ought to be. Her continued career with the CIA rested on the success of this mission; Jay had made that abundantly clear.

Princess Véronique suppressed a smile and rolled her eyes. "Lord Hugh is eighty-five and nearly blind. Lady Adela reminisces about her youth in Andorra to the exclusion of all else. Together, they can be rather tiresome. My contact with them over the years has been limited to mandatory appearances such as this one. As I am not close to them or their friends, it is doubtful any guests at this ball will know me intimately." She frowned. "The news of the assassination attempt will cause some stir, as will your bodyguard."

"That works in our favor, actually," Christina said, calm again, feeling foolish about her nerves. "If I mess up, people will assume the attack shook me up. They'll cut me some slack. I'll downplay it as much as possible, though."

Deni Van Praet, private secretary to the princess of Concordia, rose abruptly from her seat to poke at Christina's bare shoulder. "We must cover that, yes?" Her ramrod posture and carefully styled hair fit into the environment perfectly.

Twisting her head to glance at her right arm, she pulled the sleeveless shirt up to see the two-inch jagged scar. It had faded from its original angry red, a souvenir from her aborted mission in Iraq last year. It was a brutal reminder of how close she had come to dying that day.

"Yes."

Behind her, Trevor was outlining his plan for investigating the threats against Véronique. "I'll need you to make me a list. Divide it into personal friends, acquaintances, and anyone who might hold a grudge or be angry with you. Don't dismiss anyone, don't assume it can't be this or that person. When it comes to death threats, it could be a total stranger, a psychotic who has fixated on you for whatever reason. An assassination attempt is more serious. Someone's already made the decision to end your life. Maybe he blames you for his circumstances; but it could just as easily be someone you know. It will take some time to do the background checks on all of them. We'll use the time while you teach Christina."

"Should you require it, you have at your disposal, of course, the full resources of our Department of Security," Véronique said.

Trevor shook his head. "While the British government appreciates your generosity, we're assuming the threat can come from anywhere. We can't risk it."

"Then I will let you get to it, and I will work on that list." The princess rose. Trevor got up as well, recognizing the dismissal for what it was. She turned her luminous eyes Christina's way. "Will you help me?"

"Of course, Your Royal Highness," she murmured. Her body was already softening, her posture changing. She rose just as Véronique had, shoulders back, chin down, fingers touching but not intertwined.

"Please, Christina. You will call me Ronnie, yes? It is my nickname, one my friends use."

"Thank you. I'm very honored."

Trevor moved to the door. "I'll be in and out. If you need anything, or if anything occurs to you, call me immediately." His gaze included both of them. "Christina, when you're out and about, you'll have Morgan with you at all times, but you'll still get in touch with me if you see something that raises the hair on the back of your neck. Right?"

"I will." She followed him to the entryway. "Trevor?"

His expression softened as he looked down at her. "It's good to see you again."

Her shiver of unease vanished. Trevor had her back. The two of them had become friends a year ago, though at the time she'd thought she wanted more. Trevor had gently reminded her of the adrenal effects of a near-death experience, and told her to call him if she still felt the same way about him in a month. She hadn't picked up the phone.

A blush unexpectedly rose in her cheeks. "Sorry," she muttered.

He chuckled. "I didn't expect you to dial me. I value our friendship, Christina."

Curious, she canted a look up at him. "Are you seeing anyone now?"

To her surprise, a troubled look closed down his face. "No."

Christina's brows furrowed. "Bad breakup?"

Trevor glanced up at the ceiling. "It's rather complicated."

"Shelby Gibson?"

Trevor stilled. "How could you possibly know that?"

She put a hand on his forearm. "Heather told me about Shelby visiting you in the hospital when we were in Azakistan six months ago."

He winced.

"She was just scared, Trev. I only met her briefly, but Heather thinks she cares more than she lets on."

His mouth hardened. "She dumped me while I was lying in a hospital bed, Christina. Broken wrist, broken ribs, gunshot to the shoulder. Nothing life-threatening, but her timing was shite."

"I'm sorry."

Trevor forced a smile. "I am, too. Now go learn how to be a princess." Eyes sad, he touched her cheek and left.

Christina ran her nails through her hair, fluffing and settling the curls. Poor Trevor. He was courageous, handsome, and a true gentleman. Unbidden, an image of Gabe superimposed itself over Trevor. Her breath caught in her throat.

She *so* wasn't going there. Gabe might be equally brave, and as gorgeous as a fallen angel, but he was no gentleman. She peeked into the main living area. Ronnie and Deni Van Praet sat close together on a settee. Deni held the princess's hand.

Christina wandered into her bedroom and flipped open her laptop. She turned on her video-chat program. Heather Langstrom answered on the third ring.

"Long time, no chat. How're things in D.C.?"

"I'm not there at the moment. I'm on assignment."

"Where?" Heather's cheerful face dimmed. "Can you say?"

"Sorry, but no. Some of your guys are coming here, though." Heather would have no trouble reading between the lines, Christina knew. They had become friends since they had worked together in Azakistan six months before. Christina had been invited to be a bridesmaid for Heather and Jace's wedding next spring.

"Ah. I'm prepping the info for them. They're not due for another couple of weeks, though. Do you need them sooner?"

"No. I have my own prep to do. They would just be underfoot."

"I can see something's wrong. What is it?"

Christina took in some air. Where to start? With the thing pressing hardest in her mind. "This bodyguard thing. You know who's been assigned to me."

While they were on an unsecured line, neither would mention specifics about this mission. Heather nodded. "It's going to be a learning experience for both of you."

She dropped her gaze to the floor. "He doesn't like me."

Heather chuckled. "He doesn't like anybody who works for your parent organization."

"Why?"

Heather propped her head on her hand. "You'd better ask him directly. Anyway, I don't think that's going to end up being your problem."

"What do you mean?" She slumped back against the back of the chair.

Heather's expression turned from concerned to knowing. "I seem to recall sparks literally flying between the two of you in Azakistan." Her eyes twinkled.

Christina shot her a look of horror. "I can't stand him. He's arrogant and bossy and . . . and . . ." And really good-looking. His blond hair was overlong, curling around his face in a way that made her itch to push it back with her fingertips. Last time she saw him, he'd sported a ridiculously sexy two-day growth. His irises were ringed with dark brown, but the centers were a tawny gold. It was his nose, broken at some point in his life, that kept him from being too beautiful.

She sighed. "And he doesn't trust me," she finished lamely.

Heather stood. "You'll learn to trust each other. Hey, I gotta run. Briefing in five minutes."

Christina shut the laptop with another sigh. She and Gabe would be together virtually all the time. She groaned, dread twisting in her gut.

FOR THE NEXT two weeks, Christina applied herself to learning how to stand, walk, eat, and think like a crown princess. She began to wear Ronnie's clothes, speak in her lilting French dialect, copy her mannerisms. Ronnie's private secretary, whose duties had much more to do with being a staff liaison and advisor than any kind of note-taker, began to style her hair and help with her makeup.

The princess sat as heir to the throne, but Concordia was a constitutional monarchy with a parliamentary democracy. The prime minister held most of the power. She studied the significant members of Parliament, influential entrepreneurs, and foreign heads of state, and pored over the de Savoie family tree, memorizing members of Ronnie's family and ancestors that went back eight generations.

"Just focus on the important ones," Ronnie said. "Crazy Queen Bernedetta, who used tea leaves to determine the course Parliament would take. Prince Roland, who was nearly blind and walked right off the cliff at Cap de la Nau in Spain. The Marquis de Plages, who kidnapped his wife from a British household in 1528 and nearly sent the two countries to war."

Christina chuckled. "A colorful family history."

"And now, demoiselle, we must dress," Deni said. "Your bodyguard shall arrive shortly."

Ugh. Christina had been trying to forget that fact. "Do I have time for a workout first?"

Ronnie's living space mercifully included a room large enough to contain a wide variety of modern workout gear, and a large center floor that Ronnie used for kickboxing. Everything in it was first-rate. It made up for not stepping outside in two weeks.

"Perhaps after?" Deni suggested.

"All right." She followed Ronnie into the master bedroom. They sat side-by-side on the four-poster bed, the forest green bedspread soft beneath them, while Deni disappeared into the walk-in closet. She came back out and held up a garment bag with something of a flourish.

"Come. We dress, okay?"

"Sure."

The older woman's gray eyes glittered with both intelligence and wisdom. Her red hair was swept into a sleek, sophisticated style. A face lined with experience projected an air of calm authority. She opened the garment bag.

"Voila!"

Bemused, Christina changed into the pantsuit. It was clearly expensive. The silky material clung to her breasts and hips. The top was a brilliant blue, with pads to widen her shoulders, which were narrower than Ronnie's. The black pants were belted and flared widely at the bottom, which meant she was forced to wear the ridiculously high heels that the princess favored. Deni then styled her hair and watched carefully as Christina put in the contacts that turned her brown eyes green, and did her makeup.

"I don't understand. It's just Gabe Morgan, not the king coming to visit. It's *not* the king, is it?" she asked, only half-joking.

"No, miss. You will see."

Uncertain, Christina waited in the sitting room while Deni disappeared into the princess's room. Her confusion vanished at the first sight of Ronnie. Gone was the casual woman. In her place was Princess Véronique de Savoie, dressed in an exact copy of the pantsuit Christina was wearing. Their hairstyles were identical, as was the eye shadow that brought out the green in their eyes. And Christina understood. If she could fool Gabe, who had already met her, she stood a good chance of fooling the public.

They stood together by the tall windows, Ronnie on the right, and Christina on the left.

# Chapter Three

HE HESITATED OUTSIDE the door to the princess's private apartments. The guard who escorted him canted a curious eye his way. Gabe blew out a breath. Shit. This was a job, just a job, like any other. Just focus on the objective, and not the woman he'd be working beside. She was the cheese in his trap; nothing more, nothing less.

The guard gleamed with spit and polish, imposing in his red wool coat with double rows of gold buttons. The gold braid tied at his throat and fastened at his right shoulder, and the red sash draped from the opposite shoulder to hip, proclaimed him a member of the Household Guard. He'd taken Gabe past the tourists crowding the public portions of the palace, up the right staircase, and through thirty-foot-high doors into the residential wing.

Gabe banged on the princess's door knocker three times. An older woman opened the door and gestured Gabe inside, rattling off a spate of French he didn't understand. The guard grunted something in return and left.

The woman said, "I am Dame Van Praet, Princess Véronique's private secretary."

The woman could teach his men a thing or two about spit and polish. Hair smoothed back and perfectly coiffed. Flawless makeup. Tallish for a woman at around five foot seven, but she still only came up to his shoulder. Chunky gold earrings and a clearly expensive tailored light blue suit. The skirt ended three inches above her knees. Nice legs, even if she looked sixtyish. The secretary's mouth tightened and she actually managed to look down her nose at Gabe. Impressive.

"If you require anything, please come to me and I will provide it." Her voice was stiff. Clearly, this was not a woman used to being checked out. He knew who she was, of course. Her role, her family history, her political leanings. Still, his inner devil got the best of him. His lips twitched.

"If we need any fancy stationery or envelopes, I'll be sure to let you know." He started past her.

The woman planted herself squarely in his way. "I am not an administrative secretary," she said, voice frosty. "I am Deni Van Praet, Edle von Naamveld, Dame of the Order of Sint-Godelieve, Private Secretary to Her Royal Highness Véronique, Princesse de Savoie, Duchesse d'Ardes, Markiezin of Ardvaleen."

Doubly impressive. She'd managed to spit all that out without a single pause. Gabe kept his face blank and his chuckles to himself.

The woman sighed. "Think of me as kind of a chief of staff, then. You have those in America, yes? I manage Her Highness's appearances, her correspondence, her speeches, and photographs. I am communication liaison between the princess's household and the other royal households. Also between the princess and the many charities and institutions for which she is patroness. I act as a national and international political and social advisor." Her eyes snapped. "I do *not* take dictation."

Gabe felt a flush stain his cheeks. Well, and hadn't she put him in his place? What would she have said if he told her she had great gams?

"My apologies, Dame Deni. I actually do know who and what you are. Your thirty-two years of service to the royal family has been exemplary. You are a vital part of the princess's success, and everyone knows it."

She huffed, but after a moment amusement flickered in her eyes. "You are having a jest with me, then?"

"Yes, ma'am. I apologize."

She eyed him for a moment, then threw back her head and laughed. "Few dare nowadays. It is refreshing."

Deni led the way into the apartment, and he stepped inside the richest, most opulent home he'd ever seen. Apartment? The term became meaningless as he took in the forty-foot ceiling, the gray stone laced with golden tones stretching from the foyer to the entrance of what he assumed was supposed to be a sitting room, which was all curlicues of gold in faux columns and velvet-looking furniture. Totally outside his comfort zone. Still, he was here to disappear into the background. That he did exceptionally well.

He walked into the sitting room and experienced a jolt of unreality. A twin set of beautiful women stood by the floor-to-ceiling windows. One was the Crown Princess Véronique de Savoie; the other was plain Christina. So, this was a test. He strode across the floor and stopped a few feet away from them, scanning each face closely. There were minor physical differences between them—but which was which?

"Good afternoon, Your Highness," he said to the woman on

his left. A hint of surprise and even satisfaction flashed through her eyes. He turned to the other woman, who wore an identical expression. "And Your Highness."

"Please, monsieur, address me simply as Ronnie. It will make things much easier, *non*?" The first one held out an elegant hand. He took it, wondering what he was supposed to do with it. Kiss the knuckles like he was some servant? In the end, he merely shook it gently and released her fingers. The princess on his right offered her hand as well.

"We are grateful for your experience and willingness to aid us in this difficult time," she said. Surely, this was Christina? "My fiancé has been terribly concerned."

"*Oui*. Perhaps you know of him? Lord Brumley, Baron of Daversporth? He sits as a member of the House of Lords," said the one on the left.

Would the real Princess Véronique expect him to know a member of the British aristocracy? Mistake number one for Christina. Unless the princess was merely being polite? She'd said "know of him," not "know him." Maybe Lord Brumley had been in the news? Now that he thought about it, maybe he did remember hearing the name, in conjunction with a foreign aid package. Maybe.

Damn it! He'd worked with Christina. He should be able to tell them apart, but he couldn't. Their stance, facial expressions, hand gestures, and accents were all identical.

"Parliament is in session, so we are unlikely to see him," the other one said. "He will be no hindrance to our little ruse."

"That makes things easier." Well, he had a fifty-fifty shot. Gabe inclined his head to the woman on his left. "Some members of my team will be arriving shortly to take you to the safe house. They'll turn you over to Trevor's team, who are waiting for you. You have to do what they tell you, when they tell you. It's the only way I can guarantee your safety. Do you think you can do that?"

She glanced across at the other princess. "We put ourselves in your capable hands, Monsieur Morgan."

He must have chosen correctly. Whew. "Christina." He spoke to the woman on the right. "At the same time that my team takes the princess out the back, you and I are going to leave through the front. Very visible, very public. We'll leave in half an hour."

The one he thought was Ronnie gave a tiny cough. "I'll be ready."

Shit and double shit. He kept his face blank as he faced her. "Good. After two weeks cooped up here, I'm sure you'd like some fresh air."

Christina relaxed. "I'd love some. Ronnie, you must be antsy, too."

"I am not accustomed to being shut inside, it is true. However, I put myself in your care." Ronnie gave the same tiny cough Christina had given moments before. He wasn't even sure he was talking to the right woman. Damn! Christina was good.

Nevertheless, he had no intention of letting her inexperience risk his men. He wished he knew more about what had happened last year in Iraq. Scuttlebutt pointed to an error on her part that had almost cost her team their lives. That didn't sit well with him.

The door knocker banged, exactly once. Gabe swung toward the door, waving off Deni Van Praet.

"That'll be my team."

Nevertheless, he peeked out the peephole, then put his back to the wall next to the door before he pulled it open. Tag and Mace entered to the left and right, eyes already searching, focusing, cataloguing. Alex followed, scanning the hallway behind him until he closed the door. Gabe waited until they joined him near the sofas. The three soldiers dwarfed the dainty furniture.

"Your Highness—Ronnie—this is John McTaggert, Thomas Beckett—also known as Mace—and Alex Wood," he said. "They're going to take you to the safe house, where Trevor and his SAS team will take over. You'll have round-the-clock guards. No one will get close to you."

"Thank you, Gabriel. Your attention to detail is most appreciated."

Christina hugged the princess, startling him. What she said next surprised him even more.

"You're in good hands," she said. Good. She'd grasped what he was capable of.

Princess Véronique nodded, looking uncertain.

"No, really," Christina said. "I've worked with Trevor before. You'll be safe."

Displeasure shot through Gabe's gut. She hadn't meant him. She'd meant fucking Trevor Carswell. Her next words nettled him even more.

"I trust him with my life."

CHRISTINA GRIMACED. GABE glared at her from the other side of the room. Why? She'd fooled him. As much as he'd tried to downplay it, he hadn't been able to tell them apart. Satisfaction flooded her. Maybe that's why he looked like a bear.

Being with him day after day in forced intimacy with only Deni to act as a chaperone should stop her thirst to trace the muscles on his shoulders with her lips. That, and his apparent disdain.

"It's an honor to meet you," Mace said, then followed with a spate of French. He took Ronnie's hand and bowed over it, actually brushing his lips across the back of her knuckles. Ronnie laughed, a lilting, musical sound Christina had been trying to mimic for days now. She responded to Mace, and they exchanged a rush of information. To Christina, Mace's Cajun accent sounded nothing like Ronnie's French one, but they seemed to enjoy one another.

Slipping off the high heels, she stifled the urge to fling them across the room, and instead set them neatly near the sofa. She slouched against one end of it and crossed her arms under her breasts.

Alex Wood greeted the princess as well, but his body language screamed discomfort. He relaxed as he turned to Christina, looking her over with amazement. "Hey, Wonder Woman. Good to see you again."

Her eyes widened. "What?"

He grinned at her. "Azakistan? Six months ago? You were the only one who could get pics of the terrorists we took down. Thanks."

Six months ago, on the day of President Henry Cooper's visit to al-Zadr Air Force Base, a malevolent man named Zaahir al-Farouk had recruited several fanatics to help him detonate a poisonous mixture of chlorine and phosgene gas in the center of a public swimming area on the US base outside of Ma'ar ye zhad, Azakistan. Christina had talked her asset into providing photos of her brother and the other members of Zaahir's terrorist cell for the Delta Force team, including Tag, Mace and Gabe, who had gone up to the parade grounds to search for them. In the end, though, it had been Trevor, Heather, and the commander of the Delta Force team, Jace Reed, who killed Zaahir al-Farouk and prevented hundreds of deaths. Her role, though pivotal, had been rather small. Nevertheless, she smiled back at Alex. "It was a group effort."

With his light goatee and lowered eyebrows, Tag appeared to be scowling, but she knew it was his default expression and meant nothing. He prowled across the room to the windows, standing slightly to one side as he peered out.

Alex eased up next to her. "Yeah, but you were the cutest part of the group." His ridiculously long lashes enhanced his boy-next-door good looks as he lowered his head to gaze into her eyes. "Today, you could knock me over with a feather." He reached out a single finger to touch a dangling earring. "Pretty."

Christina should have felt flattered, she supposed. It wasn't her, though. It was the princess's clothes, jewelry, hair. Her normal brown curls had been straightened and lightened, streaked with a rich red, and conditioned to within an inch of its life. The cut and style would have cost more than her car payment. She touched the strands. It felt nice to be pampered for a change. And to be flirted with. Of course, the last time she'd seen Alex, he'd been mooning over one of his unit's support staff. It was hard to take him seriously.

She glanced across at Gabe, and found him frowning in her direction. He jabbed a finger at Alex, then crooked it toward himself. Alex immediately left her side to go to his team leader. Christina pushed herself off the sofa's arm and wandered into the bedroom, determined not to notice how well Gabe fit into the black suit he wore.

Deni finished packing the last suitcase and closed it with a snap. "We are ready, Your Royal Highness."

Ronnie nodded, pressing a hand to her abdomen. "I should not be afraid, but I find I am."

Christina covered the other woman's hand with her own and squeezed. "You'll be safe, I promise. We'll find this guy, and get you back to your real life as soon as possible."

From here on out until the end of the mission, Christina would eat, talk, and dress like a princess. The only time she would be able to take it easy would be here, in the princess's apartments. But really, with Gabe Morgan watching her twenty-four-seven, would she really be able to de-stress without half a dozen stiff drinks? Christina grimaced.

Ronnie picked up the shapeless gray sweats Deni laid out for her. "My costume," she said, eyes bright. "It will be wonderful simply to relax and lounge comfortably." She shed her sophisticated pantsuit and quickly cleaned her face of makeup, then twisted her hair into a haphazard knot on her head. Nothing could alter the graceful line of her jaw or her elegant collarbone, but she certainly no longer resembled the Crown Princess of Concordia. The two returned to the sitting room.

Deni appeared beside them. She pointed her chin toward Gabe, who had gathered his men and spoke quietly to them. "Your Highness, it is time. Gabriel says the cars are ready."

Christina scowled. Gabe had excluded her. By rights, she should be part of his group right now, should be hearing the details of his plan as he outlined them. It galled her to know he didn't consider her part of his team. Just as she prepared to march over and demand to be involved, the four Delta Force operators broke apart. Two went into the princess's bedroom, emerging seconds later with two suitcases apiece.

Gabe pointed a finger at Christina. "Stay here. I'll be back in five minutes."

Christina scowled and made a rude gesture. Too bad he'd already turned away and didn't see. Seconds later, Christina and Deni were alone. The huge apartment vibrated with silence.

# Chapter Four

LOADING THE PRINCESS into the black panel van proceeded smoothly. She sat on the floor, on a blanket he insisted she have, her legs crossed. Dressed as she was, she reminded him strongly of Christina.

Damn it! Why had he barked at her? She'd been distracting Alex, and he needed his team firing on all cylinders. Still, his reaction made him every bit as unprofessional as she, and that didn't sit well with him.

Now that he'd seen Ronnie and Christina side-by-side, he could never mistake one for the other. A subtle sensuality punctuated every motion Christina made. What would she be like in the throes of passion, completely abandoned, her head thrown back and her body flushed . . .

He snapped his thoughts back to the here and now. Alex climbed into the back with the princess, a radio in one hand and a Glock in the other. Gabe looked at Ronnie. "We'll get this mess straightened out," he said. "I promise you'll have your life back soon."

She pushed a stray lock of hair behind her ear. "Keep Christina safe, Gabriel. And also yourself."

Gabe gave a sharp nod and closed the doors with a snap. Mace climbed into the driver's seat, and Tag rode shotgun.

"Eyes sharp," Gabe said, leaning into the passenger window. He didn't need to say it. His men knew what they were about. Still, it made him feel better. "Ping me when you get settled." He slapped a hand onto the roof of the van and stepped away. Gabe itched to return upstairs, but he waited until the van drove to the corner of the service drive and idled. Only then did he bound up the inside staircase leading to the second floor.

Entering the apartment without knocking, he found Christina and Deni in the study. It was a silly name for an open room some thirty-by-fifty feet. The twenty-five-foot ceiling actually had a mural painted in the center, one of those celestial scenes of people frolicking among clouds, with cherubs and whatnot.

Near the center of the room, the two women sat on a weird-looking curved thing he vaguely identified as a settee, discussing the schedule of appearances to which the princess had committed.

"Tomorrow at nine, a dressmaker will be here for the final fitting. She has not been here before, so will notice nothing amiss. In the afternoon at two, you will visit the oncology ward at National Hospital," Deni said. "Wednesday at noon, you are scheduled to speak at a women's caucus. You will give a speech, in English, but answer no questions. At three, you will open the construction site for the new wing of the Veteran's Hospital." She glanced up from her notes. "Friday, we will travel to the city of Grasvlakten. It is not too far. About one hour thirty minutes to the east. We will be in the villa." She shrugged apologetically.

Christina cocked her head. "I take it the party will be at the villa? Not a hotel?"

Deni flicked her fingers to the side. "The Nabourg villa is large, with its own ballroom," she explained. "On Saturday evening at six o'clock, you will dress for Lord and Lady Nabourg's celebration. It will be small. Not more than one hundred guests. Most will be far . . ." Deni stopped, brow furrowed as she searched for the right word. " . . . erm, distant relations, and friends and neighbors of the Nabourgs."

Christina's mouth pulled down and her brow furrowed. "Sounds like fun." She settled herself against the back of the settee. "The hospital visit tomorrow. Will I be speaking?"

"*Non.* Just touring."

Gabe leaned against the doorframe and crossed one foot over the other. "The hospital visit isn't going to happen," he told them. From the way the two women jumped, it was obvious neither had heard his entry.

"Let's go," he added. "I thought I made it clear that when the princess left by the back route, we would leave publicly."

She stiffened, but didn't say a word as she thanked Deni and retrieved her heels, slipping them on. God help them if they were forced to move fast.

He stepped into the corridor ahead of her, scanning both ways before allowing her out. As soon as the door snicked shut behind her, she closed the distance between them and grabbed his forearm, wrenching him to a halt. What the hell? That was his gun hand. He yanked himself free.

She didn't seem to notice what she'd done, getting up in his face with belligerence, fists slamming against her hips. "Do not," she snapped, enunciating every word, "treat me like that. Speak to me like that."

Gabe glared down at her. This squabbling needed to stop. He couldn't protect her from outside threats if he was also trying to garner her cooperation.

Christina stood her ground. Not many had the balls to stand up to him. She was so close that the puff of her breath warmed his face as she threw her head back. Her posture also thrust her breasts forward, though he doubted she recognized her own provocative pose. Unable to stop himself, his gaze flickered down her body. His nostrils flared while breathing in the light floral scent of her perfume, and against his will, he found himself tilting his head and leaning forward to suck it deeper into his lungs.

She slapped her palms onto his shoulders and shoved, rocking him back an inch. She did it again, and he had to force himself not to react, to keep his arms at his sides rather than spinning her around and slamming her into the wall.

"Stop," he ordered, jaw tight.

"You stop!" she hissed. "Big strong he-man intimidates weak little woman. Asshole!"

He turned abruptly and put a lot of distance between them before daring to face her again. She'd misinterpreted his unexpected wash of desire as an attempt to cow her. Thank God. If she knew he found her attractive, she would waste no time shredding his ego.

"If you can't handle this, say so now," he bit out. "This isn't about you. It's about catching the person or people who are trying to assassinate the Crown Princess of Concordia."

"I'm aware of that." She crossed her arms under her breasts, shoulders so tense they were practically up around her ears.

Great. Gabe sighed. Might as well set the ground rules right now. "My job is to stop the assassin from killing you while Carswell investigates. You need to follow my orders to the letter. If I say move, you move. If I say get down, you pancake. Got it?"

Christina, predictably, lost her temper. "No, I don't *got it*," she mimicked, her voice tight with anger. "You pompous ass. I'm not a dummy. I'm a full partner in this."

He laughed his disdain. "Partner? You're a liability."

She leaned back against the wall, brows furrowing. "I've done nothing to make you doubt me. I fooled you into thinking I was Princess Véronique, and you've met me. Why am I a liability?"

It was a valid question. Gabe rubbed his chin, trying to buy some time.

"Well?"

He exhaled hard. "I don't trust your kind. I've been left bleeding once too often."

She straightened, smoothing the silk of her outfit. "Now we're getting somewhere. My *kind* being women, or my *kind* being my employer?"

He could lie and tell her he didn't want to work with her because she was a woman. He settled for a partial truth. "I've worked with the CIA before. Nothing good ever comes out of it. You coming?"

He pushed through the double doors without waiting for her answer.

CHRISTINA TOOK SEVERAL deep breaths, then several more, trying to calm her racing heart and regain some equilibrium. Suddenly, the prospect of working with Gabe Morgan for possibly weeks or months on end seemed impossible.

About to fluff her nails through her hair, she remembered the careful style at the last moment, and lowered her arm. Drat. She settled for straightening her spine, lifting her head, and gliding down the corridor.

She sailed past Gabe without so much as a glance, relegating him to the role of servant. That meant she also ignored the House Guard at the door to the royals' living quarters. Ronnie always greeted them. She forced herself to slow down.

She descended the stairs with her fingers trailing along the bannister so she wouldn't trip in Ronnie's shoes, aware when tourists and paparazzi noticed her and started to whisper. Cameras and cell phones snapped photos, and she paused, turning to accommodate them. Inside the *palais*, she felt safe, though she knew that was a fallacy. The danger could come at any time, from any direction. Still, she inclined her head and gave Véronique's gentle smile.

The Household Guard escorted her to the front entrance, through the breezeway with its rows of columns, to the waiting limousine with its double flags. Crown Princess Véronique de Savoie merited the second-largest limousine in the fleet, which bore the flags of Concordia on the hood and the royal family crest on the doors. Gabe cleared a path through the cameras. He maneuvered around her and opened the rear door. She sat at an angle, then swung her tightly closed legs inside.

The guard clicked the door closed. Gabe swung into the front passenger seat. The driver pulled away immediately.

"Where to?" he asked.

Until now, Christina hadn't given it a single thought. Gabe, however, answered immediately.

"The baroque gardens at Nanten. Take Rue de Bouclé to Rue du Destin. Follow the signs from there."

"Gotcha."

She leaned forward, checking the driver in the rearview mirror. He returned her look briefly, then turned his attention back to the road. Despite the gray suit and tie, gloves, and cap, this was clearly no chauffeur. Gray colored his temples, but his haircut, at least what she could see, was military-short. He was deeply tanned. Strong lines bracketed his mouth and slashed across his forehead and between his eyes. Christina had no doubt if she checked the fall of his suit, she would detect the slight bulge of a weapon under his arm.

"What's your name?" she asked him.

"Gavin Selle."

She settled back against the butter-soft leather, disgruntled. This grew more ridiculous by the moment. Everyone around her knew exactly what was going on. She was the only idiot in the dark.

"You and I are going to talk." She addressed the back of Gabe's head. He did not react.

As the miles unwound, Christina registered the shrewdness of Gabe's choice. The highways were long and straight, with few trees to distort the landscape. It would be difficult for a tail to remain invisible, and there was little cover or concealment for a sniper, assuming anyone knew their destination. She would bet her last dollar Gabe told no one where he was taking her.

In less than half an hour, Gavin pulled off the highway and wound his way through thick trees to a parking area. The lot was barely half full. He shut off the engine and hopped out, opening Christina's door while scanning the area around them. She drew the sweet spring air deeply into her lungs. Should she get out? Was she supposed to wait for a signal?

"Princess?"

The title caused her to start. Gavin held out a hand, a small smile tugging at his mouth. Did he know about her? Undoubtedly. No way would Gabe fail to fill in everyone on his team. There seemed to be no condemnation in his eyes, however, as she extended her arm, remembering to place her fingertips into his palm and allow her wrist to arc gracefully downward. His forearm corded under his sleeve as he helped her from the limousine.

Gabe came around the hood of the car and positioned himself to her left. "Let's go. We'll talk inside."

They left the driver behind as they entered Nanten's famed baroque gardens. Gabe paid the entry fee and ushered her inside the double set of curved columns before anyone could react to Christina's presence. They walked down a smooth brick path through more trees, then emerged into the open. Christina gave a soft gasp of pleasure.

"This is gorgeous!"

Directly in front of them was a fountain, nestled in the center of a flat octagon that was easily thirty feet on each side. Past the fountain, acres and acres of flower beds spread out before her. She stopped at one of the informational plaques.

"'Famed landscape architect Sébastien Lalor designed the gardens 1673, in the French baroque style,'" she read aloud.

"Fascinating," Gabe said. "Keep walking."

Christina barely had time to admire the vast beds of perfectly symmetrical curlicued hedges interspersed with flowers and statuary. Gabe hustled her off the main paths, avoiding groups of people, leading her away from the grand central fountain, a breathtaking triple-tiered construct of golden water nymphs, fish, cherubs, and other figures she could not identify, all spouting water or frolicking about.

He finally slowed, far from the entrance and on an unoccupied side path. Christina lifted her face to the warm sun, inhaling the mixed fragrance of greenery and blooms. After two weeks sequestered inside the princess's apartments, the fresh air felt heavenly.

"I thought you might need to get out of there for a while. Two weeks cooped up anywhere, and I'd be chewing my arm off. Gavin'll let us know if anyone suspicious comes in, but I think we're safe enough here."

Christina flicked him a look of surprise. They were here because he'd been concerned about her? "Thank you."

They ambled past an enormous urn, flowers circling its base.

"What happened in Iraq?"

The question came out of nowhere. Christina jerked, swiveling her head around to squint at Gabe. She clamped her lips over her first response: It's none of your business. It was, though, really, wasn't it? He had the right to know if she was reliable. Trustworthy. Competent.

"The mission was a bust," she said, trying for matter-of-fact.

"Keep going."

She fought the impulse to clear her throat. "My mission was to make contact with a smuggling ring, posing as an American importer who didn't care where the merchandise came from." Her hand fluttered in the air. "Every year, more than thirty-two thousand exotic birds exported from Singapore and Indonesia make their way into American and European markets. The birds are declared as captive-bred, but strong evidence suggests Singapore, in particular, doesn't have the breeding capability that the exports would suggest. It's a scam to circumvent international trade regulations."

"What *happened*?" Impatience tinged his tone.

"A lot of these birds are on the endangered-species list," she continued doggedly. If she was going to humiliate herself, she would do it her way and in her time. "The largest launderer of illegal birds is a company called Exotic Fauna Exports of Baghdad. It was run by two brothers, Yuri and Fedyenka Osinov, Ukrainian immigrants."

She stopped walking, turning to admire the statue of a maiden pouring liquid from an urn on her shoulder. Water splashed from the urn, across her carved slippers, and into a shallow basin. Christina perched on the lip of the basin and trailed her fingers through the water. Gabe did not sit. She felt him, solid and imposing, at her left shoulder.

"Birds?" Disbelief laced Gabe's voice. "Your mission was *birds*?"

"Exotic birds aren't the only thing they handle," she said. Her shoulders hunched as she looked anywhere but at him. "They also smuggle exotic animals for illegal—and extremely expensive—fur coats. Ermine and mink. Chinchilla."

Gabe exhaled an unamused laugh. "Birds. Christ Almighty."

He infiltrated hostile countries to fight terrorists, rescue hostages, train locals to defend themselves. Small wonder her mission seemed silly to him. She slapped the surface of the water, spraying droplets onto her expensive pantsuit. "Trafficking in illegal wildlife is a fifteen billion dollar a year business, second only to the drug trade. This is not a joke. Psittacines are highly profitable commodities."

He moved into view. The several feet between them might have been miles. "Go on, then. Tell me about your birds."

Instinct told her Gabe wanted as many details as possible. "This was information gathering only. Once we found what we were looking for, local law enforcement would go in for the takedown. We needed to find the holding area. The conditions in these places are awful. Rampant disease that then moves into the United States." She glanced into his face, saw no encouragement, and sighed.

Gabe propped a foot on the lip of the fountain. "Exactly what happened?"

"Bobby Roberts and I arranged to meet with the Osinovs. Bobby was in charge of the whole operation."

Incredulity colored Gabe's tone. "No way. Robert Roberts? What, did his parents hate him?"

Christina wiped her fingers dry. "Probably. Everyone else did, too. He believed in volume leadership. If he could say it the loudest, it must be true. He never admitted he was wrong, even when it was brutally obvious he was. Frankly, he was a bully. I think Customs assigned him this case just to get rid of him for a while."

"Let me guess. He threw you under the bus." A hard look crept into his eyes.

She cleared her throat and didn't answer. In fact, Bobby had vilified her. He'd blamed her for every aspect of the mission's failure. The others followed suit to save their own asses, leaving Christina holding the bag of stink. Ugly rumors spread through agency grapevines and shredded her reputation.

"Okay. Take me through it," he said after a moment.

"The initial meeting with the Osinovs was productive. We agreed on price and delivery. The next day, we were blindfolded and taken to the holding area," she said. "Yuri showed us samples of the merchandise. Everything seemed fine."

A grin tugged at his mouth. "Samples of birds?"

Her eyes twinkled. "Two Amazons, an African grey, and a cockatoo."

"So what went wrong? You said they made you."

Christina thought for a moment. "I don't know what went wrong. Shay contacted the local police. They were supposed to be standing by to arrest the Osinovs at the warehouse during the transfer, catching them in the act. And liberating the inhabitants of those cages. They never had the chance to move in. Yuri and his men drew on us. Bobby . . . well, he escaped out the back way. I used Yuri as a human shield. They started shooting anyway. I made it out the way Bobby had and went to the hotel room where we'd set up. It had been sanitized, so I went to the airfield. We had a plane standing by to extract us to Italy."

Would he care about the hours she had struggled to evade the smugglers? The terror when Yuri discovered her? Fedyenka's fury, his shouted threats?

No.

Christina's hand rose to her hair, remembered the styling gel, and dropped her arm into her lap. "The Osinovs knew about the airfield, too, because they arrived shortly after I did. There was a firefight. I . . . shot Yuri. Then a squad of SAS soldiers arrived and Fedyenka took off. I don't know how, but he escaped. The whole mission was a bust. Because of me, Fedyenka moved the holding cages and pens, and we lost the opportunity to shut them down."

When he remained silent, she added, "Next thing I know, I'm in Azakistan doing paperwork."

Her boss, Jay Spicer, had protected her by removing her from center stage to allow the rumors to die a natural death. Obviously that hadn't happened. She gave a deep sigh.

Silence settled between them. Not even the sound of the fountain broke the quiet.

"Thank you," he finally said, "for going through it with me."

Gabe straightened and took three steps back onto the path. Looking up, Christina saw a group of visitors wandering their way, chattering away in German. Their smiles dimmed as they took in Gabe's formidable posture, casting curious looks her way as they hurried past.

She waited for him to blast her, to disparage her as her own people had. When he remained silent, she finally dared to look up. He was examining her, brows furrowed, hands on his hips.

"How can you not know how you were made?"

She smoothed an imaginary wrinkle from her trousers. "That's the question of the hour. I've been over it and over it. I laid it out for Jay Spicer, my case officer. For Trevor, who led the team that got us out of Dodge. For the review board. I've examined every nuance of my behavior, and I just can't see it."

He ran a hand along his chin, deep in thought. "It's not adding up for me. All right. Let's table it for now. Later I'll see if I can spot anything that might help you."

Gabe wanted to help her? She blinked in astonishment.

When he held out his hand to her, she took it without protest. Maybe it wouldn't be so terrible working with Gabe. For the moment, anyway, he was being almost nice.

She followed him back onto the path.

# Chapter Five

"HERE'S HOW THIS is going to work."

The mild sun warmed Gabe. Even as his eyes flickered from place to place, group to group, he allowed himself to enjoy the magnificence of the gardens. His Glock snugged close and comforting under his arm, hidden beneath his suit jacket. He missed his boot knives, but at least the specially modified dress shoes would allow him to run, if needed.

"I'm going to be beside you when you make public appearances," he told her. "Gavin will man the wheel, no exceptions. He's hands-down the best driver I've ever known. Mace will have overwatch—he'll find high ground with his sniper rifle. Tag and Alex will shadow us." He glanced at her to make sure she understood. "We'll all be hooked together by Bluetooth. You'll also wear a wire as a backup, in case our comms fail. If you see anything that makes you nervous, sing out. Ditto if we do. We'll tell you exactly where to go and what to do."

Christina hesitated, but finally nodded.

Something about her story nagged at him. Maybe it was simply that she seemed so ready to accept blame for a mission that, by her own account, failed from all sides, not just hers.

"Why can't I visit the children?" she asked. "They have leukemia and cancer, for God's sake. A visit from Princess Véronique would be the highlight of their miserable stay. Lifting their spirits also increases their odds of survival, you know."

"I'm not willing to risk the children. It would be safer if we weren't there." Her empathy inexplicably warmed him.

"I disagree. Also, it's the perfect venue for my first public appearance as Ronnie. Low-profile, small audience. If your guys have the back end covered, nobody could get to me. Assuming, of course, they wouldn't blow up the hospital." Her eyes widened. "They wouldn't, would they?"

He didn't think so. He and his team had, in fact, discussed that in great detail. The original assassination attempt had been a clumsy shot from a fair distance, indicating an amateur. Either the princess or her fiancé could have been the target; and, when the bullet went wide, the assassin vanished rather than start spraying bullets into the crowd. In fact, they had concluded the hospital visit would be safe enough for the patients. He'd vetoed the visit hoping Christina would change her mind and stay inside the palace.

Could he now afford to be seen as changing his mind?

Looking into her eyes, he decided that, yes, he could. After all, he needed her cooperation. They needed to be able to trust one another; and, at the moment, trust seemed an impossibility. His decision certainly had nothing to do with the soft plea in her eyes.

"Gabe? Would the children truly be at risk?"

Eyes colored green to match Véronique's. He found he preferred her own light brown color. He jerked his gaze away from her and focused, instead, on the rainbow spray created by another fountain up ahead.

"I believe this assassin will make a play for you in the most public place possible, with lots of people and even camera crews. I'm not ruling anything out, but if he tries again very soon, the Veteran's Hospital opening or the villa in Grasvlakten would be my picks." Sweeping his gaze across the open space of the gardens, he added, "The first attempt happened in a public venue."

"Princess Véronique attended a modern dance performance at Le Monnaie Opera House in Brussels on March second with her fiancé and his sister," Christina said.

As he was well acquainted with every detail of the attempt on Ronnie's life, Gabe could only assume Christina wanted to impress upon him that she'd done her homework. She grew quiet as they passed an elderly couple sitting on a bench, heads close and hands clasped.

"They left after the performance and were walking across the street to have a nightcap at The Dominican," she continued, when they were alone again. "Princess Véronique had just stepped past the gate when the wall lamp next to her head shattered. The shot came from farther down Rue Léopold, where it crosses Wolvengracht."

"From the roof," Gabe confirmed, before she started describing the dimensions of the dome or the caliber of the rifle used. "Not far. Maybe a hundred, hundred and fifty yards. An easy shot for a professional. Since he missed, he either meant to, or is an amateur."

They wandered along paths made of white crushed rocks. Ahead of them, an enormous globe of the earth rested atop yet another fountain, water bubbling up from beneath it. All the damned water made it hard for him to hear. He led her away from it, toward the wall separating the gardens from the groves of trees surrounding it.

"But the threat came when they were outside, not inside the theater."

"Yes," he said, giving in. "If you really want to go, the hospital is probably safe enough. We can corral the kids and keep the staff away."

Her smile lit up her face and made her eyes sparkle. It took his breath away. "Thank you," she said.

Since he didn't trust his voice in that half-second, he merely nodded. "Do you have any questions?"

"Well, I have some obvious ones," Christina said. "First and foremost, I need weapons. I'd like a subcompact for my purse, preferably a Sig Sauer, and a Baby Browning with an ankle holster. Also an expandable spring baton. A twelve-inch one is fine."

That brought him up short. How could he not have anticipated that she would want to be armed? Damn. The CIA didn't arm their employees in the States, of course, since they couldn't legally operate within its borders—and she had no authorization to carry inside Concordia—but neither of them were concerned with technicalities, Gabe realized. Arming her made sense. He had to stop thinking of her as a principal.

"I'll see what I can do. What else?"

Gabe heard the noises seconds before Christina. As her head swiveled toward the sound and her mouth opened, Gabe wrapped an arm around her waist and spun her behind him, holding her there with one hand on her waist. She squeaked in surprise.

"Quiet!" he snapped. He tugged her over to the relative safety of the wall, pushing on her shoulder to indicate he wanted her to crouch, relieved when she understood and obeyed. Giving himself two steps, he jumped and caught the top of the high garden wall, pulling himself up easily and crouching as he took quick inventory of the layout before dropping lightly to the other side. The sounds came from his left; grunting and rustling as though the person or persons were trying to be quiet but couldn't quite manage it. He drew his Glock, stepping soundlessly across a bed of pine needles from the previous winter, using tree trunks to mask his approach.

"I'm close." The man's voice was a light tenor. "I'm almost there."

"Hurry." The other voice was pitched higher. "My parents will be looking for me."

A reluctant grin tugged at Gabe's mouth as he caught sight of the two teenagers locked together in a clumsy embrace, the girl's back against a tree trunk and a leg on a rock, skirt up around her waist. He withdrew as silently as he'd come, leaving the young lovers oblivious to his presence.

Christina searched his face when he dropped back down beside her. "Well?"

"It was nothing. A deer. Let's keep walking."

She accepted his explanation, following as he took them back the way they'd come. "All right. So back to our master plan. Obviously, this isn't going to be a standard protection detail. Say something happens. *When* something happens. You can't whisk me away, or leave me behind, as you did just now. That defeats the purpose. We need to draw him out, not hide from him."

Gabe stopped and turned to her, forcing her to stop as well. "I will not let anything happen to you."

She made an exasperated sound. "That's not what I'm saying. We need a plan to funnel the assassin into a trap. A predetermined net."

"We have the beginnings of a plan. We've brainstormed a lot of different scenarios."

Exasperation turned to anger. "And when are you going to fill me in?"

She wasn't being unreasonable, as much as he hated to admit it. Taking in a lot of air through his nose, he exhaled slowly, willing away his annoyance at being questioned by another damned CIA officer. "Before each appearance. I'll make sure one of us fills you in. Sound good?"

Christina nodded, apparently mollified. Jesus. He couldn't remember the last time he'd worked with an unknown entity. It was exhausting.

Rushing to put herself out there as a target made her either brave or foolhardy. She recognized that her mission in a nutshell was to be bait, and she hadn't balked or whined. That was the good news. On the flip side, she might fold under pressure. And he had to consider whether Christina or the CIA, or both, had their own agendas. Leanne had sold him out to the Reyes Cartel with the sweat of their lovemaking damp on his skin. Even four years later, it still made his gut clench.

The depressing truth was that he could not afford to trust Christina Madison.

# Chapter Six

In the time they'd been gone, the princess's home had transformed into something almost unrecognizable. The second bedroom was littered with duffel bags and rolled-up sleeping bags. The furniture in the third bedroom had been pushed against the walls, and folding tables covered with computer equipment bisected the room. Gabe's team lounged on the sofas or hunched over the computers. The huge living space seemed smaller with the seven of them. Why had she thought she would be alone with Gabe? She didn't know whether to be relieved or disappointed.

Relieved, of course.

Deni Van Praet sat at the desk in the study, tiny reading glasses perched on her aristocratic nose as she scribbled notes in the margins of a sheaf of papers. She looked up as Christina entered, looking more resigned than annoyed. A small, practiced smile graced her mouth. "Princess," she murmured, rising.

Christina ran her nails through her hair, lifting it off her neck. "It's just me, Deni. No need for formality."

"Very well. Then come sit down and we'll go over the guest list for the Viscount and Viscountess of Nabourg's anniversary party again."

Christina obediently went to sit in front of the desk. The celebration would be the first real test of her abilities. A shiver of anticipation raised goose bumps on her arms. She grinned at Deni.

The older woman pulled out a black binder and opened it at random. Pointing to the photo, she began to quiz Christina. "Who is this? What is his relationship to the Nabourgs? When did you last meet him?"

Christina realized she actually knew the answer. All that studying with the princess paid off. "That's Lord Vrejflouw, MP of Meestragen North. His title comes to him by marriage, and he has very little influence, even as a member of Parliament. He became a widower three years ago."

"How do you know him?"

Christina felt the corners of her mouth twitch. "Trick question. I've never met him, nor very many other members of Parliament. The queen alone has the honor of sitting in the royal box at 6 Rue de Nobles."

A curious stillness in the air made her look up. Gabe leaned against the doorjamb, thumbs stuck in his belt loops and his ankles crossed. "How's it going?"

Such innocuous words, but Christina knew from one look into his eyes what he was really asking. "I'll be ready."

"Good. There hasn't been a lot of mission prep time. The damned thing's in two days."

"I'm a quick study." Christina turned back to the book. Flipping the page, she said, "Nessandra Florentine. Socialite. Been on the cover of *Le Sommet* three times."

Gabe wandered up to peer over her shoulder, and gave a low whistle. "Holy smokes. As what? Sexiest cougar of all time?"

"Just divorced husband number four." Christina's lip curled. "Obtained her wealth through her ex-husbands' generosity. She's probably looking for ex-husband number five, if you're into that."

Gabe lifted the binder from Deni's desk and peered at the photo. "Damned straight. Are we going to meet her at this shindig?"

Unaccountably nettled, Christina snatched the binder from him and snapped, "Maybe you could roll your tongue back into your mouth long enough to remember that your job isn't to hit on women at this *shindig*."

He gave a low chuckle, and she realized he'd been teasing her. She groaned and dropped her head to the back of the chair. "Go away. I'm working."

The chuckle turned into a laugh. "I just came in to tell you Tag's looking for you."

"Seems you found her first," Tag said, tramping into the room. "You got a sec? I need to test your microphone."

"You bet." She followed him into the third, smaller, bedroom and over to a Louis XV table, carefully covered to protect it. An array of equipment littered the table and the sofa next to it.

"Sit down," Tag said. "I need to measure you."

She found out what he meant a moment later when he held up a tiny coil of wire.

"You'll have to either pull your shirt up, or take it off."

She snorted a laugh. "Yeah, right. I can do it myself. I've attached wires to my clothes before."

"To the back of your bra?" came Gabe's voice from the doorway. What was it with him, appearing like unwanted magic in doorways? "You'd have to be pretty limber for that."

His eyes were on the electronic gadgets, not her, but Christina found herself turning beet red. Fortunately, neither man seemed to notice. "I can attach it to the front, under the dress," she said.

"Won't work," Tag said. "Too close to your heartbeat. That only works if it's outside your clothes, like they do on air or whatever."

Tag poked among the various wires, looking at Christina's breasts with apparent professional detachment, then came to perch beside her, reaching for the back hem of her blouse.

"I can do it," she said, her laugh good-natured. She batted his hands away.

"I have to measure the width between your shoulder blades, and the width of your bra at the clasp. Then we size the wire and the microphone so they'll fit under the strap, but on your back." Tag waited, hand outstretched.

She hesitated. It was his job. He was a professional. And so was she. "All right. Go ahead."

The expensive silk slipped through Tag's fingers as he gathered it and slid it up her back. She reached over her shoulder to grab it, holding it up so Tag could measure her. She glanced at Gabe. Her back faced away from him; he couldn't see anything, yet he stared at her with an intensity that was unnerving. He swallowed several times.

Christina froze. The naked hunger in his gaze paralyzed her. He followed Tag's touch like a physical caress against her skin. She was shocked when a rush of heat flooded her. Her lips parted on a breath. Their eyes caught, suspending her in a timeless moment. It became Gabe's long fingers, scorchingly hot against her skin, lightly touching her back under her bra. Her tongue touched her lower lip. His gaze zeroed in on that tiny movement. He didn't seem to be breathing.

He yanked his gaze away, expression closing down with a finality that jarred her. He hadn't meant for her to see his desire, that much was clear.

What the hell had just happened?

"What . . . what if I wear a different bra that night?" She forced words past the constriction in her throat. The tenuous thread between them vanished, and she could breathe again.

The two men looked at one another, brows pulled in. Apparently, it had not occurred to either of them.

Christina swallowed a laugh. "I'll go get the one I'll be wearing," she said.

Gabe moved away from the doorway as she passed him. Making sure there was no contact between them, she thought. Anxious to get this over with, Christina hurried to her bedroom and dug into the underwear drawer. Véronique de Savoie favored silky, sexy underthings more daring than anything Christina had ever attempted. She'd purchased a dozen sets similar to Ronnie's, since the maids would find it odd if the princess started wearing plain white cotton. Christina was wearing one of the more conservative sets now, plain black but edged with lace. She rooted through the contents, looking for another comparatively plain set.

Her nails snagged on a sheer pink bra, deeply cut and barely there across the nipples. The panties were equally scandalous. A deep V started at the top of her thighs and dipped to just above her mound. Anticipating the look on the operators' faces, she chuckled and scooped up the bra. *Let's see Gabe look at* that *with no reaction.*

TAG FINGERED THE tiny microphone. It would nestle between her shoulder blades without a telltale bulge. Once under the bra strap, no one would be able to tell she wore a wire at all.

Christina walked back into the room. No, she swaggered. Her tight, athletic body was curvy in all the right places, and Gabe couldn't stop the stirrings of his body. His attempt to jerk Christina's chain had apparently worked a little too well, and not the way he'd intended.

Damn it! Why couldn't he be attracted to that cougar— whatever her name was? Yes, she was beautiful, but how could men miss her greed? The cold and calculating gleam in her eye. Gabe preferred the understated sexuality he was certain Christina did not know she exuded.

Although, at the moment, there was nothing understated about the sway of her hips as she approached them. What was the blasted woman up to? He had his answer a moment later, when she dropped a tiny pink bundle into Tag's outstretched hand. As Tag straightened the fabric, Gabe felt all the moisture leave his mouth. Holy God! There was barely enough fabric for Tag to grasp, and what was there was like gossamer. A picture of Christina wearing the scraps of barely-there and sprawled across his bed had him sitting abruptly and shifting forward on the chair, hands clasped in front of him to hide the bulge in his pants.

"Here you go," she said, voice husky. "Do you need me to put it on? Or can you manage?"

"No problem." Tag sounded strangled. "I can just, um, use this."

"Oh, good," she purred, eyes on Gabe. "I have work to do, so . . ."

She was playing with him, that much was obvious. The question was, could she see just how affected he was? He wiped all expression from his face but could not stop his eyes from dropping to her breasts. Watching Tag do nothing more than lift the shirt up her back had gotten him so revved up he hadn't been able to hide his reaction from her. Damn it! He dragged his gaze back up to her face. Satisfaction flared in her eyes, and he silently cursed.

"We're leaving at one o'clock tomorrow for the hospital," he said, striving for matter-of-fact. He kept his eyes fixed on Tag as his teammate attached the wire to the bra he held in his large hands. "Wear shoes you can run in, if you have any. The team will be stationed along the route in unmarked cars. You and I will take the goddamned unarmored piece of shit state limo."

Her brow furrowed. "That doesn't work for me. We should convoy in three cars, one in front of us and one in the back. Let people see us. Otherwise, what's the point?"

He couldn't stop the irritation flashing across his face. This wasn't her area of expertise. He knew what he was doing, and he'd be damned if he'd allow any harm to befall her.

"The more visible we are, the more likely the assassin will make a play for me. Isn't that the point? Don't you think this"—her arm swept in an all-encompassing arc—"is overkill? If you keep me too safe, you practically invite the assassin to make a play that might get civilians killed."

He took in a lot of air through his nose. She was part of his team, he reminded himself. He couldn't shut her out. "Sit down," he said finally.

She hesitated, but finally came to settle on the sofa next to him.

"I don't bite," he snapped, annoyed with her reticence and knowing he was the cause. But wasn't it better to keep her at a distance?

"Are you sure?" she shot back. Tag laughed.

"Not unless that's what you're into." Damn it! That had sounded flirtatious. He controlled his own damned body, not the other way around. He glared at her. "God knows what they teach you at Langley."

Surprisingly, humor lit her eyes. "I don't recall biting being taught as a self-defense technique."

He couldn't manage a chuckle, but his irritation faded. "We'll leave you more exposed, but in the future. I don't disagree with anything you said, except that we don't have positive control over the environment. We've barely had time to vet the attendees, and this has been advertised on the princess's website for weeks. We want to draw the assassin out, yes. But on our terms, not his. And we sure as hell don't want any civilians caught in the crossfire."

To his relief, she dipped her head. "I understand. I'll be ready."

He stood with her, searching her eyes, for what he had no idea. His unwilling attraction would go nowhere. She was the principal, and therefore off limits.

No, she wasn't. Nor was she truly part of his Delta Force team. She was Christina Madison, CIA.

# Chapter Seven

CHRISTINA CHANGED INTO shorts and a T-shirt and headed down the wide hall to Ronnie's private gym. Since the team had arrived, someone was always in there. This afternoon, it was Gavin, Alex, and Tag. One of them had hung a heavy bag in a corner—miracle-worker Deni must have acquired it for the team—and Gavin worked it steadily, sweat dripping down his face. Tag ran on the treadmill, and Alex pumped free weights.

Tag lifted a hand in greeting. Christina flopped onto the floor to stretch.

"What's your poison?" Alex asked. His biceps bulged from the eighty-pound dumbbells in each hand, but he wasn't even breathing hard.

"I'd really like to do some speed training. I'll probably need to move fast rather than hit something. Are you up for some sparring?"

"I could do that." He looked doubtful. "We didn't bring any pads, though."

"No problem," she assured him. "We'll just pull our punches."

Shrugging, Alex set the dumbbells neatly back in their rack and came to the center of the floor. It was covered in a thin layer of foam, making it a soft landing spot in case he took her to the ground.

She moved her right leg back a few inches and raised her lightly closed fists. Alex mirrored her move, and they started to circle. Christina threw two jabs and a left cross. He slipped them easily, throwing a halfhearted punch toward her center. She faded left, and he let her. Taking two steps in, she executed a combination of kicks and jabs. He fended her off, but didn't return with an attack of his own. She frowned. Executing a perfect spinning side kick, which should have dumped her on her ass as Alex scooped her leg, she made light contact with his thigh as he simply moved back.

"Alex, this is only helpful if you actually engage with me," she complained, stopping and dropping her hands.

"I am . . . I just don't want to hurt you . . ."

"She's right," came Gabe's voice from the doorway. He strolled in, followed by Mace. "You're being a pussy. Shove over, Junior."

Alex shrugged and went to sit sideways on the stationary bike. Gabe took his position in the middle of the mat. "Let's try this again."

She again took up a light sparring stance, putting her weight forward onto the balls of her feet. He did the same.

She felt the difference instantly. Gabe came at her with intensity, faster than she could have believed a man could move. She slipped his first punch and parried the second, stepping close to his side to land a punch to his ribs. He spun to deliver an elbow jab to her face, barely brushing her nose, and completed the turn with a rigid hand that flicked the side of her head as she ducked under it. She slapped his arm aside and came up with an uppercut, but he was no longer there. His fist bumped her temple from the right. She spun, kicking toward his knee, and he danced away. They circled again.

"Come on, Christina, take him apart!" Tag called.

"Show him how it's done." Gavin draped a towel around his neck and came to watch.

Their casual inclusion warmed her. Determined to prove herself, she drove forward, faking a punch to Gabe's face. She thrust her leg between his, locking it behind his ankle, and pushed on his shoulders. The inner reaping throw should have put him on his ass, but he whipped his right foot and body back, and she missed the sweep. From his perpendicular position, he wrapped his left forearm around hers, bracing it on his right, his fist pushing upward on her elbow, locking out the joint. She couldn't move without hurting herself. He released her, and they parted again.

Point for him.

"Not too bad," Gabe allowed, stretching his neck a little. His eyes twinkled. "But don't forget, we help teach combatives at Camp Peary. You're going to have to do better than that if you want me on my back."

Was he trying to distract her? Or was he actually flirting with her?

Either way, it made her even more determined. "I'll put you on your ass."

He grinned, and her eyes narrowed. Damn it! She twisted to throw a roundhouse kick, anticipating that he'd move right to avoid it. Settling her weight on her front foot, she flicked a backhand toward the face sliding into her view. He used her own momentum to push her arm past her face, using his other hand to dogleg her arm into a lock. They stared at one another, faces close, until he released her arm.

"Had enough?" he asked.

"We've just started. Have I exhausted you already?" He was right. Using standard tactics taught during her training would get her nowhere. She needed to take him to the ground, where her size would work to her advantage.

The team called out suggestions and encouragement.

"Elbow to the solar plexus," Gavin called out. "That'll shut him up."

"Kick him in the nuts," Tag suggested. "He don't need 'em."

"Bite me," Gabe said.

They circled again. Christina spun, bringing her leg up as she'd done with Alex. As expected, Gabe caught her leg and lifted, throwing her off balance. As she fell, she kicked upward, scissoring both legs around his arm and twisting. Both of them spun to the ground. She slapped the mat with one arm as she hit, trying to pin his neck between her legs.

And then something happened. Instead of immobilizing him, she found herself flipped onto her back, his hands under her thighs and his head very nearly between her legs. He didn't so much as twitch, but the look he sent up her body widened her eyes and sent scalding heat coursing through her.

"Damn it!" She yanked her legs. His grip held her still, but he loosened his fingers by increments, allowing her to wrench free and scramble to her feet.

He got up more slowly. "Nice move. Where'd you learn that?"

"I have a few tricks up my sleeve."

He came at her almost before she was ready, throwing a flurry of combinations that had her scrambling to react. Finally, she threw him back a few steps, just enough to get inside his guard and smack her fist alongside his temple. His head rocked back, and she realized her control wasn't where it needed to be. Before she could apologize, he spun her around and wrapped his arms over hers, gripping both her wrists.

She twisted her head, looking over her shoulder at him. His head was closer than she'd expected, and they ended up nose to nose. His breath fanned her face as his eyes dropped to her mouth. Without thinking about it, Christina brought her elbow straight back into his floating ribs. He grunted, and his grip loosened. She didn't move.

"Ow."

"Had enough?" she mocked.

He slowly shook his head, eyes dark on hers. "Not nearly enough."

"Nice shot," Mace said. "Any harder, and you'd'a broken him."

"I'm tempted." She glared at Gabe as her voice dropped to an intense whisper. "What happened to helping me with my reflexes?"

Gabe also lowered his voice. "I'm trying to. I needed to see what you could do before I—"

Alex snapped a towel in their general direction. "Get a room."

She pulled free of Gabe's embrace and moistened her lips, glancing around. "Unnecessary. He's an ass."

Mace hooted with laughter. "That's the God's honest truth."

"Assholery does seem to be the general consensus," Gabe agreed.

Even Tag's normal scowl lightened. "Shit, I like you, Christina. You're damned good at reading people."

"I'm not an ass," added Alex. "If I'd known what you meant, I'd'a thrown down with you, too." He didn't mean it, though. Despite the nature of his comment, sexual undertone was absent.

She turned innocent eyes to Alex. "You had your chance, farm boy. Toss me some water, would ya?"

Alex grabbed one of the bottles and lobbed it at her. She caught it one-handed, twisted it open, and drank deeply. They simply accepted her into their midst. It's what usually happened to her in new groups, and she was relieved to see it happen now.

Except with Gabe. He remained untrusting and wary.

And yet something had happened during their sparring match that, as much as she wanted to, she couldn't ignore. The spark Heather mentioned had unexpectedly burst into flame. They'd both felt the pull.

She shifted her new awareness into aggression. A much safer emotion.

"Gavin, are you done with the bag? Seems I have some hostility to work off." She kept her tone light, teasing.

He half bowed, his sweeping arm inviting her to take his place.

She taped up her hands with practiced ease. For the next fifteen minutes, she worked her way around the heavy bag, funneling all of her doubts and insecurities into powerful punches, jabs, and kicks. At last, exhausted and sweaty, she dropped her hands to her thighs and bent over, sucking in air.

"Impressive."

She turned to see Mace in the doorway. At some point, the others had finished their workouts and left. "Thanks."

"You've got great form. A lot of boxers don't get that right hook in there, but you really dig in. Are you finished with the bag? I don't want to interrupt you."

"Yeah, I'm done. I'm going to work some free weights."

Mace slipped on a pair of light boxing gloves, tightening the laces with his teeth.

"Here, let me do that," she said. "No point in struggling with it."

Mace looked pained. "Struggle? Me?"

She laughed, tying the gloves into place. "Now try, hotshot."

While Mace took over the bag, Christina sat on the free-weight bench, but made no move to pick up the dumbbells. What the hell had happened here? As much as she wanted to deny it, she had reacted to Gabe physically. That just couldn't be allowed. He was a jackass, and he had no faith in her abilities.

"Everything okay?" Mace stopped pounding on the bag and regarded her.

"Yeah, sure. Of course. Why wouldn't it be?"

He gave her a chiding look. "As long as you're part of this team, your problems are our problems. Spill."

No way was Christina telling Mace about her absurd attraction to Gabe. The first thing the sniper would do is tell his team leader. She thought fast.

"I had an interesting experience with a gray panel van in D.C. a couple of days before I flew out here. I need to call my boss to follow up."

"Were you in an accident? Hit and run?"

Christina chewed her lip. "Not exactly."

"What van?"

She couldn't control a start of guilt. Closing her eyes for a moment, she reluctantly turned to where Gabe leaned against the doorjamb.

"Uh . . ."

He straightened and planted his hands on his hips as his eyes narrowed. "What van?" he said again.

"Um, nothing, really. A training exercise. Probably." She coughed to clear the frog in her throat.

"What. Fucking. Van." His voice had dropped to a low growl. Crap. This is what she'd been afraid of.

He closed the distance between them. Anger darkened his eyes.

"Someone tracked me the day before I flew here," she said in a rush. "I reported it, per standard operating procedure, but when I checked with the Surveillance Center, no recruits followed me that day."

Gabe's brows snapped together and his mouth flattened. "And you didn't think this was important enough to mention?"

"Truthfully, I'd forgotten about it until just now. I've thrown myself into this role a hundred percent." She glanced to the side, unable to meet his eyes. Her mouth drooped.

She felt the weight of his glare. In her periphery, she saw the same expression of disapproval on Mace's face.

"Did you get a look at him?" he finally asked.

"I saw the driver. I didn't get much of a look at the second guy. They put a stolen plate on the van. But nothing else happened." She forced herself to breath. "Fairfax County police investigated it, but do you know how many gray panel vans there are in D.C.?"

Gabe rubbed a hand along his forehead. "This is exactly why I don't work with alphabet agencies. You all have your own fucking agendas, and you withhold vital information."

Christina forced her spine straight, resentment flooding her. She'd screwed up; she knew it. But she hadn't concealed it on purpose. "I don't have an agenda! Except to finish this mission and never lay eyes on you again!"

She brushed past him as she exited the room, surprised when he let her leave. Stalking back up the hallway, she cursed herself for every kind of a fool. Why had she expected anything different from him? He didn't and never would see her as an equal.

Deni looked up as she stomped into the bedroom. "What is wrong?"

"Nothing. Just a disagreement. I'm going to shower."

"As you wish."

What she wished was never to see Gabe Morgan again. Since that seemed unlikely, she scrubbed, rinsed off, and wrapped herself in one of Ronnie's silk robes. She stretched out on the bed and closed her eyes. "Just for a few minutes."

# Chapter Eight

CHRISTINA FORCED HERSELF to remain still while the dressmaker pinned and sewed the satin gown. She gripped the speech she would give the following day at the joint Austrian-Concordian caucus on equality of women's pay, practicing it aloud in English while Deni and the seamstress chatted. This polyglot event conveniently made sense of her rehearsing in English—and negated the need to join their conversation in French.

Dinner the previous evening had been strained. The camaraderie she'd been developing with the team withered under Gabe's disapproval. He continued to believe she'd deliberately withheld the van incident from him, but it had never occurred to her that it and her mission here might be related. How could they be? Only a select few people even knew she was here. Her call to Jay Spicer had yielded no new information. This morning, she'd eaten breakfast in her bedroom, unable to face Gabe's censure.

Princess Véronique's ball gown needed to be altered slightly to fit Christina, taken in slightly to account for her smaller breasts and longer waist. The dress was a gorgeous burgundy wine color, and Christina had fallen in love with it on sight. The halter neck-line was embroidered with a silver thread design. A crystal spray decorated her stomach. The full skirt started just below her navel, and was gathered at various points with crystal clips.

The seamstress had taken one look at her scar and tut-tutted, then whipped out a sheer silk material in the same color and had sewn, on the spot, a scarf-like drape for her shoulders that con-cealed her upper arm.

The fitting and alterations took two hours. At the end of it, Christina looked at herself in the full-length mirror. "*Très bien*," she murmured, touching the seamstress's shoulder with genuine appreciation. "*Merci beaucoup*."

If the woman noted anything odd about her accent or was sur-prised by the scar, she did not show it. Discretion was part and parcel of working with the royal family, Deni had told her.

Christina gave a regal nod as Deni escorted the woman from the apartment. When she was alone, she slipped out of the dress and hung it up carefully, then pulled on a pair of yoga pants, a sports bra, and a loose, drawstring top over it—and felt like her-self again. She spent the next half an hour in the gym stretching, thought about changing, and decided she deserved to be comfort-able for some part of this mission.

By the time she entered the dining room, the Italian cook had laid out lunch and vanished. One by one, the operators drifted into the room behind her. The lunch menu consisted of clam chowder, lasagna, a grilled vegetable salad. Red wine. And—what on earth was that?

"Red wine marinated escargot over bowtie pasta," Deni said, seating herself. She laid her napkin across her lap. "Apparently, it is one of Lorenza's specialties."

Christina sniffed at it. It smelled wonderful. "All right. I'll bite."

The rest of the team filled their plates and sat down.

"Comms check at thirteen hundred hours," Gabe said. "We don't want any surprises at the hospital. Departure at thirteen-thirty."

There were nods all around. The teammates shoveled food into their mouths at incredible speed.

"It's actually good," Alex said, swallowing the escargot pasta. "I mean, I've eaten snails before. They didn't taste like this."

Christina simply shook her head. "Maybe if you took the time to taste it?"

"So," Mace said briskly, rubbing his hands together. He smiled at Christina. "I'm bored of Alex going on and on about farming equipment, or Tag talking about his horses. Tell me an interesting story."

"What?"

Gavin speared a slice of squash from his salad and waved it at her. "Tell us about yourself."

She frowned. What could she tell?

"How did you come to work for the CIA?" Gabe asked. His tone was casual, but she saw the hard look in his eyes.

She cleared her throat. Was she really going to do this? Give Gabe more ammunition to use against her?

"Well, I was recruited right out of high school, so I haven't known anything else."

"They recruited you? Isn't that unusual?" Mace looked genuinely interested.

"Yeah, it is." Christina closed her eyes, remembering her initial conversation with the recruiter. "The normal application process is long and drawn out. Background checks and polygraphs, interviews and exams. They only recruit when someone has a special-ized skill. A talent they need. In my case, it's complicated."

"I like complicated," Alex said. He threw a snail at Mace, who caught it one-handed and popped it into his mouth. "Like the ma-chinery parts on my thresher."

"All right." How could she sanitize the story? "My parents got involved with some . . . stuff. I got them out of trouble, but just after we . . . moved to a new city, a CIA recruiter visited me."

The interview had been bizarre from the start.

"I hear you're brilliant. Are you?"

"Um, no. Not really."

"Do realize what you did? The degree of difficulty, especially at your age?"

"I know what I did."

"Was it merely a fluke? An act of desperation? Did it excite you? Thrill you? Bore you?"

"It was kinda cool."

"Could you do the same thing again, if your parents' lives weren't at stake?"

"Sure, would be a lot easier that way."

"Do you realize how much danger you were in? I want to make it very clear. What I'm suggesting would be just as dangerous, and you couldn't tell your parents anything at all about what you're doing. You game?"

"The case officer who visited me sent me into a rough high school in a mostly minority neighborhood. His daughter's school. He knew major narco-trafficking was going through the school. He gave me the starting players, then told me I had six months to tell him how the trafficking worked. No one could know what I was doing. I had no official cover. He gave me his contact data, but the CIA can't operate inside US borders. I was on my own."

*"If you pull this off, I'll do three things for you," the case offi-cer promised her. "One, your parents will win the lottery and earn $50,000 from a ticket you will buy. Two, I'll offer you a full-ride scholarship to college, to study whatever you want, provided that three, at the end of getting your education, you come to work for us for a minimum of five years."*

"What if I fail?"

*"I walk away and you never see me again. Most likely if you fail, you'll be dead. Your parents will get $10,000, and I'll put roses on your headstone."*

"I managed to fit in. It's my chameleon thing," she told them. She tucked a leg under her.

"Chameleon?" Alex asked, forehead wrinkling.

Tag sniffed the wine in his glass and put it down. "It's a lizard, numbskull."

Alex lobbed another snail, this time at Tag. It bounced off his chest and rolled onto the floor. Tag didn't react. "I know what a chameleon is, asshole."

"But you asked—"

"You've fooled everyone around you so far." Mace said, ignor-ing them. "You're a good actress."

"Thanks. But I took acting in high school, and I bombed at it. What I'm doing here, it's not an act. When I'm in a role, I am that role. I fit into my surroundings, like a chameleon." She couldn't help the glance toward Gabe, who watched her without expression.

"So you were the marshmallow in the hot chocolate," Mace prompted. "Did you figure out who the dealers were?"

She scooped up the last of the pasta, chewing to give herself time to frame her words. "I did. It took me four months. I went back to the case officer with my information. The D.C. police raided both the school and their homes the very next day. I was arrested along with the dealers, because no one knew me from Adam. My father bailed me out, I got a huge lecture, and then the charges against me were dropped. I've always assumed the case officer pulled some strings.

"From there, it was exactly as the case officer promised. My parents retired after the money showed up. The Company sent me to college. I studied political science and international economics. When I graduated, I went to work for them."

"Any regrets?" Surprisingly, the question came from Gabe.

She could lie, but what would be the point? "Only that I screwed up in Baghdad last year. I took a life. I could have cost a teammate's life."

Silence surrounded the table.

Discouraged, Christina dropped her gaze to her empty plate.

"You failed to rescue your birds." Gabe's voice sounded surprisingly benign. He squinted at her, as though he could pull the truth straight from her brain. "Okay, maybe you made a mistake. Depends on how you were made as an operative. But things happen on missions. Things go FUBAR—fucked up beyond all recognition—and plans get chucked. You adapt and survive."

"Sounds to me like you're not the only one who screwed up," Mace added. At her surprised look, he grinned. "Gabe filled us in, obviously. We only work as a team if we all have the same info. We're so tight, if Tag gets indigestion, Alex farts for 'im. Sorry, ma'am." He nodded to Deni, his cheeks reddening.

"Your team leader abandoned you." Tag sent Mace a chiding look. "There was no contingency plan if it all went sideways. Sounds like you did the best you could under bad circumstances."

Christina felt her mouth drop open. Everyone around her had blamed her exclusively for the mission flop. At some level, despite not being able to see where she went wrong, she had accepted that, as the junior operative, the mistake must have been hers.

Gabe quirked a small smile at her. "Hey, now," he said, voice almost teasing, "we finally found out how to shut you up. Give you a compliment."

A shaky laugh surprised Christina, but it felt good. "Those weren't exactly compliments, but I'll take it." She suddenly felt lighter, as though some of the guilt she carried with her daily sloughed away. "You're the first people to say that."

"So I gather."

"We heard a different story in Azakistan," Tag said. "Sorry, but when you stepped in to help, we wanted to know who you were."

"Of course." Her cheeks heated. To hide her reaction, she drained her water glass. Wine with lunch was the norm in this country, but to her it felt unnecessary.

Alex pushed back from the table. "Excellent grub. I'll go lay out the Bluetooth. Bluetooths? Blueteeth?"

"Knucklehead." Mace rolled his eyes.

Deni excused herself as well, and the rest of the team drifted out one by one, until only Gabe remained. Christina rose, anxious to leave as well.

"That was a carefully sanitized story you just told," he said just as she reached the doorway. "I'm more curious about the parts you conveniently left out."

# Chapter Nine

CHRISTINA TURNED HER head, but he noticed she didn't bother to deny it. "What I left out was irrelevant."

His voice dropped as his temper rose. "I'm your team leader, however temporary this arrangement is. I decide what's relevant."

Anger flashed through her eyes. "So what about you, hotshot? Did it ever occur to you that I might also want to know who the hell I'm trusting with my life? What's your story, huh? Where did you grow up? What made you decide to join the Army? Did *you* ever mess up on a mission?"

His head reared back. What?

She laughed her fury. "No, I can see it never even occurred to you. It's all about you, isn't it? As long as Gabe Morgan gets his way, everything's fine."

She turned to stalk out, and slammed headlong into Gavin. He steadied her with his hands on her arms, a carefully neutral expression on his face. Christina took a step back.

"What?" Gabe snapped.

Gavin actually had the nerve to shoot him a grin. So much

for keeping his emotions to himself. "Time to rock and roll, boss. Unless we're scrubbing the hospital visit?"

Christina hurried through the door. "No. I can be ready in ten minutes."

He didn't even know what to say about her accusations. If he was being honest with himself, the criticism had validity. Sure, he liked control. What operator didn't?

Christina had changed into her princess clothes by the time the team was done with their communications checks. This time, she made no protest as they exited the back way and climbed into an unmarked car. Apparently, she realized how close the toss-up had been about allowing her this visit.

They wove through narrow streets, taking lesser-known roads and doubling back several times to see if they were being followed. Their destination was public knowledge, but a tail would give them more data to work with. Possibly even a look at their enemy. Christina spent the time staring out the window, commenting on the architecture and the variety and beauty of flowers blooming in window boxes. He muttered something about the town being pretty. Clean and well-kept, despite its age.

She surprised him again when she obeyed his command to stay in the car until his men were in place. Mace settled into the overwatch position they'd identified, and the rest of them cleared a path through the journalists and cameras.

Once he was satisfied, he held her door open and offered her his hand. Before his eyes, she transformed into Princess Véronique de Savoie. She placed the tips of her fingers in his palm, swinging her sleek legs out and rising with regal presence. Constantly scanning the small group, he urged her forward even as she smiled for the cameras.

She swept through the automatic doors. He and his team stepped far enough back to give her room, but close enough to react should anything happen. A tall man with classically Italian features stepped forward and bowed.

"Your Royal Highness," he said, eyes bright. "I'm Elia Magnoli, hospital administrator. We are honored by your visit. Um, I was assured by the Private Secretary's Office that we could speak in English? I don't speak French and Felicity is Welsh."

"Yes, of course." Christina offered a graceful hand. "I 'ave been looking forward to spending time with the children."

The bureaucrat shook it gently, then turned to the other two people in the foyer. "May I introduce our Chief of Medicine, Francois d'Ammet, and Chief of Oncology, Felicity Bevan?"

Christina shook each hand in turn, smiling warmly at them. "It is a pleasure to meet you. I am very interested to see what you 'ave created here."

The oncology wing of the hospital had opened only three months before. His team had compiled detailed bios of the three standing in front of him, but Gabe still did not relax as they walked toward the elevators.

Christina lifted a hand in his direction. "This is my bodyguard, Gabriel Morgan."

The administrator's face creased in concern. "I was distressed to hear about the attack. It's terrible. Just terrible."

"But I am unhurt," Christina said, laying a hand along Magnoli's forearm. "And Gabriel, 'e shall ensure that I stay that way, yes?"

Over the next two hours, she toured the facility, making the appropriate approving noises. When it came to the wards of children fighting various cancers, she moved among them, taking the time to get to know them. Sitting down with a group in a common area, she read stories to them and answered questions about the life of a royal, even fabricating a story about a dancing tree that had the children giggling. In the end, she distributed the plastic crowns the chief of oncology provided, declaring each and every one a prince or princess. They departed among beams and hugs and kisses.

If she was playing a role, she was the best damned actress in history. Gabe staked his reputation he was seeing the real Christina. Which worried him, because she'd shown herself this afternoon to be sensitive, kind, and caring. He could like this side of her, if he let himself. Maybe she was different?

His inner laugh felt bitter on his tongue. Yeah, right.

It wasn't until she was safely back in the limousine that she lost her smile.

She stared out the window at the hospital until it faded from view. Even then, she kept her face turned away from Gabe. A finger discreetly dabbed the corner of her eye.

"Sad, huh?"

She nodded, finally turning to look at him. Her face was solemn. "It's heartbreaking. If I came back next year, a third of those sweet children wouldn't be there anymore."

What could he say? She was right. Cancer devastated the body, and watching children fighting for their lives caused a churn in his gut. There had been moments during the afternoon when his heart had clenched and tugged, as well. "They're getting great care, though, and medicine makes advances all the time. There could be a breakthrough."

It was inadequate, but she nodded anyway. Before he could think about what he was doing, Gabe reached out and drew her into his arms. She tensed. He started to pull back, but then she relaxed against him.

Gavin, in the driver's seat, met Gabe's eyes, then pushed the button that raised a dark window between them. He simply held her, not speaking. Anyway, he doubted could have croaked out anything meaningful in that moment. Her softness snuggled against his hard chest felt unbelievably good.

But that changed nothing. Preternaturally strong Samson of biblical fame had two weaknesses. Sure, his hair. But he also had the misfortune to be attracted to untrustworthy women. Both his first and second loves had betrayed him. Gabe had thought Leanne loved him, but she'd sold him down the river. He wasn't giving Christina the chance. Liking children didn't mean he could rely on her.

Still, he stroked her hair, careful not to muss it. It felt soft and silky in his hand. She rested against his chest for another moment, then pulled back far enough to look at him. The troubled look in her eyes nearly undid him.

He used a thumb to tuck a strand of hair behind her ears. So subtly he almost missed it, she leaned into his touch. His fingers stilled.

Her lips parted as she looked at him. What was going through her head? He couldn't tell. Expecting her to pull free of his arms at any moment, he waited, fingers resting beside her ear. Was he supposed to say something?

Her gaze dropped to his mouth. The air left his lungs with a whoosh; he was too experienced a man to mistake this new expression. Her sadness caused her to seek other comfort. Would it help her? Knowing her, she would no doubt blame him and castigate herself later. Though it pained him to do it, he forced himself to push her back gently and let go. "It's okay, Christina . . ."

The air between them electrified. He forgot what he was saying as her body softened and his mouth dried out like the Gobi. Her breath came in small pants as she dropped her stare to her lap, hands twisting together. "I'm sorry. I shouldn't be . . ."

Cursing himself for every kind of fool, Gabe slipped a finger under her chin, raising it until she looked into his eyes. Then, lowering his head, he kissed her.

ALL RATIONAL THOUGHT fled. Christina's head dropped back onto his shoulder as his lips, warm and soft, brushed across hers. When no second kiss came, she peeped up at him. He stared at her, frozen, conflict written all over his face. Without thinking about anything but the fragility of life, she nipped his chin. His breath blew warm on her face as his mouth parted.

She slipped a hand around the back of his neck, her fingers shaking. His eyes closed on a groan as their lips met, urgent and scorching, his heart hammering triple time in her ear as he enticed her to open for him. She did, and his tongue immediately stroked into her mouth.

He tugged her onto his lap. Her bottom nestled against him, where she could feel the very large proof of his desire. His hands came up to frame her face, tangled into her hair, and angled her mouth so he could plunder it more thoroughly. He licked along the roof of her mouth and she shuddered at the intense sensation. She traced his shoulders and flattened her palms on his chest. What the hell was she doing? He lumped her in with the rest of the CIA as an adversary. But her traitorous body shook with the need to get closer to him. His hands slid down her arms and pressed her hands into his chest.

"God, Christina, you are so damned sexy," he groaned.

Before she could respond, the car slowed. They must have arrived back at the palace. Horrified, Christina wriggled back to her side of the car, ignoring his hiss as she dragged her bottom across his erection. Frantically, she smoothed her hair and clothes, praying no one would be able to tell.

Gavin seemed slow to come around to her door. Did he know what they had been doing? Heat rose in her cheeks. When Gavin finally opened the door, Gabe slid out the other side. Tourists and journalists hovered around the limousine. She forced herself to slow down, to behave as Ronnie would. This time, though, she could not force herself to acknowledge the crowd's applause. Walking with what dignity she could muster, she did not stop until the House Guard opened the princess's apartment door for her. She sailed inside and made a beeline to her bedroom, where she shut the door and locked it.

What the hell had she just done?

She'd made some boneheaded moves in her day, but kissing Gabe Morgan had to take the cake. He would use it against her, no doubt. But he'd kissed her back. Why had he? To comfort her, maybe. Seeing her upset, he'd been moved to offer solace.

She plopped down on the sofa and curled her legs under her, heedless of the expensive outfit she wore. And then she tore it off and threw it onto the bed. The underwear followed. Stepping into Ronnie's shower, she scrubbed herself to within an inch of her life, but it did very little to alter her sour mood. Changing into her own casual clothing helped.

She was tempted to ignore the knock when it came. The person at the other end of the door persisted, and she finally yanked it open.

"What?"

Deni Van Praet actually took à step back. "I'm sorry to disturb you," she said stiffly. "I need to pack your wardrobe for our trip to Grasvlakten."

"I'm so sorry," Christina mumbled, grabbing the older woman's hand and almost yanking her into the room. "I didn't mean to snap at you."

Deni disengaged her hand and straightened her suit jacket. "Did something go awry at the hospital?"

Tempted to say yes, to blame the hospital administration, the children, anything, she instead shook her head. "No, the children were fantastic," she said, her innate honesty coming to the fore. "Upbeat, optimistic, no matter how bad the prognosis or how much pain they were in. It was humbling, and I'm so glad I went. It seemed to mean a lot to them."

Deni's face relaxed. "I'm so pleased. The cause is dear to Ronnie's heart."

Overwhelmed with the need to confide what she'd done, she collapsed onto the sofa. "I kissed Gabe."

If Deni was surprised, it didn't show. She came to sit next to Christina. "You regret it?"

"Hell, yes! He doesn't like me. Deni, I don't know how I'm supposed to work with this team," she admitted. "Gabe makes his dislike plain. I was making headway to being accepted as one of them, but . . ."

Deni made no comment about Christina's casual sweat pants and camisole, nor about the heap of Véronique's clothes on the bed. "He watches you all the time."

"He's just doing his job."

Deni chuckled. "I do not mean he follows you. I mean, his eyes are on you. Constantly."

That brought her up short. What? "Maybe he's checking to make sure I don't mess this up."

Deni patted her hand and stood. "I have no reservations whatsoever about your ability to accomplish this ruse as the princess. You have her kind heart, her grace, her intelligence. You have adopted her mannerisms as your own. Your bodyguards have devised a plan to, 'ow you say, smoke out the bad guys?"

It was ridiculous the amount of relief she felt at this affirmation. "Really?"

"Yes, truly."

Christina blew out a breath. "I'm in this for however long it takes, I promise."

"And I will aid you in whatever way I can. Together we are formidable, eh?"

Christina beamed at the secretary. "Well, then. Let's get packed for Phase Two. Operation Nabourg."

For the next hour, Deni helped her pick and choose the outfits she would bring. One for the journey to Grasvlakten. One for dinner that evening, another for the next day. The crowning jewel, her gown for the anniversary party. Then there were handbags, shoes, makeup, and jewelry. By the end of it, Christina was exhausted.

"Being a freaking princess is a full-time job," she said, sinking with a tired sigh onto the bed. Three large cases and a small jewelry box sat near the door.

Deni gave a small smile. "And now, it is time to rebuild your strength. Shall we go to dinner?"

# Chapter Ten

"And therefore, we, as leaders and champions of Europe's economic growth, must support initiatives that will secure a stable future for our next generations. I urge you to vote in favor of expanded oil drilling in Europe's north-central regions. Thank you."

Almost as one, the room rose to their feet, the applause genuine. Gabe restrained himself from joining in. Christina had perfectly captured Ronnie's vivacious passion. The speech had been well-written, but she'd brought it to life. He could almost believe she supported the princess's cause. Like the hospital visit the previous day, she commanded attention while remaining gracious and charming.

As planned, the senior librarian at the Bibliothèque Nationale de Concordia shook her hand and took over the podium, thanking Princess Véronique for her patronage both of the library and of the Women's Caucus on Economic Diversity. Christina inclined her head, gave a regal wave to the room at large, and followed Gabe and Deni out of the room.

"Very well spoken," Deni said. "Princess Véronique herself could not have done better."

Gabe nodded to Tag, whom he'd placed in the corridor outside of the auditorium. Tag fell in behind them. They picked up Alex inside the front door. "Any change?"

"The crowd's gotten bigger," Mace reported in his ear. "They're itching for her to come out."

"We should go out the back," Alex said.

Gabe hesitated. That would be the move if this were a real protection detail. Christina had nailed it, though, when she insisted they put her out there as bait for the assassin. He knew she was right; it was the whole point of the deception. Still . . . he didn't like it. Not one bit.

"What's going on?" Christina asked.

During the speech, she'd taken off the Bluetooth earpiece, so she hadn't heard Mace's continuous reports of the anti-drilling protestors gathering outside the National Library. Now she inserted it into her ear and repeated the question.

"A group of farmers are protesting your stance on oil drilling," Gavin said. "I guess not everyone here loves you."

Gabe grimaced. "Anyone stand out?"

"Negative. I've been watching them the whole time. There are reporters, too. Whoops. Police just showed up. At least we'll have crowd control."

"Gabe," Christina said firmly. "Mace has overwatch and Gavin has the limousine. We discussed this. I'm ready."

Respect for her courage grew inside him. He made his decision. "Okay. We're coming out the front door now. Alex, go coordinate with the police."

About a hundred protesters milled around outside the library, carrying flags and signs, chanting and singing the Concordian national anthem. They surged forward as they caught sight of their princess, and the shouting increased.

Gabe and Tag pushed Christina behind them, closing in so she could barely see between them. The half-dozen police officers ran in front of the crowd, arms outstretched to keep them back. One spoke into his shoulder mike. Calling for reinforcements?

"Save our food," Gavin translated. "No more drilling. That sort of garbage."

Christina said, "It's not garbage to them. It's their livelihood."

"There are too many of them," Gavin said. "They're all around the limousine. I haven't had to break any heads yet, but the afternoon's young."

A reporter rushed forward, thrusting a microphone toward her, the cameraman right behind. Others followed. Gabe stepped two paces forward, barring the reporter from access. Rapid French followed.

Gavin translated. "How do you respond to accusations that you're in bed with big oil co . . . dammit! You get off my hood! Now!"

"Gavin, bring the limo up," Gabe ordered. "We can't walk out with this crowd in the way. They're too rowdy. We can't stay here."

The crowd started pushing forward, the voices becoming angry.

"Four o'clock," Mace said tersely. "Woman, red coat, pulling something out of her pocket."

"Shit." Tag leaped the steps four at a time, zeroing in on the woman and bearing down on her like a freight train. She saw him coming and turned to run. He caught her by the back of her coat, spinning her around and grabbing her hand. Dipping into her pocket, still controlling her movements, he came up with an apple, bruised and moldy. Swearing, he released the woman, pointed a finger at her nose, and said, "Go home."

"Target neutralized," Mace reported dryly. "Fruit of choice is a rotten apple. Better than a tomato. At least it won't splatter."

"This crowd's pissed. What the hell's setting them off?" Gabe asked, frustration in his voice. "We can't stand out here forever. Gavin, where are you?"

"Target." Mace's voice tensed. "Eleven o'clock. Man, five-eight, goatee, burn scar on his left cheek."

"What's he doing?" Christina asked. She scanned the crowd.

"Nothing. He's across the street, sitting in his car. Watching."

"Snap a pic," Gabe ordered. "We need to know who it is."

"Doing it now. And . . . emailed it to Trevor."

The chanting grew louder. Emboldened, the crowd pushed closer and closer to the library steps. It was getting ugly.

"I think if the assassin were here, he would have done something by now," Christina said.

"What the hell are they saying, Gavin?" Tag asked, returning to Christina's side.

The limo came into view from the parking lot, creeping along, Gavin laying on the horn. Men and women began to bang on the hood and roof. "'No big oil. Farmers unite. Don't let us starve.' That's a good one," Gavin reported through the Bluetooth. "And then there's one poor little old lady in a walker, directly in front of me, who wants to save the wildlife from oil spills. I think I'll run her over."

Before Christina could open her mouth to protest, Gavin gunned the engine and let the limousine jump forward a foot. The woman, bent over in a bulky coat, dove out of the way, her wig coming off as she scrambled to her feet. She began to scream obscenities as she shook her fist.

"Magically no longer needs the walker," Christina said in disgust. "What's she? Twenty? Twenty-five?"

Several more police cars arrived, driving directly onto the cement and blocking the steps as they angled in. The crowd milled about. Several lobbed apples or potatoes in their direction. Gavin stopped the limousine and jumped out, physically shoving several people out of the way until he was able to open the rear passenger door. With Gabe shielding her with his body, she climbed down step by step and ducked into the car.

Uniformed police began to swarm the area, pushing the crowd back. Someone on a loudspeaker told them, Gavin reported, to disperse or be arrested. Gavin didn't wait to see if they obeyed. He drove them straight across the concrete apron and onto the street.

Christina turned to look out the back window. "Well, that didn't work. Where's my assassin?"

# Chapter Eleven

GABE KNOCKED SOFTLY at Christina's bedroom door. Everything was set. Cars packed, team deployed, path cleared of all unwanted onlookers. It was time for Christina to resume impersonating the Crown Princess of Concordia.

After Wednesday's confrontation with rioting farmers, he'd scrubbed the construction site ribbon-cutting. Christina had grit, he'd give her that. She'd stayed calm and focused, despite the impending riot.

Yesterday had been peaceful, but now was time for what he considered to be the most dangerous part of this mission—the drive to Grasvlakten, where they would be out in the open and exposed.

There was no answer. When he tried the knob, he found the door had been locked. To keep him out?

He'd dreamed of her last night. Eyes sparking, fast-talking and perceptive, she'd visited him in his sleep, sliding in next to him like warm silk in a sizzling fantasy. Whispering hot promises in his ear, she tormented him until he twisted and thrashed in the sheets. He woke frustrated and unfulfilled.

Shit.

He pulled a small leather case from his jacket and went to work on the lock. In a few seconds, the lock on the door snicked open. Without apology, he walked into the room. Tough if she didn't like it. She should have answered the door.

He found her sprawled across the bed, clad only in a silk robe that had parted at the waist, arms outflung, dead asleep. Her face was smooth and soft. Gabe resisted the urge to climb onto the bed with her and pull her into his arms again. Jesus, he was becoming obsessed with her—it had to stop. He'd thought her beautiful back in Azakistan, but this forced proximity was so much better—and so much worse. Reluctantly, he bent down and stroked a hand across her hair. Her eyes opened, confused by sleep.

"Why are you dressed?"

Startled, he jerked back. "What?"

As she fully woke and awareness returned, her face closed down, leaving him with no idea what she was thinking. "Nothing. I was dreaming. Nothing. Is it time to go? Let's go." She swung her legs over the side of the bed and stood, wobbling a little. His hand shot out and gripped her upper arm, steadying her.

She'd been dreaming about him? Naked?

"I'm awake now," she said, easing her arm free. "Sorry. Thanks. Give me five minutes to dress." She closed the door in his face.

When she finally emerged, she had transformed once again into Princess Véronique, wearing a silky white blouse, peach wraparound miniskirt, and six-inch heels. She slid designer sunglasses onto her nose. He discovered he preferred plain Christina.

This woman was above him in every way. Inaccessible, regal, untouchable. And he knew he wanted very much to touch her again.

They made their way down the back staircase to the limousine. This time, Gabe sat in front, riding shotgun. He'd put Alex in the follow car. Tag guarded the midpoint of their route, and Mace sat overwatch at the three-quarters mark. They were as ready as they were going to be. Christina slid into the back next to Deni, and the two vehicles pulled out.

They made the drive in virtual silence. While Gavin focused on the road, Gabe continuously scanned the countryside. The route he had chosen and scouted wound through farmland, avoiding the forests and high areas. It took them a bit out of the way, but it was worth it for the security advantage it gave them.

As they drove, he processed the information being relayed by Alex, behind them, and Tag, miles ahead. He'd positioned Mace at the critical point, where two highways and three local roads crossed. That was still half an hour away.

"Nothing unusual headed your way," Tag said. "Small cars, farmers. A tractor going like thirty miles an hour. Thing's booking."

In his earpiece, Alex choked out a laugh. "That's nothing. I got passed by an old farm truck piled to the rim with crates of chickens. Cluck, cluck."

"Sounds like dinner to me," Gavin said.

Gabe ignored them. His primary worry were the windmills that dotted the countryside. Three of them would be close enough for a good sniper to fire on them.

Ahead of them a herd of sheep milled around the road, a harried young shepherd trying to get them out of the way. Gavin braked. Three cars behind him, the farm truck with the chickens laid on his horn. The shepherd gaped at the official flags adorning the limousine. Gabe tensed, hand clenched around the shotgun at his feet. It was doubtful this was any sort of trap, but he couldn't afford to let his guard down. Finally, the shepherd coaxed and bullied the sheep off the road far enough for the limousine to drive around them. Gabe did not relax until the herd was far behind them.

"Black Renault just passed me," Tag reported. "Driver alone in front. Tinted windows, so I couldn't see if anyone was in the back."

It didn't necessarily mean anything. There had been any number of vehicles on the roads, and Renaults were common enough in Europe. "Speed?"

"Normal. Staying with traffic."

"Roger that. Alex, close distance to one klick." At one kilometer, he would be just over half a mile behind them. Close enough to react if an attack came from either direction.

"Got it."

He checked the rearview until he saw Alex's nondescript Audi. With the oncoming traffic, he seemed to be having trouble getting around the damned chicken truck. The Renault appeared ahead of them. "Christina, Deni, get down, please."

"Okay." A glance in the rearview showed them shifting to lie sideways on the back seat, with Christina covering Deni's body with her own.

The road had cleared behind him. Alex pulled into the left lane, but the farm truck drifted left at the same time to straddle both lanes, making it impossible for him to pass.

"Fuckwad," he said calmly. "If you're going to go that fast with crates full of chickens, learn to stay on your own side of the road."

Christina poked her head above the seat to look out the back window. "Alex," she whispered into her earpiece. "That truck is matching your speed."

It was true. In the other direction, the Renault was slowing. "Alex, get past that truck. Now. Whatever it takes." Gabe unholstered his Glock and passed it through the divider to Christina, who left the back seat long enough to accept it. "Keep your head down. This is just in case." He canted an eye at her, a flicker of humor in it. "Careful, champ. Don't shoot me by mistake."

Despite the worry in her eyes, she arched a saucy brow. "Don't worry. I'm an excellent shot. If I shoot you, it won't be by accident."

As he turned back to face what he was certain was an attempted ambush, Gabe found a grin tugging at his mouth.

SQUASHED SIDEWAYS IN the back seat and practically lying on top of Deni, Christina could only follow what was happening by the terse communication flowing through Gabe's team. She touched her earpiece, grateful that Gabe had given her the Bluetooth.

"Chicken truck is blocking me," Alex said. "Keeps swerving in front of me."

"Renault is speeding up again," Gavin bit out. "I can't take this beast off road here. There are ditches on both sides."

Gabe cursed. "They couldn't have timed it better."

In other words, someone either knew or had researched the terrain well enough to set a trap for the limousine. Christina shivered, gripping the handle of the Glock a little tighter. She debated risking another peek. As though reading her mind, Gabe twisted in his seat and pinned her with a look. "Not one muscle."

She hated not seeing for herself what was happening. Reluctantly, though, she nodded. The team could not be distracted by her actions right now. Still, if push came to shove, she could help. She popped the magazine on the Glock. Fifteen rounds of .40 caliber ammunition. Not a lot, but it could be a lot worse. Like, if she weren't armed at all.

"What is happening?" Deni asked. Without a Bluetooth device, she could only hear the two in the front.

"Shh," Christina murmured. "Just hold on. We're going to be fine." She hoped.

"Gavin, floor it." The stately old limousine leapt forward, shaking and groaning as it hit sixty, sixty-five, seventy. At the same time, Alex swore. There was a squeal of brakes through her earpiece, the unmistakable sound of metal impacting metal, and then the wild clucking of what seemed like hundreds of chickens.

"Alex, report." Gabe's voice was calm in her ear, a direct contrast to her own pounding heart. "Alex. Are you mobile?"

"Yeah," Alex said finally, voice slightly unsteady. "Damned car's covered in chickens. Gimme thirty seconds to . . ."

"Shit! Brace for impact!" Gavin shouted, pushing the old car to further acceleration. "Asshole blocked the road."

Christina slipped out of the shoulder portion of the seat belt so it wouldn't cut her neck when the two cars collided, and braced her arms to cover Deni. The ripping sound of gunfire preceded the driver's window shattering and a lurch as the limousine swerved. She closed her eyes briefly. Deni squeaked.

Gabe levered the shotgun out his window and fired, the blast nearly deafening her in the enclosed space. He pumped the action and fired twice more, then the limousine swerved, skidded, and slid. Deni cried out, a terrified sound, and covered her head with her arms. Somehow the tires found traction again, even though the limousine seemed to be moving sideways. Christina brought her forearms vertically in front of her face to protect her head. The impact, when it came, slammed her forward. Another rip of automatic fire. She heard the bullets slam into the metal of the car. There was shouting, and a scream.

"Got him on the other side," Alex said. Christina caught the flash of blue as the Audi reached them. "Nope, they're moving. You swung them around enough. Veer left to get back to the road. Gavin. Left."

The limousine shuddered as Gavin wrestled it around and got it back onto the asphalt. "They're not pursuing."

"Nope," came the cheerful reply as Alex moved in behind them. "I almost clipped one, but the fuckhead jumped out of the way too quick."

"You're still twenty minutes from me," Mace broke in. "Do you want me to come back?"

"Negative. Maintain position. They left the chickens. Three men. The Renault's heading back toward Parvenière."

Christina brushed a hand over her hip and down her leg. Glass slid from her skirt to the floorboards. She lifted herself off Deni and slipped her hand into the older woman's, pulling her upright. "It's okay, Deni. It's over."

Gavin slowed to a more reasonable speed, so the air rushing through his shattered window didn't roar. Deni slowly uncurled herself and sat up. Her normally coiffed hair stuck out in all directions, and her suit was rumpled. Of all of them, she looked the most like she'd been to war.

Gabe turned in his seat to look the women over from head to foot. "Are you all right?"

"Yes." Christina brushed more glass from her hair. "Deni?"

"I am uninjured."

Gabe turned back toward the front, leaving her to deal with Deni's pale face and shaky voice. She gave the woman's hand a squeeze. "You were very brave."

"Rally point echo, guys. Let's regroup."

"Here?" Mace asked, startled.

"Yeah. Clearly our route was compromised. Taking the back roads didn't work. I want us out in the open now," Gabe said. "With you on overwatch."

Christina agreed with his strategy. However the men had found them, they couldn't afford to be boxed in anywhere. Alex followed Gavin in the limousine. About five miles down the road, Tag eased in ahead of them.

Rally point echo turned out to be a BP gas station and Exki grab-and-go restaurant on a small hill at the juncture of Route Provinciale 23 and Route Nationale 12. There was no sign of Mace or his car, but Christina took one look around and knew he was on the roof of the restaurant, either behind the cornice or the decorative raised area over the front entrance. Gabe directed them to the far end of the parking lot, where they parked and gathered around him. Mace listened in from his overwatch position.

"What happened?" Gabe asked. Christina thought it was obvious, but his team knew exactly what he was asking, and each outlined the events from his perspective. He listened intently and without interruption. When they were finished, he nodded.

Christina rubbed her arms, though it was a warm day. Gabe gave her a searching look. She lifted her chin. No, she wasn't going into shock. One side of his mouth quirked up. Deni stood quietly beside her, seemingly composed but for a fine trembling in her hands.

"Our security was compromised," Gabe said. "Someone knew

exactly where to come at us so we couldn't get off the road." There were nods or mutters of assent. "Gavin, that was a hell of a maneuver with what's basically a refrigerator on wheels. I don't know anybody else who could've pulled that off."

"Aw, shucks," Gavin said, ducking his head. "It's true. I'm the best driver you'll ever know."

Gabe shot him a chiding look. "On the other hand, no one knew our route. Only us." His glance encompassed all of them, which both gratified and surprised Christina. "So how did they find out?"

Christina could only think of one way, but she couldn't seem to gather enough moisture in her mouth to utter the words. Gavin did it for her.

"I checked for bombs on the limo. I didn't check for trackers." No amusement tinged his tone this time. He sounded as grim as all of them looked. "The Household Guard placed a man outside the garage. No one in without authorization. I checked the list myself. Only cleared personnel went in. Fuck."

Gabe looked unsurprised. "We have to reassess the situation. Unlike the first attempt, which was clumsy and amateurish, these guys were sophisticated, and clearly had access where they shouldn't have. Gavin, find me that GPS tracker."

Christina's brows pulled in. "They were trying to stop the limousine. Not blow it up. Not kill the princess."

"Yeah," Tag said. "But they were trigger happy, quick enough." He glanced pointedly at the limo's shattered window and the bullet holes. "And they had to know we'd check for incendiaries."

"How could they have set this up so quickly?" Christina asked.

"They reconnoitered the routes," Gabe said at once. "It's the only explanation. Once we hit this stretch of road, the car following us must have signaled to the Renault. Alex, you didn't make a tail?"

"There wasn't one." Alex said, a faint defensiveness in his voice. "I'd've spotted it."

Gabe gave him a reassuring squeeze on the shoulder. "I know, kid. I shouldn't even have asked. They must have come from one of the other roads once they knew which way we were headed."

Gavin wriggled out from under the vehicle. The GPS device was no more than four inches tall and barely an inch thick. He wrapped his hand around it and squeezed, as though he could crumble it into dust. "Tucked in behind the exhaust manifold. Clever."

Christina grimaced. "So one of the Household Guards took a bribe and let someone in, or someone the Guard trusted went in."

"It could have been someone from my office." Deni looked more shaken at that prospect than from the attack. "Perhaps I inadvertently revealed something?"

"I doubt it," Gabe said. "You didn't know our route. The most your office could have let slip is that we were making the trip to Grasvlakten instead of canceling it. Besides, there are only a handful of ways to get there. For all we know, they had an ambush set up on each one." He pulled his phone from his front pocket and hit a button.

"Carswell."

"It's Gabe."

"Afternoon. All right?"

"Yeah, good. You're on speaker. We had visitors."

"Was anyone hurt?"

"No. Anything unusual at your end?" Gabe kneaded the back of his neck.

"Not a thing. What happened?"

Gabe filled him in. "Any updates on Ronnie's list?"

"It's a long list, but we're making progress. So far, nothing stands out. I did identify your mystery man from the protest, however. Ronnie knows him. His name is Émile Bonnet. He's heavy into agriculture and the preservation of natural resources, particularly of endangered species found only in the mountains. Influential, but not a groundbreaker. He got the scar on his cheek in the field artillery during Operation Granby in the Persian Gulf. What you Yanks call Operation Desert Storm."

Gabe frowned. "So he opposes Ronnie on oil drilling."

"He's an activist." Trevor sounded apologetic. "He has no history of violence. I don't see him as the shooter. I'll dig deeper, though."

"Good," Gabe said. "All right. Let's check in again tomorrow before the party."

"Cheers then." Trevor hung up.

"All right. Let's mount up and head straight to Grasvlakten. Secrecy didn't work. Now let's have a show of force." Gabe curled his lip at the limousine. "Starting by replacing that piece of shit with a vehicle with some actual security protection."

Christina didn't point out that Concordia probably didn't have Euros in the budget for new, expensive limousines with bullet-proof glass and heavy armor. In all their long history, there had been very few violent attempts against any monarch or member of the royal family. The country was peaceful. Still, maybe Véronique's fiancé, Trevor's cousin, could persuade the British government to make a gift of it.

Gavin used an Asp tactical baton to clear the rest of the glass from the shot-out window. On cursory glance, it simply looked as though the window was open. There wasn't anything they could do about the bullet holes, however. Mace appeared behind them, carrying a rifle case. Gabe circled his finger near his shoulder, and his team dispersed to their cars. Christina and Deni once again slid into the rear of the limo. In moments, their four-car convoy was on the highway, the gas station receding behind them.

IT NEARED SEVEN o'clock when they pulled up to the wide, circular drive, past a comparatively simple single-level fountain with nine spouts shooting water skyward. The estate house loomed, venerable and pitted, and Gabe groaned. Mace echoed the sound.

"Gawd damn," he said. "Dat moodee goan make de misere."

"English, Cajun," Gabe said. "I don't speak gibberish."

Mace cursed. "Where the hell am I supposed to find overwatch in *that*?"

From what Gabe could see in the front, six arched windows thrust toward them as they pulled up, connecting two enormous wings of the stately old mansion. Each wing sported gabled dormers and multiple chimneys. Mace was right; the roof was made up of hills and valleys as A-frames butted up against one another and the chimneys. Footing would be treacherous, and finding a tactical position with good visibility would be difficult.

An army of footmen swarmed the cars, faces showing varying levels of shock and horror at the damage done to the limo. They muttered to one another as they lifted out suitcases and duffel bags, carrying them inside and forcing Gabe's team to hurry to catch up. One held the door for Christina, and she dipped her chin in gratitude, sailing past the servants as though she'd been born with the proverbial silver spoon in her mouth. An angular man dressed in formal livery met them just inside the entryway, his thin mustache giving him a vaguely sinister look. He bowed to Christina, but his eyes darted between the damaged vehicles and the Delta Force operators.

"*Welkom bij Stenen Huis*," the man intoned, training overriding curiosity.

"It would please me if you speak English while we are here," Christina replied, her gentle words nevertheless an order. "My bodyguards speak neither Dutch nor French. I do not wish them discomfited in any way."

"Your Highness," the man said, bowing again. "Yes, certainly. I will ensure the servants are made aware." He turned to the small group of men, and raised his voice. "Welcome to Stone House," he said, enunciating each word. "We are honored to have Her Royal Highness, and her guests, in attendance." By the end, he was nearly shouting.

Gabe stopped himself from rolling his eyes, and caught Christina biting the inside of her lip. He grinned, sharing the joke, and her eyes twinkled back at him. Even severe Deni Van Praet was struggling not to smile.

Christina stepped forward and placed a hand on the man's forearm. He immediately shut up. "You are Meneer Hendrik Rietveld, *ja*?"

An almost worshipful expression transformed the man from villain to champion from one second to the next. "*Ja, mijn prinses.* I mean, yes, Your Royal Highness. I am honored and humbled that you would know who I am."

"With respect, Meneer Rietveld," Gabe said. Enough of this kissy-ass shit. "Would you be so kind as to show the princess to her room? The journey has been . . . tiring."

The butler immediately complied, turning to lead the way into the left-hand wing. "Of course. But what in heaven happened to your automobiles? Was there another attack? My princess, shall I fetch a doctor?"

"No one is injured, Meneer Rietveld." Before Gabe could motion her to zip her mouth, Christina continued smoothly, "We did have an unfortunate incident with a truckload of chickens. I am happy to say that we fared better."

Clever girl. Put just the right amount of truth into your lies. They probably taught her that at Langley. His lip curled at the thought of that den of liars and thieves. And she was part of it, he reminded himself. They all lied for a living. He'd learned that lesson the hard way.

He found himself hesitating. She'd been up front with him about her mission in Baghdad. She hadn't shied away from taking blame, or calling him out when she thought he was wrong. He respected those traits.

His mother certainly had no respect or regard for her family. She'd traveled constantly, often gone for months at a time. Never there for his Little League or football games, or when he won State in track-and-field. His father had used her absence as an excuse to drink and throw Gabe and his brother around. Around the time he became a young teenager, he'd become convinced that she was having an affair, that she even had another family in a different city. The truth had been so much worse.

The butler pulled his face in doubtful lines. "I understand, Your Royal Highness. But . . . those holes . . ."

"The garage will have to be off limits to everybody. Drivers, staff, friends, everyone," Gabe said. "I'm very sorry, but starting now. If you need transport, you'll have to park it outside."

"Outside?" Rietveld drew himself up and widened his eyes. "I have never heard of such a thing. Lord Nabourg's driver will not be happy."

"I'm concerned about someone tampering with the limousine. We're here to keep the princess safe. I know you want that, too. I'm counting on your help, Mr. Rietveld." Gabe's patience was wearing thin. The butler stopped gaping at him, thank God, and moved farther into the building. They went up a set of stairs to an open balcony.

"My Lord and Lady Nabourg will receive you for dinner at eight-thirty," Rietveld said to Christina and Deni. He stopped at the second door and opened it with something of a flourish. When Christina would have walked in, Gabe put an arm out in front of her, shooting a warning glance over his shoulder. He motioned Gavin and Alex inside. As they cleared the room, he turned to the butler.

"I'm afraid Princess Véronique will eat in her quarters this evening."

"Certainly." The butler's voice and face fell. "They will be disappointed. Not many visit anymore."

Gabe ignored him. They'd have plenty of guests tomorrow night, at the party. "As we discussed yesterday, sir, we're going to need full access to the villa."

"Of course. I'm happy to show you around."

According to his research, one nurse aide, the butler, and the driver lived here full time. Three others came in daily; two maids and a cook. "Thank you. We'll need to verify what you've already shared; where everyone sleeps and works, daily routines, and so forth. One of us will always be with the princess."

The butler kept his face expressionless. "Yes, sir."

Gavin returned to his side. "All clear."

"Where do you have my team, Mr. Rietveld?"

The butler motioned to the room to the right of Christina's. "Your man was quite specific when we spoke last week," he said, nodding toward Mace. "You are to surround the princess at all times." He drew himself to his full height, nearly eye-to-eye with Gabe. "You must not do so when you are in the presence of the Nabourgs, however. It would be improper."

Gabe didn't give two shits about offending some semi-important has-beens. Christina, however, inclined her head sagely. "Of course. I will not insult my grandaunt in such a way, you can be assured."

The man's eyes widened, and he practically hopped from foot to foot. "Princess Véronique, I meant no disrespect. I have only the highest regard for the royal family, and for you. I would never—"

"Meneer Rietveld, please relax. I took no offense." Christina's hand rose, then dropped. Gabe recognized the gesture. She'd been about to ruffle her hair.

Christina ended the awkward conversation by entering her room. Deni Van Praet went into the room to the left, footmen following her with what seemed like a mountain of suitcases.

Gabe turned to Rietveld. "Mr. Rietveld, I need to know if there are any last-minute changes to the guest list."

"Of course." The butler's lip curled ever so slightly as he met Gabe's eyes, in sharp contrast with his conversation with Christina. Guess the royal treatment didn't extend to the bodyguards. "There have been three changes. Mrs. Hawrelak is ill, so her husband will attend on his own. Lord Bonnet had originally declined, but found himself free to accept as of this morning. The third is Emma Van Beveren, the Lady Nabourg's great-granddaughter."

Something in the butler's voice alerted Gabe. "Coming or going?"

"Not attending. She has refused to come to an anniversary honoring a man who, erm, has not honored his wife."

"He had an affair?" Gabe choked out a laugh. "What is he, ninety?"

The butler allowed himself a small smile. "Well, he is rather elderly. How do you Americans put it? There is snow on the mountain, but a fire in the hearth?"

Close enough. Gabe whistled. "I'd take being that randy when I'm his age." Not that he condoned the infidelity. He gave his head a quick shake and got back to business. "What about the new arrival? Tell me about him."

Rietveld's face turned respectful. "He is Émile Denis Javier Bonnet, Second Earl Bonnet. He is one of the Prime Minister's most trusted advisors. It is a great honor that he's attending the Nabourg's soirée."

Gabe's instincts went on full alert. "He wasn't expected?"

"No. The king and queen were invited, naturally. Perhaps he is acting in their stead, as . . . as stand-up?"

"Stand in." Gabe nodded a dismissal. "Thank you, Mr. Rietveld. I know the princess appreciates both your help and your discretion."

The butler inclined his torso. "Both are my pleasure."

He stepped into Christina's room. The guest quarters, though spacious, were much smaller than their rooms at the palace. The main area was decorated in muted shades of green and gold, tasteful and modern. The furniture had clean, simple lines. A bookcase unit dominated one wall, with a large flat-screen television mounted inside. Rectangular end tables gave the room a distinctly twenty-first century look, as opposed to Ronnie's baroque style. An overstuffed leather sofa and love seat nestled together in the center of the room.

Gabe peeked into the bedroom. Good God! The thing was decorated wholly in deep yellows. Golden textured wallpaper, gold bedspread. Chandeliers, armchairs. Even the frame on the portrait was gilt. His lip curled. He much preferred the living room.

Christina stood by the bed, hands on her hips, looking around with an expression identical to Gabe's. "Barf," she said. "I'm sleeping on the sofa."

"Might be a tad crowded," Gabe said. He appreciated the sentiment, though. He wouldn't voluntarily sleep here, either.

"Excuse me?"

The hostility in her tone alerted Gabe to the fact that he hadn't told her about his decision to sleep in her room. "Uh—"

"No. Nope. Nuh-uh," she said. "You sleep with the rest of your team. I get some privacy."

Gabe ran a hand along the back of his neck. He needed to coordinate with her better. "You're not going to be alone until we catch this guy. Might as well resign yourself to it."

Christina's movements were jerky as she stalked past him. Gabe moved back, allowing her out of the barf-worthy room. Against his will, his gaze dropped to her ass as she strode away. Damn, the woman had a delicious body. His breathing deepened and a light sweat popped out of his pores. He adjusted himself discreetly as he followed her into the much calmer tones of the living room.

"I don't even want to see the bathroom," he said, trying to lighten the mood. "Probably all purple or orange or some shit."

"You can't sleep in here." Christina swung around to face him.

"I am." But he knew he'd get no sleep with her so close by, tucked under yellow blankets, dreaming of him. Naked. He dreamt about her, too.

"But why?" There was an edge to her voice that Gabe could only identify as desperation. "I want to be alone."

"I'm sorry; I should have told you. Just ignore me. I'm pretty good at disappearing."

She snorted. "I'd notice you no matter what." She clamped her mouth tight, as though sorry she'd let the words out. "I mean, you make a big road bump. And you annoy me."

No, he didn't. She felt as drawn to him as he was to her. Neither were comfortable with that reality, but there it was. She'd probably slap his face if he said it, though.

Hell, he'd had worse from a woman.

"Christina," he said carefully, "I think we have to acknowledge the elephant in the room."

Alarm flared in her eyes, and he knew he'd been right. She didn't want them to be alone, in close proximity.

"This isn't a conversation we need to have. Ever." She crossed her arms under her breasts.

"If it helps, I'm not happy about it, either."

That got him a surprised look. He watched the play of emotions across her face. Would she retreat? Argue? Deny the attraction between them altogether?

She settled on battle. He waited, anticipation curling in his belly.

"Why do you hate the CIA so much?"

The question wiped the smile off his face. "That's none of your fucking business."

It was the dead last thing he'd expected from her. He'd never tried to hide his distrust of her employers. And, by extension, her. So why was he surprised that she'd confront him about it? He backed away and turned, stalking toward the door, familiar feelings of rage and impotence swamping him.

It wasn't an unreasonable question.

Maybe she deserved the truth. He'd felt himself growing to like her, respect her, and it scared the holy hell out of him. He couldn't go through that kind of betrayal again.

No, she definitely deserved the truth.

Forcing himself to stop, to unclench his fists, he slowly turned to face her. He tried to pry his jaws apart to speak. "No, it's exactly your business. You have a right to know. Why I can't afford to trust you."

She regarded him somberly, not saying a word.

He forced the words through clenched teeth. "The second CIA operative I trusted sold me out to a Peruvian drug cartel. For money. After . . . she was done seducing me."

He found he couldn't meet her gaze, unwilling to see pity in her eyes.

"God, Gabe. I'm so sorry . . ."

He whipped his head up to glare at her. "Don't."

She had moved forward, but now she stopped. "All right," she said calmly. "Tell me."

He took in a lot of air. Was he really going to confide in her? He took a step toward her, then another. "I'd been a Delta Force operator for about two years. I was sent to Huaraz to gather information on cocaine production by the Reyes Cartel. I linked up with two relief workers. Leanne Parker and Anthony Davidson." He couldn't help the bitterness in his voice, but she didn't react. Just listened.

"Leanne and I . . . we became lovers. In love, I thought." He had to stop, clear his throat. "Anyway, when I had what I needed about the cartel, I asked her to come back to the States with me."

He forced himself to look at Christina. To finish it. "She, uh, left to go tell Anthony that she'd decided to go home with me. Next thing I knew, the Peruvian National Police broke down my door and threw my ass in prison."

"Maybe it wasn't a betrayal." Her voice was soft. "Maybe . . ."

"It was," he said as matter-of-factly as he could manage. "I found out after I was released that Leanne and Anthony were actually CIA. The cartel bought them. They fed the cartel intelligence. They sold me out."

She came right up to him, putting a hand on his arm. "Those two were despicable. That's not the norm. We're not all like that. Some of us believe in what we do."

He shook his head, unable to speak.

"Gabe . . . you said Peru was the second time you trusted someone from the CIA. What was the first?"

He couldn't seem to get it together. He knew his face showed his vulnerability, his frustration, his anger. What good would come of telling her? And why the fuck did he even care, after all these years?

"The first admitted she only had me to secure her cover."

Christina inhaled sharply. "Your mother? She—"

"Lied to us for years."

"No." She shook her head in denial. "That's awful!"

"That's life."

"No," she said again, more strongly. "It's not. That's not how normal people behave."

He tried a smile, but knew it came out as a grimace. "The CIA isn't normal."

Her hand was still on his arm. He looked down at it. Her fingers tightened briefly, then dropped. "We're not all liars, Gabe."

"Yeah? What is it you're doing here?" His arm swept out, encompassing the room. "Pretending to be something you're not."

Hurt flashed through her eyes. Feeling like as ass, he pinched the bridge of his nose. "I'm sorry. I know I'm being unfair."

She cocked her head to one side, a hand on her hip. "You know as well as I do that people don't want to know the reality of gathering human intelligence. They'd rather pretend we get all our info from our allies or from satellite pictures. Your missions rely on intelligence gathered by agents downrange, right? But you're okay with that."

He knew that. Still . . .

"All Uncle Sam asks of you is to die for your country," she said bluntly. "And no one questions your patriotism. If I'm asked to go undercover and play a role, lie for my country, steal or cheat to accomplish my mission if necessary, I'm evil? I'm no less a patriot than you. I believe in my country and the good it can do in the world. Are you telling me you've never had to do those things on a mission?"

Of course he had. He couldn't count the number of times his team had slipped into a hostile area undercover. Things went sideways in missions. They adapted, improvised, and got the job done. No matter what.

She paced away from him. "I have a unique talent. I can blend in with the people around me. I go into a club and become a wild party girl. In class, I'm a serious student. At the gym, I fit in with the jocks. I am, or seem to be, what those around me are. I adopt their mannerisms, their speech patterns, even their habits. If they smoke, I smoke. If they slam back jello shots, so do I."

Gabe folded his arms across his chest. "So no one ever knows if they're seeing the real you."

She frowned. "When I'm on a job, that's who I am. It's all the real me, and none of it. It's how I'm pulling this off, and how I intend to succeed in keeping us all alive."

Would she do anything to make sure an operation was a success? He knew he would. So how could he blame her for having the same dedication? Her honesty struck him in his gut. She was every bit as much a professional as he was.

She stared at him across a gulf that seemed impassable. He had to admire her spunk. Not many had the stones to stand up to him; yet here she was, in his face.

"Gabe? What happened to the two officers who betrayed you?"

One look in her eyes told him she already knew. He took a breath. "The Company promoted them. They work cushy desk jobs in Langley now."

"How were you released from prison?"

He snapped his jaws together. "Why are you asking questions when you've already figured out the answers? My mother pulled strings."

He'd been in that pigeon shit of a prison for close to a month. His teammates were gearing up for a prison break when word came down that the Associate Deputy Director of Latin American Operations, Judith Morgan, had arranged for his release. When he'd refused to see her upon his return stateside, she'd come to him, cornering him as he left the house. The conversation had been short and brutal.

*"I'd rather have rotted in my cell than owe you anything."*

*She'd looked at him with cool eyes. "People know you're my son."*

*"Do me no favors. Ever."*

He'd gone back to his unit vowing never to work with the CIA again. Yet here he was. Again.

"Gabe. Where did you go?"

He looked up to find her directly in front of him. "Nowhere."

"Mistrust compromises our job here. We have to work together, no bullshit. I've been honest with you from the start. But how about this? I promise I'll only tell you the truth from now on."

She waited, her eyes steady. He edged closer to her. Her unique lime scent reached his nose.

"Do you wear perfume?" he blurted, surprising himself.

"No. It's probably Ronnie's shower gel." She arched a brow. "Does this mean we've reached a temporary cease-fire?"

One corner of his mouth tipped up. "Yeah."

He leaned forward. The closer he got to her, the calmer he felt. She put out a hand, which bumped against his chest. Gabe forced himself to stay still but couldn't stop his body from swaying, allowing her palm to brush back and forth across his pecs. Damn, that felt nice. "How about a cease-fire hug?"

He'd meant to sound teasing, but his voice came out hoarse and needy. Straightening abruptly, he took two steps away from her, turned, and bumped into the stupid lamp by the door. The thing looked like a salt shaker with a triangle of stained glass at the top. It teetered, toppled, and fell to the floor with a crash. Shards of glass flew everywhere. Christina gasped and jumped, clutching her hand.

He whirled back to her. "Are you all right?"

Blood stained her palm. "I'm fine. Just a scratch."

The door to the suite slammed open, and eight hundred pounds of muscle swarmed in, weapons out. When they saw the tableau, they pulled up.

"What's up?" Tag asked.

"Broke a lamp." Gabe stated the obvious. "No worries. Call it a drill."

The four men shrugged and the weapons disappeared. They plopped down onto various surfaces. Christina went to the telephone.

"There seems to be a direct line to housekeeping," she announced to no one in particular. Punching the button, she said, "This is . . . yes. I see. I have very clumsily broken a lamp. Would you . . . thank you. Oh, yes? *Merci bien*." She hung up. "Someone's on their way up."

Gabe crossed to her and grabbed her wrist. Her arm tensed. He gently but firmly pulled her fingers apart. They were bleeding. "You're cut," he said.

"It's nothing. Some glass."

"Embedded." The shard wasn't huge, but it needed to come out. Mace came to examine her palm. "I'll need tweezers."

"I have one in my makeup bag," Christina said. She tugged her wrist free. "I'll go get it."

Gabe followed her through the bedroom and into the bathroom. Unlike the awful yellow room, it was tasteful in off-white tones, larger than normal, with granite countertops, a walled shower, and a separate Jacuzzi tub. Christina shot a startled look over her shoulder.

"I can do it," she blurted.

"It's easier if someone else does," he said. "Trust me. I've been there." Granted, his had been a two-inch long chunk of wood lodged in his thigh, shrapnel from an RPG attack. Tag had the bedside manner of an elephant with a bullet in its ass, but he got the job done.

She ducked her head and opened a large case, extracting the tweezers and turning slightly toward him, all without ever lifting her face.

"Sit down," he said, gesturing to the toilet. Her face pinked, but amazingly enough she sat, perching gingerly on the closed lid. He placed the back of her hand on one rough palm, spreading her fingers so he could get a look at the glass sliver. It was long and sharp, but embedded shallowly. He worked it out by increments, careful not to break it off under the skin. When he had extracted the sliver, he held it up. "Pretend it's a bullet. You have a battle scar now."

It was a clumsy attempt at teasing, but he knew it had failed when frost touched her eyes. Without a word, she slipped out of her expensive silk jacket and twisted on the toilet seat so that he could see the puckered red scar on her upper arm, about four inches below the sleeveless shell. Without volition, he reached out and traced the jagged flesh. A bullet had plowed through her skin there. Too deep to be called a graze, it had taken about two inches of flesh with it, leaving a scarred indentation. But there was no mistaking it. Christina had been shot.

It shook something deep inside him. He'd been treating her like a kid, he realized abruptly. Someone playing a grown-up. A member of a despised organization. Suddenly, his view of her changed. She was a fully-trained operative, and she had been wounded during a mission.

He'd been an ass. Guilt churned in his gut. He deserved her condemnation. How would he have reacted if their roles were reversed? He tossed the glass shard into the porcelain waste-basket.

"Guess you don't need this one, then." It was equally lame, but he was still processing this new information. Fortunately for him, she didn't say a word as she wiped the blood smears from her palm and slapped on a Band-Aid. She slipped on her jacket and walked out.

He followed her out to the main room, unsettled and restless. Looking around at Tag, Gavin, Alex and Mace, he said, "We might as well review the plan, as long as we're all here."

His gaze slid to Christina, who stood by the window with her arms crossed. Refusing to stare at her breasts, he kept his eyes firmly on hers. Only too late did he realize he might be coming across as aggressive when her eyes narrowed and her mouth flattened. He turned away.

"I'll be by your side at all times," he told Christina. "Gavin will stay with the car, to make sure no one tampers with it. Tag and Alex will wander and make sure no trouble's brewing. They're our advance eyes and ears. Mace will maintain overwatch as our sniper. He'll cover us when we have to be in the open, which we'll keep to a minimum. We'll all be hooked together through Bluetooth, like we were on the way out here."

Christina didn't move from the window. She absently stroked her scar. It must have happened in Baghdad. Conveniently, she had left being shot out of her story back at Nanten's baroque gardens. Was she reliving those moments?

"Okay," she said. "I see the protection routine. What I don't see is how we're going to draw out the hitman."

Mace nodded. "That'll come next," he said, Cajun accent

strong. Women responded to those velvety syllables. He'd seen it time and again. Gabe narrowed his eyes. Mace had the gall to wink at him. "This is the last time we won't have positive control over the environment."

"We need your input," added Tag. "Need to know what your comfort zone is."

Christina strode over to the team. "I can handle it, whatever it is."

"Ain't no doubt," Mace said.

"You got this," Alex said at the same time.

Gabe rotated his neck. Where had all this tension come from? "Right now, let's focus on this shindig tomorrow. I just found out from the butler that Bonnet's going to be there."

"The activist? I'll stay away from him," she said at once.

"He's probably here just to talk to you. We'll keep him at bay."

Tag prowled around the room. "Maybe that's not the best approach. Like you said, we have to create a hole the assassin can get through. Carswell doesn't think Bonnet has it in him, but I'd like to see for myself."

Gabe didn't like it. What if something happened to her? "Why don't you guys go get some grub? I'll stay here."

His men rose. Mace approached Christina, speaking to her in a low voice. She responded, eyes sparkling. Mace let out a low laugh. Gabe ground his teeth.

"Get out of here," he snapped. One by one, the four operators filed out.

Christina glared at him. "What was that for?"

"I don't need my team distracted. Let's keep it professional, all right?"

She laughed her outrage. "Oh! *I'm* being unprofessional? When you're the one growling and snapping at your men because one of them dared to speak to me?"

Ouch. She'd noticed that, had she?

"I'm putting my life into your hands, don't forget. Why is it a bad thing if I get to know your team?" She put heavy emphasis on *your*. "I get you don't see me as an equal. Fine. But don't get in the way if I want to establish a relationship with someone who does."

She wanted to . . . with Mace . . . ? His brows snapped together and a muscle ticked in his jaw.

She came right over to him, hands on hips, fire shooting from her eyes. One long index finger poked him in the chest. "Friendship, asshole. Friend. Ship. I'm not looking to hook up with him. All he said was he's happy we get to work together again, and told me I did a good job in Azakistan. Which is more than you've ever done."

Gabe's head jerked back. "What?"

"All you've done since I met you is belittle me. Fine, I'm no special operator. But the CIA trains its officers well. I know what I'm doing."

"Do you?"

"Yes." Her voice had a hard edge. "We learn from our mistakes."

True. And he was about to make a colossal one. He closed the distance between them, unable to stop himself. Closing his arms roughly around her shoulders, he pulled her to him. She resisted.

"I'm sorry. That was asshole-ish of me. You got your asset in Ma'ar ye zhad to open up about her brother. You got her to send us photos of the terrorist cell. You're the reason we knew who to look for. Mace is right."

She relaxed against him. Gabe pressed an openmouthed kiss to the pulse in her neck, the rush of blood beneath her skin pounding against his tongue. "You've kept your cool here, too. Don't think I haven't noticed. And you just promised to be honest with me."

Mouth sliding up her neck, he touched his tongue to the tender skin beneath her ear, enjoying the quick inhale that told him she felt something for him, if only unwilling sexual arousal.

"I've never been dishonest with you."

"Good." He nipped her earlobe, then traced the tip of his tongue around the delicate shell of her ear. She shivered against him. Her mouth turned, blindly seeking his. Before he could touch heaven, a sound at the door made him leap away from her, drawing his weapon from his shoulder holster in one smooth pull.

The knock came again. Christina cleared her throat. "It's probably the maid. Don't shoot her, okay?" She walked over to the door and opened it before Gabe got his vocal cords working enough to tell her to wait.

A girl in—no kidding—a French maid's outfit came in with a broom and dustpan. Gabe focused on her cleaning up the glass to avoid looking at Christina. When the girl had gone, he looked around and found that Christina had retreated into the awful yellow bedroom. Just as well.

# Chapter Twelve

CHRISTINA LOCKED THE door behind herself with unsteady hands. What had just happened? His impulse to comfort her, if that's what it had been, had turned swiftly to something carnal. His hands had trembled, his mouth hot as he nibbled her neck. She hadn't been able to stop the rush of heat as her skin sensitized. She'd wanted him to settle his mouth onto hers. Wanted his hands on her body.

Bad move.

She let out a shaky breath, pressing a hand to her abdomen. This assignment wasn't going to work if she had to guard against her attraction twenty-four/seven.

Her mind shied away from an unwanted image of him above her. Down that road led nothing but heartache. Determinedly, she picked up the binder of guests for tomorrow's gala. Better she use her energy making sure she could pass for Véronique.

A brisk knock at the door startled her some time later. She pushed the binder away and rose, realizing all at once how stiff she was. What time was it? She stretched as she crossed to the door, pulling it open just as a second knock sounded. Unsurprised, she looked up at Gabe.

"Dinner," he said, looking searchingly at her. She deliberately kept her expression blank.

"Thanks." Moving into the main room, she saw that a temporary table had been set up, covered with plates under dome lids. She lifted one, inhaling greedily. "It smells great."

"It's *stamppot*, so I'm told. Dutch stew, served with *metworst*." He raised another lid. "A selection of cheeses. Edam, Gouda, Leyden. I don't remember what those two are." Picking up a bottle of red wine, he sniffed, then looked at the label. "Bordeaux. There's also a bottle of white to go with the cheese. Viognier, whatever the hell that is."

The table had been angled so that both chairs had a clear view of the door. Coincidence? She doubted anything that happened around Gabe came about by accident. She sat down and dropped the linen napkin into her lap. Gabe poured the red into both wine-glasses and handed her one. His fingers brushed against hers as she took the stemware. She looked away, nonplussed.

"Is your team joining us?" she asked, looking pointedly at the plates, clearly intended for two.

"No. I thought it was time you and I reached an understanding."

What did he want from her? Surely, he wasn't going to force a conversation about their almost-kiss. "In reference to what, exactly?"

Gabe tipped his glass back and took a healthy swallow of wine. "You said it yourself earlier. We have to learn to work together. And we have to do it now, before you make any more public appearances."

Christina picked up her fork and took a bite of the stew. It was delicious. "Mmm," she mumbled around the mouthful. "God, that's good." She cut a piece of *metworst*, a dried sausage. It had a strong flavor that wasn't nearly as appealing as the *stamppot*. Shrugging, Christina sipped from her wineglass.

Gabe tucked into his own meal. Around a bite, he said, "So, let's lay it on the table." He swallowed, then pointed his fork at her. "You said I belittled you. Maybe that was true, when we started this charade."

Christina bent over her plate. Where was he going with this?

"But not any longer," he said, voice low. "About Baghdad. I think you got thrown under the bus. If so, that doesn't sit well with me."

"I was persona non grata until Jay took me to Azakistan," she blurted. Gabe couldn't have surprised her more if he'd said caterpillars were aliens. "My boyfriend dumped me as soon as he heard the rumors, like even associating with me would hurt his career. I guess maybe you have a point about the CIA. Frank the Fink taught me not to date inside the Company."

She fiddled with the stem of her wineglass. Oh, what the hell. She could indulge in another glass. She poured, and topped off his as well. "So . . . now what?"

"Now we eat dinner. We talk. Get to know each other." He slouched back, flipping his fork around on the tablecloth with one finger. "Figure out your strengths and weaknesses, so we can compensate."

Don't get defensive, she told herself. Probably he didn't realize how insulting that sounded.

"Um." Gabe cleared his throat abruptly. "I meant, maximize your strengths and compensate where needed. Nobody's good at everything. We all have strengths and weaknesses. That's all I meant." He glanced at her, apology in his eyes. "Christina, I know my teammates better than I know my own brother. We're tight. Tactically, we think the same." He sighed, glancing up at the ceiling. "I'm not used to having a . . . a teammate I haven't trained with for thousands of hours. So . . . so I apologize if I haven't included you. That stops now, okay?"

Christina almost forgot to chew and swallow. Gabe was apologizing? To her?

"I need to know what you can do, do you understand that?"

The *stamppot* stuck in her throat. Quickly, she washed it down with a huge gulp of wine, feeling the warmth of the alcohol spread through her system. "I understand. And vice versa, okay?"

If he were surprised by that, it did not show in his face. Instead, he inclined his head solemnly. "Agreed."

Her fork scraped the bottom of her plate. Eyebrows raised, she saw she'd eaten everything, even the *metworst*. Gabe chuckled. Christina felt her face heat. "Guess I was hungry," she mumbled.

His eyes glittered at her as he rose and served the salad. She pushed it aside, uninterested. What the hell did that speculative look mean? Her gaze dropped to her plate, willing the flush to subside, then jerked her head up. *No weakness, remember?*

"Frank the Fink was an idiot."

Hearing her nickname for her jerk of an ex-boyfriend coming from Gabe's mouth made her smile. "I might have called him another F-word a time or two. He still has my leather jacket, the louse. My favorite. It's got diagonal zippers that make me feel badass."

"I'd like to see you in badass." He captured and held her gaze. A peculiar warmth settled in his eyes.

She was so not having this conversation. "I'll go first."

Gabe didn't miss a beat. "Okay, then. What do you bring to this mission?"

He cleared the untouched salad plates. Fresh stemware waited by the white wine chilling in a bucket. Gabe offered her the cheese tray while he opened the second bottle and filled both their glasses. She used the delicate tongs to transfer tiny wedges to a small plate, using the time to marshal her thoughts.

"We both know I have this assignment because I look like Ronnie." She shifted around, uncomfortable. He clearly wanted more. "I'm a skilled marksman. I scored highest in my class in defensive driving. I have the usual training in weapons, small team tactics, house-clearing operations. Hand-to-hand." What did she know that might help them? "I know a lot about money laundering and smuggling operations. I've completed all the training for clandestine operations. But, as you know, I don't have a lot of field experience."

"Do you speak any languages?"

"Uh-huh. Russian."

"That's a tough one to master," he said.

Christina pulled a face. "I grew up with a variation of it, but it was such a bastardized dialect that I think it hurt more than helped."

"Were your parents Russian?"

It was a reasonable question. Christina tried to think how to answer. "Not really. My father was from Kem, on the White Sea, but he was Latvian. He met my mother in Kuusamo, Finland, but she was Greek, not Scandinavian. We spoke Pomor in our home, which is a dialect from the far north, where they were from. There tends to be a smattering of Scandinavian in it, which makes it tough to be understood by anyone who doesn't speak it. So when I studied Russian, I had to unlearn everything I thought I knew about it."

"That's quite the ethnic mix. You took the best of all of them." He emptied his wineglass. "More?"

"No, thanks. I'd better keep a clear head."

"Tonight's the only night when you don't have to," he told her. "Take the down time when you can get it." He held the bottle out, waiting, and Christina gave a small laugh as she held out her glass. "Why not?"

He gave her an approving smile, and her insides softened. "Live dangerously," he said, clinking his glass to hers.

She took the opportunity while he nibbled on a piece of cheese to look at him. He still wore his suit, though he'd slipped off the jacket and tie. The white shirt clung to the hard planes of his body, the open buttons giving her a tantalizing glimpse of his chest. He had shaved off his usual two-day growth, and her gaze followed his cheekbone to his slightly off-center nose. His golden eyes gleamed with amusement, and she realized he'd caught her staring. Infused with liquid courage, she refused to look away. Something molten flared to life in the depth of his eyes.

What had they been talking about? Oh, yeah. Russian.

"We always wrote in English," she said, sipping hastily. "So when I was first learning, just mastering the alphabet was hard. It's easy to trip yourself up. Cursive *M* is a *T* in Russian. A cursive *G* is a *D*, a cursive *N* is a *P*. After a while, I couldn't write English cursive any more. And the accents!" She raked her nails under the hair at the nape of her neck, and raised her voice an octave. "'No, listen to me. 'E' and 'E'—hear the difference?' All of us would look at each other, and we'd all have the same dumb look on our faces."

"I'm sure you figured it out quick enough."

She blinked in surprise. "Oh. It took a while, but I started to get the hang of it. I bombed the first quizzes. I did well enough on the reading, but they were speaking so fast I had a hard time following. But immersion works wonders. After forty veee-eerr-rrry long weeks, I did fairly well on the final proficiency exam." Her wineglass was empty again. How had that happened? She poured, and topped off Gabe's glass as well. He nodded his thanks.

"So you grew up in Russia?" he asked.

"No. It's complicated." How much could she safely reveal? "My parents emigrated to the States and settled outside of Chicago after the Wall came down. They figured if the Cold War was over, they'd rather live in the land of baseball. My dad loves baseball. He can quote you stats for every player the White Sox ever fielded, as far back as 1900, I bet."

"And you?"

She made a noncommittal sound. "I pretended to be a fan."

"That's an odd way of putting it." When she didn't say anything else, Gabe tipped his head to one side and raised his eyebrows. "Didn't you just promise to tell me the truth?"

She blew out an annoyed breath. "That doesn't include revealing all the skeletons in my closet."

His smile was lopsided, his eyes shrewd. "Maybe not, but now I'm very curious. Would you tell me the story? Please?"

She thought about it. She could trust his discretion, she decided. Whatever she told him in confidence would remain there. "All right. Parts of it anyway. Parts are still classified."

"Okay." He dipped his head in agreement. "So, your parents emigrated . . . ?"

"In 1990," she took up the tale. "My mother was pregnant. She wanted me to be born in America. They came legally, but even legal papers were bought and paid for back then. There was an air base outside of Kem, run by a corrupt major general, and the emigration documents cost my father. At first, it was small things. Contact so-and-so. Pass on information. Then it was smuggling small pieces of art. Pottery, mostly—ancient artifacts from Greece."

She glanced at Gabe. His expression was thoughtful rather than outraged, so she continued.

"Over the years, he became the middleman for a variety of different kinds of stolen objects. He'd keep them for a few days or weeks, until he received instructions on where to send them. He tried multiple times to get out of the business, but the threat to his family back in Kem kept him in line. By the time the major general retired, though, his replacement had enough on my father to send him to jail for the rest of his life, if he chose. My father's great-aunt passed away shortly after that and the children moved to Moscow, but Dad still couldn't get out.

"Then the girls started showing up. In ones and twos, from Russia, China, and Indonesia. Dirty, and usually crying. My parents cared for them, bought them new clothes, got them medical attention if they needed it. After a few weeks, they'd disappear."

"Let me guess," Gabe said. "The traffickers threatened to kill you and your mother if your father didn't cooperate."

She nodded. "At first, it was a game to me. Not the girls. Before that, I mean. I started noticing it when I was twelve, I think. Packages arrived from time to time. My father would store them for a few weeks, then repack them into a backpack or box and drive somewhere. When he returned, he no longer had the item. The next day, my mother would meet a friend for lunch and come home with a purse full of money. I, uh, might've skipped school to follow them, then followed whoever they were meeting. I just wanted to know."

Both Gabe's eyebrows raised at that. "You mapped their network?"

"Yeah. I didn't know that's what I was doing, of course. I was just a nosy kid." She ate a wedge of cheese.

"At twelve. Color me impressed." He sounded like he meant it, too.

She flashed a grin. "But wait. There's more."

He returned her smile, and for a moment they simply stared at one another.

"Christina . . ."

"So I decided to do it again," she rushed on, tearing her gaze away. She didn't want to know what he'd been about to say. "I followed my father to the pickup point, and then followed his contact back to a warehouse. Over the next several months, I observed the arrival and departure of girls via boat and van, and got pictures, including the girls. Especially the girls."

Gabe had lost his smile. "And then you had to map the downline."

She toyed with the stem of her wineglass, twirling it slowly around and around. He already knew what she was going to say; she could read it in the shock and dismay in his eyes. "Yes. It took a lot for my parents to agree to it. I bought a button-sized tracker from the office supply store and sewed it into my clothes. My father tracked it on his Palm Treo phone. And then I substituted myself for one of the girls."

"Holy Christ, Christina! Were you out of your ever-fucking mind? Women disappear forever into that cesspool of depravity! What the hell—"

She thrust her plate away. "Ditch the outrage. How was that any more or less dangerous than going undercover in Baghdad? These were *girls*, Gabe. Fifteen, sixteen years old. I needed to stop it, if I could."

He shook his head slowly, eyes never leaving hers. "How old were you?"

"Seventeen."

"Seventeen." He repeated it in disbelief. "No training, no backup, no resources. What in God's name were your parents thinking?"

She quirked a small smile, which he did not return. "I didn't really give them much of a choice."

"I'm assuming you knew how incredibly dangerous it was? That girls are often kept drugged to make them compliant?"

Of course she'd known that. "Fortunately, the . . . customers for these girls wanted them clean. I memorized the faces of the sellers and buyers. I was . . . sold to a billionaire as housekeeper and nanny to his three children. He put an ankle monitor on me. There was another slave in the house, a young boy, who had"— she had to stop to clear her throat—"more intimate duties. I convinced him to leave with me, which wasn't easy, believe me. Ted had walls around his mansion, and guards with dogs patrolling it. We managed to escape, though, and I went straight to the FBI.

"I told them I'd hand them a human trafficking network, but not until they gave my parents immunity and protection. They threatened and blustered, but agreed in the end. It all worked out."

Gabe gripped the hilt of his butter knife so hard his knuckles were white. "Holy hell. Why wasn't any of this in your file?"

She couldn't stop the smirk tugging the corners of her mouth.

"After the trials, we went into Witness Protection. Madison's not my last name by birth."

Without warning, he scraped back his chair and stood. Striding to his Army duffel bag, dropped near the sofa—where he would be sleeping—he unzipped it and withdrew a small bundle, which he brought to her. "Here," he said. "If you'll do something that dangerous, you need to be armed. It's a baby Sig for your purse. The P238 subcompact. We might be able to rig something for small-of-back carry, but, honestly, with you in those princess clothes, it would show in most of what I've seen you wear."

She took the Sig Sauer from him, automatically checking the magazine. "Seven rounds," she said. "Not a lot of firepower."

"No," he agreed. "Look at it this way, though. You having to use that means we're all dead."

She frowned up at him. "Jesus, Gabe."

"No, I mean it. That thing doesn't come out of your purse except as a last resort. If you pull it and someone sees, your cover's blown."

"I get it." She set the handgun on top of her discarded napkin. "Are you familiar with it?"

"Yes." She truthfully wasn't any more familiar with it than the dozens of other semi-automatics she'd fired, but a handgun was a handgun, and she was a good shot. She rose from the table, taking herself and her wineglass to the sofa. Where Gabe would be sleeping.

A hand fluttered to her throat. All six-foot-plus of hard muscle, sleep-mussed hair, and bedroom eyes. She swiveled to face him as he sat next to her on the sofa, curling one leg under her but not quite able to meet his eyes. After a moment, a long finger touched her chin, nudging it up.

"Look at me." Christina obeyed the soft command. "I'm an expert in my field. I've done executive protection work before, and so have the guys I handpicked for this team. That's what I bring to the table. I shouldn't have said that before, about all of us being dead. Because it's not going to happen."

She didn't doubt that. Delta Force operators were some of the best trained men in the world. They were very hard to kill.

Gabe shifted closer to her, taking her wineglass and leaning past her to set it on the side table. He smelled clean and somehow light, and the scent of wine on his breath made her slightly dizzy. "I'm having trouble wrapping my head around this. You were incredibly lucky. Now you're trained, but at seventeen . . . ? Experienced undercover agents go missing and are either found dead, or never found at all. I . . . Jesus, you could have . . ."

She couldn't seem to catch her breath as his palms came up to cradle her face. He was upset about something that, years ago, might have happened but hadn't. Flutters moved from her stomach to her heart.

His lips were soft as he brushed them over hers, eyes closing on a sigh. She found herself leaning into him, letting her head fall to his shoulder as he turned his head and captured her lips. Soft, drugging kisses. He tugged her closer, his fingers running up and down her arm. She shivered as his other hand cupped the back of her head.

She had not expected him to be gentle. It disarmed her like nothing else could have, and silenced the voice at the back of her mind shouting that this was the very last thing she should be doing. He kissed her like they had all the time in the world, rubbing his lips back and forth on hers for the sheer pleasure of it. He licked the corner of her mouth, and did it again when she gave a soft moan. Frissons rippled across her shoulders as his fingers brushed her skin.

Dipping into the hot recesses of her mouth, he slid his tongue across hers, tangling them together in gentle union. She shivered, angling her head to deepen the kiss. Taking it for the invitation it was, he tugged her onto his lap. Where she became very aware of the bulge in his trousers as it nestled against her bottom.

"Christina." The soft note of entreaty did strange things to her stomach.

Humming with feminine power, she pulled his dress shirt from the waistband of his trousers; he helped her. She ran her hands under it, finding bare skin. Finally! The fingers that had itched to touch him for days smoothed across his stomach. He was silk over steel, his abs clenching as her nails ran across his skin. A sound sloughed out of him.

"Again," he muttered, bringing one of his hands over the top of hers. "Do it again."

She did, fingers shaking with the need to surround herself with his scent, his feel, his taste. She ran her fingertips up his rock-hard chest. His light hair was springy, but the look he gave her was dark and carnal. His hand followed hers up his body until he found her breast pressed into his side, and he paused there, his fingertips brushing across it so lightly she found herself pushing closer, wanting his hand hard on her breast. Instead, he reached down to tug her blouse from her skirt. His long, tapered fingers unfastened the last button first, then moved up her body, his knuckles brushing against sensitized flesh as he worked each tiny stud loose. His concentration was absolute. She felt the heat of his look like a physical caress. When he reached the top, he rubbed his knuckles across her collarbone as he slowly spread the material.

Resisting the urge to cover her chest, Christina instead forced herself to meet his eyes. His gaze scorched her, approval glittering in their depth. Emboldened, she straightened her shoulders, slowly thrusting her breasts forward. Dark promise poured from him as he swept a tongue across his lower lip. Without thinking, she leaned forward to capture that tongue and pull it into her mouth, drawing a hiss from his lips. He crushed her to him, his arms strong bands, his mouth voracious as he ravaged her mouth with kisses. His hands slid up her spine, under the material of the blouse she still wore, and paused at her bra strap. The material loosened.

"Do you have any idea how damned sexy you look, half naked and in my arms?" His voice was hoarse. The truth was, she felt wanton and wild with her blouse open and bra undone. Her hands went to the tie of her wraparound skirt. His beat hers there, nudging hers aside so that he could tug the clip free.

"Come here," he commanded, picking her up by the waist and turning her so that she straddled him. The wraparound skirt parted and slid up her thighs, allowing her to sink onto the smooth material of his trousers. She rocked against him, and he responded by gripping her hips. "Kiss me."

Their lips met and dueled. Christina felt feverish as his hands slid to her breasts, cupping them through the peach lace. His thumbs brushed across her nipples. They hardened instantly. She swallowed a moan, bracing her hands on his shoulders, pulling back to look at him. His eyes were wild, almost desperate, and he closed them on a groan.

"Gabe. Look at me."

# Chapter Thirteen

GABE CLOSED HIS eyes, resting his forehead on her shoulder, shaking as he struggled for control. Finally, he simply wrapped his arms around her and held on. She stroked his hair.

Her fingers sliding against his scalp felt amazing. But he couldn't do this. Not again. Was it cowardice, this need for control? The need to limit lovemaking to the physical? No emotions involved. It wasn't fair to Christina. Women needed affection. Reassurance.

He couldn't give her those things. Wouldn't, no matter how much he might later regret the lost opportunity.

He could give her pleasure, but never his heart. Leanne's betrayal had hardened him. He'd loved her, or thought he did. Never again.

He pulled back, not quite meeting her eyes. Pulling her blouse off her arms, he snagged her bra as well, leaving her naked from the waist up. Sliding his hands up her ribs, he cupped her breasts again, bending to lick across a nipple. She shuddered. He did it again, then drew it into his mouth and suckled, teasing and rolling the nub with his teeth. She gasped and arched.

Inching his hands up her thighs, underneath her skirt, he tortured them both with his leisurely exploration. She reached down, pulled her skirt away and let it fall to the floor. His thumbs reached the apex of her thighs and lingered there, scant millimeters from where he wanted them, but he held himself still as she squirmed and uttered a noise of protest. Finally, he allowed the pads of his thumbs to brush across her core. She cried out, pushing forward, and he pulled his hands away, teasing her. He wanted her wild for him; too wild to realize he'd closed his emotions down. She was incredibly perceptive, and he didn't want her to know.

"Gabe?" She looked uneasily at him. "What is it?"

"Nothing." He tried to make his voice teasing. "You have my undivided attention."

She was nearly naked, while he was still fully dressed. Bringing her hands up, she tried to cover herself, but he gripped her wrists lightly and pulled them down again.

"Let me look at you. Your body is a miracle." He hadn't meant to say it; it just slipped out. She just flat out did it for him. He just couldn't let her know how vulnerable he felt.

She burrowed close, cuddling into his chest. Damn it! She felt that something was off; she just didn't know what.

To distract her, he nibbled along her neck to her ear, and ran his tongue lightly around the delicate shell, pulling another shiver from her. Then, so fast she barely had time to register it, he reversed their positions, laying her along the sofa and nestling between her legs with a groan of delight. Even as she tried to slow him down, tried to still his hands, he pulled her knee up and ground into her.

"Stop. Gabe, stop. I need to . . . . think . . ."

He ran his fingers up into her hair, controlling her head for a long, lingering, seductive kiss. "The absolute last thing you need to be doing right now is thinking," he said in a rough voice. Him, too. "Let me make you feel good."

That evidently wasn't what she wanted to hear. She pushed against his shoulders and levered herself partway from under him. He stilled his hands and let them drop away.

"What is it?" he asked. But he knew. And, somehow, she did, too.

Christina covered her breasts with shaking hands. "What are we doing here, Gabe? What is this?"

"Christ," he groaned, his head dropping down to rest on her stomach. "It's been too long for you if you can't figure out what I'm doing." He ran his hands down her hips to her thighs, hoping her desire would cloud her mind, but she yanked her feet free and pulled them to her chest.

"I'm serious."

"I was afraid of that." He pushed himself upright, again not quite meeting her eyes. "What's the problem?"

Christina looked like her head might explode. "What's the *problem*? For starters, we work together. Don't you have rules about that?"

He adjusted himself, trying to get comfortable. His face burned. She had every right to be upset. It was for the best anyway. Getting involved with her physically on any level was a piss-poor idea. Now he just had to fix their working relationship so there wouldn't be any fallout from tonight's activities.

"Nah. I'm allowed to screw Tag if I want to. Which I *so* don't."

He tried a smile, but Christina glared. He realized she sensed she was being played. "You're thinking of an executive protector getting involved with his principal, like Kevin Costner did with that singer in that movie."

"Whitney Houston," she said absently.

"Yeah. That one. It's bullshit. A professional would never do that. But you're not my principal. You're my teammate."

"So, what?" she said, head rearing back. "Tag's not available, so you jump me instead? Is that what this is?"

"Why does it have to *be* something? Why can't we just be two people enjoying a night?"

Her expression of hurt nearly undid him. He forced himself to release her when she stood, grabbing her bra and putting it on. "No, thanks."

He ran a hand through his overlong hair, scraping it back from his forehead and then letting it flop forward again. "You're turned on. I did that to you. Let me take care of you."

"Just sex?" she asked. He kept his face expressionless. "Just two teammates relieving stress, no emotions involved?"

His eyes narrowed and his teeth clamped together. "It's not like that," he snapped, but his eyes shifted away from her because that's exactly what it was like. What he'd made it, because that's not how it had started out.

"Get out."

He stood to face her. "It would be good between us. Why deny yourself?"

Only pleasure. No strings attached.

She planted her hands on her hips, but she looked like she might cry. "Dinner's over. Dessert just got canceled."

A muscle moved in his jaw. "Have it your way. This couch is occupied, though, so unless you want to finish what we started, I suggest you get the hell out of here and go to bed."

"You're an ass, Gabriel Morgan."

She scooped up her clothes, turned on her heel, and stomped into the bedroom. It was for the best, he told himself. But he knew he would get no sleep tonight.

# Chapter Fourteen

THEY SPENT THE next day exploring the villa, mansion, whatever it was. It was old, and that meant lots of hallways, lots of rooms, and plenty of places to hide. Gabe had them run through scenario after scenario, getting to know the layout and the exits. To his relief, Christina did not argue or fight him on any of his tactics, though she treated him with icy disdain. He'd tossed and turned the night before. The tactile memory of her smooth skin, scorching heat, and passion-glazed eyes were seared into his brain.

He'd royally screwed the pooch last night. The sheer overwhelm of his emotions swamping him had scared him to death. He couldn't remember ever feeling that way before. Instead of admitting the intensity of his feelings, of opening himself to her, he'd pulled back, locked himself away, and tried to make it just about sex. It hadn't worked, and he'd hurt Christina on top of it. He was a jerk, no doubt about it.

All seven of them trooped into the informal dining room for luncheon. Well, he and his men clumped in, looking ridiculously out of place in their plain clothes and practical shoes. Deni Van

Praet strode in, an air of authority surrounding her. And Christina presented her grandaunt with a bouquet of flowers, kissing her cheek and seating herself next to the Viscount and Viscountess of Nabourg like she'd done it a hundred times before. He and his team were relegated to the bottom end of the long mahogany table, away from the nobles. That suited him just fine. It gave him the opportunity to watch Christina.

Calling the room informal felt silly to him. The table could easily seat fourteen. Table arrangements of fruit and candles decorated its length. Red oak paneling on the walls, dignified portraits, a chandelier above the table. Informal? His ass.

There was the slightest echo in the Bluetooth earpieces they all wore, due to their close proximity. The situation was unique. Normally, the principal wouldn't hear the bodyguards' chatter. It distracted Christina. She finally flicked the tiny earpiece into her napkin, fast enough that the Nabourgs didn't notice. Gavin followed suit. "Don't make sense," he muttered, "we all being here." Gabe nodded, and the rest took them out or turned them off.

Lunch consisted of a lamb-and-vegetable stew, followed by chilled shrimp salad and another selection of cheeses. As he ate, Gabe only half paid attention to the conversation going on around him. Mostly he watched Christina.

There was something different about her, some small thing about her demeanor that pinged at the back of his head. When she ducked her head and chuckled, he realized what it was. Sure, she still acted like Princess Véronique. But a subtle difference manifested itself: she fit in. Her body language mirrored the Nabourgs', her inflection, her facial expressions. Despite the Nabourgs' stilted English and Christina's pretense, he almost forgot that she wasn't a royal joining her relatives for an intimate luncheon. It impressed him.

Come to think of it, she'd done the same thing with his team, when she hadn't been arguing with him. She had adopted their mannerisms. She had blended. They had accepted her easily.

After lunch, the Nabourgs retired to their rooms to rest. Gabe took his team onto the grounds and through the wild gardens, and they repeated the drills of the morning. Before they knew it, it was time to dress for the anniversary ball. Gabe escorted the ladies back to Deni's room, where Christina's glass slippers awaited. Then he went next door, reflecting that he fell far short of Prince Charming.

IT TOOK THE better part of an hour to dress Christina. Deni had already changed into a floor-length sheath dress with matching jacket.

"You look beautiful," Christina told her. Deni only smiled, and went to work.

She swept Christina's hair back from her face and into a series of larger and larger intertwining rolls. It wasn't a bun, exactly, but it was neatly coiffed and elegant. Deni placed a hair comb made of a spray of crystals just above the rolls of hair.

Then came makeup—more makeup than Christina had ever worn in her life. Deni would not allow her to look in the mirror.

"Just wait, *petite*. You will see soon enough, eh?"

Before she slipped on the dress, Deni covered her scar in a sheer bandage, then blended it into her skin with more foundation.

"It is virtually undetectable," she pronounced. "No one will notice this."

The jewelry Deni presented to her took her breath away. The

diamonds in the necklace echoed the crystal spray of the dress, teardrops dripping into an inverted triangle. Deni added square-cut diamond earrings and a triple-banded diamond bracelet.

"Holy crap. What if I lose these? What if a diamond falls out? What if I decide to steal them and retire to Rio?"

Deni quirked a shaped brow. "Then I should miss you very much."

Finally, butterflies flitting through her stomach, Christina stepped into Ronnie's Manolo Blahnik satin pumps, dyed to match the dress.

Deni guided her over to the full-length mirror. "Now you may inspect."

Christina felt her mouth drop open. "My goodness."

"I echo the sentiment," Deni said, giving a rare smile. "You will, 'ow you say, knock their socks off."

"It's too fancy," she said. "Aren't I going to stand out like a sore thumb?" The dress had not seemed so overwhelming when she had tried it on before, but now, with hair and makeup, she looked like she should be attending the Oscars. Next to her, Deni almost disappeared.

Deni gave her a puzzled look. "Sore thumb? I do not know this idiom. But no, you are not too fancy. The Nabourgs are a very old family, and very traditional. All will dress like this." She slapped her hands together briskly. "And now, *princesse*, we face the fire together, yes?"

Taking a deep, cleansing breath, Christina smoothed her hands down her waist. "Yes."

Deni preceded her out the bedroom door, clearing her throat to alert the team. And then it was time. She stepped through the doorway.

All conversation ceased. The team, spread throughout the room, came to their feet as one. Christina's gaze unerringly found Gabe. Her stomach roiled with conflict; hurt and anger sat at the fore, but confusion shifted in the back of her head. He stared at her with the same stupefied expression as the rest of the team. No one moved or spoke. Then, a slow wolf whistle broke the silence. Mace stepped forward.

"*Magnifique*," he said. "You are truly magnificent." He raised her fingers and brushed his lips across her knuckles.

She felt her shoulders relax and she gave his hand a tiny squeeze before letting go. It was good of him to reassure her. The tension in the room broke.

"Holy Christ," Tag muttered.

Gavin gave her a thumbs-up.

"Boo-yah." Alex grinned at her. She grinned back at him.

Gabe still stared, not moving a muscle. Maybe not even breathing. She couldn't even hazard a guess as to what he was thinking. Her gaze slid down his body, and she found that she, too, was speechless. He—like most of them, she noticed—was wearing a tuxedo. The black fabric hugged his shoulders and emphasized his lean waist and hips. The black bow tie over snowy-white shirt should have made the rough, tough operator look silly, but instead he reminded her of James Bond.

"You all look very handsome," she said to the room at large, but she couldn't tear her eyes from him.

Gabe finally took a ragged breath and exhaled hard. "I'll be fighting off every man under eighty. You look . . . amazing."

She looked down. He shouldn't say things he didn't mean. He wouldn't fight for her. "We should go."

"Wait. Let me check in first." He pulled out his phone and hit a button. "Who's this? Archie? What's wrong? Where's Trevor?" He laughed. "Hell of a time to take a leak. Any updates?" He hit another button and an Irish voice came on the line.

"Conall can't stop gawking at Her Highness's diddies. It's true she's a fine bit of stuff, but she's sound. He's a fecking eejit. Ow! Leave off, Conall. I was just having a bit of fun."

Mace laughed. "You're on speaker, asshole."

"Ah, Christ. Tell a fella next time. Your pardon, ladies."

Gabe spoke with exaggerated patience. "Are there any updates on Her Highness's list of possible enemies?"

"One or two." Archie's voice deepened as he got down to business. "There's a gent named Escamilla who lost Her Highness's patronage for his halfway house because of liberties with the accounting. He was skimming. Also, FYI, the Nabourgs are broke. Heavily in debt to any number of businesses. God knows how they're funding that fancy hooley you blokes are popping into. Any use?"

"Yes," Gabe assured him. "Do we know where Escamilla is?"

"Aye. His wife left him and he went back to Madrid. Interpol is keeping an eye on him for us."

"Thanks. Call if anything comes up."

"See ya after," Archie said. The line went dead.

There was complete silence for a moment.

"We're bound to catch a break," Christina said. She kept her expression bright and optimistic. "Trevor's team will find answers for us."

Alex shrugged. Gavin muttered something too low for her to hear. Tag grunted.

"We work with what we've got," Gabe said, slapping his hands together and rubbing them briskly. "We've done more with less intel."

"True. Let's get this party rolling," Mace said. He showed Christina a tiny Bluetooth device. "To keep us all connected. The wire you're wearing is only a backup." He made as though to insert it himself, but Christina put out a hand. He dropped it into her palm. She slid it into her ear canal, and they did a brief comms check.

"I'll be in your ear translating, if necessary," Gavin said. "But I only speak French, not Dutch."

"I understand. I'll be fine. Deni will be with me."

Mace and Gavin, who wore suits but not tuxedos, peeled off. In a few minutes, they checked in. Mace found a spot on the roof that he grumbled "sucked less than the others," and Gavin was with the cars, just in case they needed a fast exit.

The rest of them descended from the open balcony, where a liveried footman escorted them to the ballroom. Panels of light wood separated cream-colored walls. Chandeliers gave the room a warm air. The dance floor dominated the room. It was formal and grand, just as Deni had said.

She joined the line waiting to go in, Deni beside her. Tag stood at the doors to the great hall. Alex and Gabe had slipped inside the ballroom. When it came her turn, Christina stepped through the doors and into the ballroom. The receiving line was to her left. Deni addressed a stiff man in formal livery at the head of the receiving line.

"Dame Deni Van Praet, Edle von Naamveld," she told him. "Presenting Her Royal Highness Véronique, Princesse de Savoie."

The herald turned to Lord Nabourg and repeated their names

and titles. The viscount shook Deni's hand, turned, and introduced her to his wife. Then it was Christina's turn. As Ronnie had instructed her, she offered both hands to the viscount, then kissed both cheeks. She did the same with the viscountess, who then introduced her to the woman standing beside her, Lady Nerys Nolin. Lady Nolan curtsied to Christina, saying in French, "It is a pleasure to make your acquaintance, Your Royal Highness." Gavin murmured a translation into her ear.

"I am pleased to meet you, as well," she replied in English. "For tonight, I am practicing my English." She leaned forward, eyes twinkling, as though sharing a secret. "It's for my bodyguards, so they do not feel unwelcome. Will you oblige me?"

Lady Nolin hastened to assure Christina of her cooperation. This routine continued down the receiving line, which was mercifully limited to six. By the time she and Deni stepped free, Christina felt calmer. This was going to work. She could do this. *Was* doing it, with no one the wiser. Gabe fell into place one step behind her and to her left. Alex drifted from spot to spot, looking tense and uncomfortable.

A waiter in a black tuxedo with blue bow tie and cummerbund offered her a tray of champagne flutes. She took one simply to have something to do with her hands. "We can't sit yet, not until the Nabourgs do," she said into her earpiece. "I'm going to find somewhere out of the way to stand." Deni nodded, not realizing Christina wasn't talking to her. "Alex, relax. You look like you're about to be devoured by raging lions."

"I'd rather fight lions," the farm boy groused. "These people stink."

Christina knew what he meant. Dozens of different perfumes and colognes swirled around them, mixing poorly into a soup of fragrances. The ballroom was already filled with chatting couples, all dressed like movie stars. Women wore full-skirted ball gowns like hers, or, less common, sheaths such as the one Deni wore. The jewelry glittered. A number of the men wore military uniforms. The brilliance stunned her.

Her plan to fade into the background failed almost at once. The guests were eager to meet her. They expressed outrage over the attempt on her life, wished her well in her marriage, and passed on tidbits of gossip. No one was crass enough to mention the viscount's infidelity in her hearing, but she noted the bright, curious looks sent his way.

She disengaged herself from several women discussing the next elections, to be held in the fall. She'd barely taken a step when a man strode up to her. Gabe stepped in front of her. Surprise and displeasure flickered across the man's face.

"Pardon me," he said stiffly.

The man had a sharp, lean face, close-cropped hair, and a goatee. The burn scar swept up his left cheek to just above his ear, puckered and shiny. Christina recognized him from the photo taken at the anti-drilling protest. Anxiety spiked. This man knew Ronnie.

"Good evening, Lord Bonnet," she said, in Ronnie's lilting, musical voice. "Is this not a lovely party?"

The man bowed very slightly. "Yes, Your Royal Highness. I wonder if I might have a word?" He eyed Gabe, who had not moved.

Was this her potential assassin? He certainly looked the part, which made the notion that he might be one ridiculous. She touched Gabe's arm, pressing firmly. He scowled and didn't budge.

"Gabriel," she said. She'd meant to sound firm, but her voice quavered at the end. He half turned to look at her. "Please step aside."

Alex appeared behind the man. "I got your back."

Gabe took a step back, allowing the man close enough to talk.

"*Merci bien*," he said to Christina, ignoring Gabe. He began to speak rapidly in French. Gavin translated. "I know we've been on opposing sides on your idea to open up our northern regions to exploration for oil and natural gas. But the damage . . ."

Christina gave a gentle smile and placed a hand on his forearm, stopping him in midsentence. "We 'ave all made a pact tonight to practice our English. It will be fun, yes? Do you speak English?"

Bonnet scowled. "*Naturellement*. Of course, if it please you, ma'am. I was saying that . . ."

"*Non*, Lord Bonnet," she interrupted. "My grandaunt's anniversary ball is hardly the place to discuss this. Enjoy the evening, and we will speak at the Vienna summit in three weeks."

A frown pulled his stern face down even more. "This is very important, and I've been unsuccessful in making an appointment through the private secretary's office." He glared in Deni's direction.

The Nabourgs ambled toward the head table, signaling it was time for guests to take their places. Relieved, Christina stepped back. "I'm sorry, Lord Bonnet. Our hosts are beginning the seating for dinner."

He reached out toward Christina, glanced at Gabe, and lowered his hand. "May I speak with you later, then? It's urgent."

Not if she could help it. The man gave her the shivers. "Yes, of course." She turned to Deni.

"You will sit beside Lady Nabourg," Deni said at once. "I am assigned to sit at a table with Lady Nolin and Mrs. Boeckman."

"Oh," Christina said, eyes rounding. "But . . ."

Deni patted her arm. "I do not have the rank to sit with the nobles. You will be fine."

Butterflies returned to her stomach. She relied on Deni's knowledge and, when needed, intervention. She felt chilled, knowing she was on her own.

A warm, calloused palm slid into hers. "We're here," Gabe said. "You're doing great."

Grateful, she squeezed his fingers. When he stepped away again, she missed his solid presence beside her. She moved to the head table and found her name on a simple white card. A footman held her chair. Gabe nudged him aside, gentle but implacable. When he'd seated her, he fell back several steps, until he almost blended into the wall.

"Bonnet," she murmured, lips barely moving. "He's a politician, right? A public figure. It's odd that he wasn't in front of the cameras at the protest. Usually politicians want the spotlight."

"Trevor will find something, if it's there to find," Gabe said reassuringly. "Focus on the here and now."

Dinner was a long, tedious affair. At the start of each of the seven courses, several guests would stand and offer a toast to the Nabourgs, to their wedding anniversary, and to their continued health.

At last, the toasts dwindled and stopped. Lady Nabourg rose, presumably to give her own speech of thanks. Before she could open her mouth, though, a man entered the ballroom and made straight for the head table, a footman following him with a small box and a bouquet of roses. He stopped about fifteen feet from the table and inclined his head. His dark hair was cut short, but would be curly if allowed to grow. Thick brows slashed over grayish-blue eyes. His nose seemed slightly rounded and too large for his face, but fit well with his broad shoulders and long legs. He looked familiar, but she could not immediately place him.

"My lady, you look lovely," the man said. "My apologies for appearing uninvited, but I very much wanted to wish you both many more years of happy marriage."

The viscountess beamed down at him. "Lord Brumley, you honor us. And I am thinking your surprise visit might have more to do with my grandniece, your beautiful fiancée, is it not so?"

Christina's heart stopped. Ronnie's fiancé? What was he doing here?

"Abort," Gabe said into her ear. "That's Julian Brumley, the fiancé. Get ready to move her out."

TREVOR HAD WARNED him it was too dangerous for them to be together until the shooter had been neutralized. Why had he ignored the warning? Christina, the 'her' in question, raised her napkin and pretended to blot her lips. "Wait. He can't get near me until the dancing starts. It will look too suspicious if he appears, and I immediately run away."

"It's too risky," Gabe said.

Christina intensified her whisper. "You're in charge of protection, but I'm in charge of the pretense. I'll move when it won't look odd."

He'd positioned himself between wall sconces so that his face was in shadow, but she felt the fury in his gaze. Half expecting him to lunge at her and drag her away by the hair, she was astonished when he didn't move. And didn't move.

"Thank you," she breathed. There was no response.

Julian Brumley indicated the box the footman held. "My lord and lady, a small gift to celebrate your anniversary."

Lord Nabourg peered at it. "Excellent. Lovely." He gestured, and the footman bowed and placed the box on the table beside the other gifts.

Julian lifted the roses into his arms. "And now, my lord and lady, if you will permit me?" He strode to Christina, sitting beside Lady Nabourg. Christina tensed. He smiled into her eyes, warmth and affection pouring from them, and handed her the bouquet. "Beauty for my beauty," he said. The crowd murmured approvingly.

Nonplussed, Christina bent her head to sniff the flowers, then set them on the table. "They're beautiful, Julian. Thank you." She stumbled almost imperceptibly over his name. He smiled again, then the footman was back, guiding him to a table halfway down the room, where there was an open seat. Christina began to breathe again.

Conversation began again in the room, perhaps a touch more animated than before. Her appetite gone, Christina picked at the *spekkoek*, a traditional layered spiced cake. Her gaze kept skittering to Julian Brumley, even as she asked Ronnie's great-aunt questions about her youth in Andorra. Lady Nabourg spoke animatedly about her childhood, slipping from Dutch to English and back again. Christina nodded and smiled and murmured at appropriate intervals, and made herself look interested.

"When they get up, come toward me," Gabe said in her ear. "Nod so I know you heard me."

She hesitated, but finally inclined her head. It wasn't the right move. In order to reveal the shooter, she had to remain exposed to a certain extent. And where would she be safer than at a party with a bunch of old noblemen? Gabe was being reactive, but there was no way to communicate that to him.

The room became restive, and Lady Nabourg finally raised her head. "Well, my dear, it is time to start the dancing." She rose, and her husband followed suit. They came together on the dance floor, and the orchestra began to play a waltz. They were elderly and not spry, so they did little more than sway, but it released the rest of the guests to dance as well, or move about the room to chat. The dance floor filled quickly, mostly with the younger guests. Christina rose, intending to withdraw quietly, with no one the wiser. Instead, Émile Bonnet waylaid her as soon as she stepped from the table.

"Your Royal Highness," he said. "I was distressed to hear about the attack in Brussels. Your life is in danger. Perhaps it would be better if you didn't attend the Geothermal Exploration conference in Vienna next month?"

Ronnie had mentioned the conference several times. In fact, she and Trevor had argued about it, in their very polite way. Even if the "situation," as she called it, was not resolved by them, Ronnie still wanted to go. She was scheduled to speak on economic responsibility, supporting an initiative to lure oil companies into Concordia. "I speak for future generations," she'd said. "Our economy cannot sustain itself on farming and tourism alone. We import seventy percent of our food from other countries as it is. There are many ways to mitigate potential damage that oil production and distribution might have in certain rural areas."

Christina spoke as she believed Ronnie would, hoping she got it right. "It is too important an issue for me to stay away. All geological reports indicate there are huge deposits of oil in our northern, rural regions."

Émile frowned. "With respect, ma'am, that's shortsighted. Importing oil does no damage to our land, which sustains some very rare animals. It's irresponsible to destroy natural animal habitats."

Ronnie had discussed this with her at length. "You refer to the sheared mink in the Ardennes. You need not worry. They will be very carefully monitored and regulated. Every effort will be made to insure their survival."

Gabe stepped to her side. "I'm sorry, Lord Bonnet. The princess is required elsewhere."

Before she could move, Julian strode up to her and caught her up in an embrace, swinging her around in a tiny circle. Christina could do nothing but clutch at his shoulders until he set her down again.

"Ronnie," he said, hands on her shoulders. "I know you told me not to come, but I had to see you." He wanted to kiss her, Christina could see it in his eyes, but the famed English reserve took precedence. "I missed you, little cabbage."

"I . . . I missed you, too." She forced a smile. Gabe was right; she had to leave now, before Julian realized the woman before him was not his Ronnie.

Émile extended a hand. "I am pleased to meet you, Lord Brumley. I am Émile Denis, Earl Bonnet."

"Lord Bonnet." Julian gave a polite nod and a brief handshake. "I appreciate the English. My French is atrocious."

"It was Her Royal Highness's wish for the evening."

Gabe and Alex had moved in, one on each side of the men, near enough to tackle them if things went south.

"May I introduce Gabriel Morgan and Alexander Wood?"

Julian looked them over and opened his mouth to speak. Deni appeared beside her. "Julian," she said. "How wonderful to see you again." She kissed both his cheeks.

Émile turned back to Christina. "Ma'am, I beg you to listen to reason. Oil and gas exploration is invasive. We cannot afford to lose fertile soil in our farming areas."

"Her Royal Highness's position has not, and will not, change, Lord Bonnet. You will have to persuade others at the summit," Deni said.

Émile's nostrils flared and his mouth flattened. Brows pulled down, he said brusquely, "Saner voices will prevail." He dropped his voice and leaned closer to Deni. "What is this awful business of someone firing a rifle at our princess?" he said in French. "It must be a madman; she is a compassionate champion of our people. See how she fights for our country's health. Perhaps naïve, but well-meaning all the same." Gavin translated in her ear, though she doubted she was meant to hear the low conversation.

"*Oui*," Deni agreed. "This is the reason for the bodyguards, until they catch this madman."

Julian laughed suddenly, wrapping an arm around Christina's shoulders. His hand came to rest directly on top of her bandage. He did not seem to notice, addressing the group at large. "No more politics," he declared. "I want to dance with my fiancée."

"First things first," Gabe said. "The princess was just mentioning she really needed to go, uh, go powder her nose. Why don't we let her do that, and then you can dance."

Christina eased free of his arm. "That's true. I'll be right back. Julian."

"In a moment." He grabbed her hand and walked toward the

dance floor. She had no option but to follow him or cause a scene. "It's been weeks, darling. Let me hold you."

Once on the dance floor, he swung her into his arms and led her expertly across the floor. A good dancer herself, she had no problems following his lead. She forced herself to relax. One dance, then she would get the hell out of there.

"I know Trevor said we'd be safer apart," Julian said. "But I can't focus on anything else, knowing you might still be in danger, and me so far away. Your texts and phone calls aren't enough, darling. I need to be with you."

Ronnie called and texted Julian? That was news to her.

"I want to be with you, too. But what if Trevor is right, and you being here puts me in danger?"

He smiled at her, eyes full of mischief. "I don't think it will." He gathered her close, banding his arms around her. His head dipped, and he whispered into her ear.

"Now, my dear. Just who the hell are you?"

# Chapter Fifteen

GABE CURSED. DAMN it! He should have hauled Christina's ass out of there as soon as the freaking boyfriend walked in. Fiancé. Whatever.

"Abort," he hissed, knowing they were too late. The jig was up. Any minute now, Brumley would pull out his cell phone and call the police. If they were lucky, he wouldn't make a scene while he did it.

"Well?" Brumley asked. His voice was calm and even; he could have been asking about the weather, for all the excitement he betrayed. "Darling?"

"I know how to handle this," she said, and Gabe realized with a jolt she was talking to him. God fucking dammit. She was putting herself in danger. Not disengaging.

"Negative," he clipped out. "Abort. Gavin, bring up the car. Tag, Alex, to me."

But as he closed in on her, Christina did the unthinkable.

"My name is Christina," she told him. She *told* him. Freaking unbelievable.

Gabe could see Brumley's hand clench around Christina's fragile one, hard enough to turn her fingers white. For a moment, all he could think about was getting the bastard's hands off her.

"Where is she?" the man's voice was icy. "If you've harmed her in any way . . ."

"Ronnie is safe, I promise." Christina wiggled her fingers. "Please. Let me explain."

"What is this? Kidnapping? Extortion?"

"Neither. We're . . ."

Tag and Alex reached him, both ready for action. "Break trail," Gabe snapped, and clamped a hand around Christina's upper arm. "Walk with me, princess, if you would, please."

When he guided her none-too-gently by the arm, she moved with him, thank God. Tag and Alex stayed two steps ahead of them, clearing a path. It wasn't until they hit the front door that he realized Julian Brumley had followed them. His hand dipped into his tux to his shoulder rig, touching the butt of his Glock.

"Back inside," he said, pointing with his other hand. 'Course, that meant he'd let go of Christina's arm, and she halted, turning back toward the freaking fiancé, who should have been two countries and a Chunnel away from them.

"Gabe," she started, "we have to . . ."

"No," he grated. "We do not." He took the four steps he needed to get into Brumley's personal space, and dropped his voice almost to a growl. "Go. Back. Inside."

"Gabe, stop. Julian's not the assassin. He's not involved."

Brumley drew himself up to his less-than-impressive five foot ten. "I will not," he said, somehow managing to look down his nose at Gabe. "However, I will call the Federal Police and have you arrested."

"Stop, both of you. We're causing a scene." Christina stepped past Gabe to slip her arm into Brumley's. "Darling, let me show you the garden. It's a bit overgrown. We'll have some privacy," she said, loud enough for those nearest to hear.

Shit. He'd been so focused on the fiancé that he hadn't even noticed the groups and couples strolling on the lawn, enjoying the evening. And Christina was right; they were starting to stop, to stare.

She settled the matter by walking that way.

He gave himself a mental shake. He'd better get his act together, and fast. Seeing her dancing with Brumley had thrown him off his game. It was a good plan. It got them out of view, and, if Brumley tried to hurt Christina, he could disable the fiancé with no one the wiser. Without being told, Tag led the way and Alex brought up the rear in their fun little parade.

"Ronnie is safe," Christina said quietly. "We're not extortionists. We're part of the plan to keep her alive."

Brumley dipped his head closer to hers, the better to hear her, probably. Gabe clenched his fists to stop himself from physically tearing the two apart.

"I talked to her just last night. She said she was looking forward to the ball tonight." He sounded more puzzled than hostile. "Is she here?"

"No. Trevor put her in a safe house. I don't know the location; it's better that way. I can't tell anyone what I don't know."

Brumley tugged on his earlobe. "Why didn't she say anything? Is Trevor with her, at least?"

"Yes," Gabe cut in. "He's investigating the people around her. Including you."

Displeasure flashed in the other man's eyes. He stopped,

turning his head to pierce Gabe with a stare. "Surely, Trevor cleared me."

Without warning, without a sound, three dark shapes swarmed them. Tag grunted in front of him and collapsed. Gabe registered the spit of a silenced handgun as he drew his Glock and dove for Christina.

The figure on the left raised an arm to shoot Brumley. Christina spun aside, crashing into Ronnie's fiancé. They went down in a tangle of arms and legs. The muffled shot went wide.

Gabe leapt over them, using his forearm to knock aside the man's handgun—with silencer—and tag him in the throat with the webbing between his fingers and thumb. The man staggered back, hand on his windpipe. Before Gabe could relieve him of the weapon, the crack of a rifle sounded, and the man spun and fell.

"Target down," said Mace.

Behind him, a second man reached down to grab Christina by the hair, and hauled her to her feet. Gabe whirled back, already reaching for the man's wrist to break his hold.

The third man fired at Gabe. He felt the wind as the bullet passed within millimeters of his ear, reflexively ducking and missing his grab for the bastard holding Christina. Her hands flailed, trying to reach the top of her head, unsuccessful as he yanked her backward by the roots.

Alex returned fire, the crack of his handgun loud in the almost silent struggle. The man jerked, but didn't fall. Alex leapt toward him as the man shifted to aim at him. The kid swept an arm up and over, knocking the gun aside, then closed with his target, sliding his hand down to the man's wrist to control the gun. The other hand snaked around the man's neck, and Alex smashed the man's face into his knee several times.

The bastard holding Christina pressed a gun to her temple. Controlling his rush of adrenaline, Gabe steadied the barrel in his palms, slowing his breathing. The coward was hiding behind her, using her as a human shield. He couldn't get a clear shot without risking hitting Christina.

"Drop your guns," the man ordered. "Or I blow her brains all over the ground."

The third man broke free from Alex, panting heavily. He spat out a mouthful of blood and dove for his handgun.

Gabe edged sideways, trying to get the man holding Christina to turn and follow him. If he could get Mace a clear shot . . .

A second crack, this one pitched lower, and the gunman fell sideways and lay still. Christina scrambled away from him, tripping over her long skirts.

"What the hell?" Mace said. "That wasn't me. There's another shooter up here."

Gabe snagged Christina's wrist and dragged her into a crouch, covering her with his body. He watched as the third man reached his gun, only to have Alex smash into him and take him to the ground, where the young operator flipped him over and twisted his arms high onto his back. The man cursed. Gabe stayed where he was, head swiveling as he watched and listened. Other than the screams and running of the Nabourgs' guests, the grounds were silent.

Brumley got to his hands and feet, and crawled over to Christina. The whites of his eyes were showing. He added his bulk to Gabe's, covering Christina from the other side.

"Where's the second shooter?" Christina tried to rise, but he kept her where she was. "Mace?"

There was a long pause. "Got 'im." Gabe heard the sound

of a bolt snapping back, ejecting a shell casing, and then being slammed forward. "Freeze! Hands where I can see 'em." Then, "Put the rifle down. Step back. Back! Get on your knees, ankles crossed. Hands behind your head. Lace your fingers. Do it now!"

"Mace, report."

"White male, early fifties. He was in another goddamned part of this fucking maze of a roof. Pardon my language, *chérie*."

Gabe pulled Christina and Julian with him to the relative shelter of a tree.

"Stay put." He ran, crouching, over the uneven ground to Tag, who was groaning and starting to rise. "Is he alone?"

Mace cursed again while he passed the question on to his captive. "He says so, but who the hell knows up here?"

Gabe pushed Tag down flat and checked him over. His teammate was muttering profanity. "It caught your vest, dickhead," he said, relief thick in his voice. "Whatchoo doing, taking a nap out here?" He tore Tag's jacket off and helped him remove the ballistic vest.

"Figured . . . figured I'd take the night off."

Gabe supported him while Tag caught his breath. "Gavin," he said. "Did you see anything?"

"Blacked-out van. Didn't come onto the grounds, which is why I didn't see it earlier. It stayed on the road and took off the second it saw me."

"All right. Head up to the roof."

"Already on my way."

Julian left the safety of the tree, followed closely by Christina. He knelt beside Alex. "I can take him, if it would help."

Alex looked to Gabe. He shook his captive as he squirmed and fought.

"No. Thank you, but we've got it covered." Gabe glowered down at their prisoner. "We're going to talk, you and me. You can do it with your face full of leaves, or I can let you up. Which'll it be?" It felt good to vent his anger on someone.

A single eye blazed up at Gabe, hostile and far from cowed. "Let me up."

Gabe's nostrils flared. "Maybe not. How many of you are there?"

"Eat shit."

He twisted the man's arms higher on his back and increased the pressure. The man hissed in pain. "How many, asshole?"

"And die."

He wasn't going to get immediate answers here. Hauling the man to his feet, he kept the hammerlock tight as Tag staggered over to search him. A folding knife, a strip of cloth, a map.

"I found duct tape on one of the dead men," Christina reported, coming over to him. She kept well back from his captive.

Gabe didn't dare release even one hand to take the tape. "Can you come over here and bind his wrists?"

The awkward positioning meant that Christina nearly had to wedge herself in front of him to reach the man's wrists. As she wrapped the tape around and over, Gabe tried to scan down her body. "Are you hurt?"

"No." She finished securing the man's hands and stepped away.

Mace reported in from the roof. "No one else up here, Archangel. We're coming down."

"Let's go." Gabe's command encompassed them all. Tag, Christina, Julian, and their captive marched back to the house and assembled on the wide, curved driveway. Alex and Gavin came around a corner, each holding the arm of a balding man wearing black fatigue pants and a black pullover. Mace headed up the rear, carrying a rifle slung over a shoulder and another in his arms.

"Who's in charge here?" asked the second shooter. He tried to shrug off the arms holding him, but neither man let go until Gabe gestured to them.

"I am." He jerked his head at Alex, who came to take charge of their captive. "And just who the hell are you?"

The man drew himself up to his full height, which was still inches short of Gabe's own six foot one. "I am Commissaris Jansens, Federal Police."

Gabe's eyebrows went up. "You're a cop?" He didn't bother to try to conceal the disbelief in his voice.

"*Ja*," the man said. He had a round baby face, but experience lined his skin. Large ears and thin lips should have made him look silly, but the man carried himself with absolute authority. "I have been assigned to protect Princess Véronique." He turned to face Christina and bowed formally. *"Prinses, ben je gewond?"*

# Chapter Sixteen

CHRISTINA FROZE FOR half a second, then squared her shoulders and shook her head. Was that the right answer? It seemed to satisfy the man for the moment.

"I don't suppose you've got any ID on you?" Skepticism rang in Gabe's tone.

Jansens reached his left hand back, and five handguns rose as one to cover him. "Naturally, I have identification," he said, huffing a little.

"Slowly," Tag said. "Two fingers."

When the badge wallet was visible, Gavin took it from him, flipping it open while Jansens's jaw tightened and his right eye twitched.

"Deputy Police Commissioner Aart Jansens of the Special Missions Unit of the Concordian Federal Police," Gavin said. "Badge and everything."

"Tag, check out his story. Make sure he's legit." Gabe's eyebrows pulled down until they nearly met in the center. "Who the hell assigned you to protect *my* principal?"

Jansens extended his hand, ta[...]
wallet. "The Minister of Interna[...]

"We coordinated with the m[...]
Concordian bodyguards, at Lor[...]
he go back on his word?" Gavi[...]
commissioner returned it to his[...]

"Princess Véronique is impo[...]
foreigners could never understa[...]
will one day be our queen."

Mace hefted the second rifle. "So you just thought you'd hop up onto my roof?" he snapped, nearly frothing at the mouth. "If I'd seen you, I'd've shot you. Did you think of that?"

A corner of Jansens's lip curled. "I am a highly decorated police detective. You will find I am not so easily killed."

Mace looked like he wanted to rip the man's throat out. Gabe held up a hand. Mace backed off a step, but no more. Gabe willed his own wrath down to manageable levels.

"Why didn't you coordinate with us?" he asked.

"Why?" The man puffed up like a blowfish, trying to look larger than he was. "Why would I? We Concordians protect our own. We don't need any help from hired thugs."

Something about this felt . . . off. And not just because some bureaucrat in the minister's office had assigned one or more policemen to protect Véronique without his knowledge. Before Gabe could put his finger on it, Jansens said, "It is a good thing I was on overwatch. Without my actions, the princess would have been killed."

Gabe couldn't argue that one. The shot, fired in the dark, into the midst of battle, with Christina and her attacker in such close proximity, required a master marksman. He wasn't a hundred percent sure even Mace, one of the Army's best snipers, could have done it.

of you are there? So we know who not to kill," he
_____tically.

_____nough," Jansens said, chin lifting with arrogance. "Who
_____you to interfere in our affairs, anyway?" He turned to Chris-
___a, and a spate of words flowed from him.

Christina met the man's eyes squarely. "English, please. I am
the only one here who speaks Dutch. And I have no secrets from
my bodyguards . . . or my fiancé."

Jansens looked like he wanted to argue, but finally gave a
grudging nod. "Yes, Your Royal Highness." He glanced around. "I
asked why foreigners protected Princess Véronique, instead of her
own trusted countrymen."

Brumley stepped forward. "I'm responsible. I am Lord Julian
Brumley of the English House of Lords. I asked for their help."

That wasn't strictly true, but Gabe let it slide. Brumley had
asked his cousin Trevor Carswell for help, and Trevor had reached
out to Delta Force.

"You must understand that my first priority is to keep Ronnie
safe," he continued. "Since we didn't—and still don't—know
where the threat is coming from, it seemed logical to me that we
use professionals whom we knew to be uninvolved. The fewer
people who know her whereabouts, the safer she is. I thought the
minister understood that."

Enough of this. They needed to get out of here. He could hear
sirens wailing in the distance, heading toward them. "Tag, search
the bodies again and then the area for anything they might have
dropped. Any clues. Gavin, find us an unmarked SUV. No flags,
no decals. Mace, give me Jansens's rifle and take yours up to the
house. No need to alarm the locals."

His men scattered.

"I must insist that you return my weapon."

Gabe barely glanced at Jansens. "No."

Jansens looked like he wanted to argue.

"I'm turning you over to the police," Gabe said. "They can figure out what to do with you."

Alex shook his captive. "What about him?"

"I guess the police will want him, too." Maybe they could take him somewhere? Get him to talk before the police took him? Gabe reluctantly let go of the thought. They were almost out of time. "Why did you attack us?"

He didn't really expect an answer, but it would be foolish not to ask. The man glared sullenly.

Police cars began pulling into the wide drive.

"All right," Gabe said, working his shoulders. "Alex, look harmless."

He held the sniper rifle out from his body by one hand, muzzle down. Alex held their captive by a shoulder, his other hand out and open. Predictably, the police took one look at them and began shouting. He needed no translation. He set the rifle on the driveway, stepped away from it, and knelt, hands interlaced behind his head. Alex followed suit. Their prisoner tried to run, made it ten feet, and was tackled by a blue-uniformed cop. Jansens flashed his badge, which earned him in equal measures respect and hostility. Apparently, the rivalry between locals and Feds wasn't limited to the United States.

Guests swarmed the police, gesturing and talking at the same time.

"Princess, Brumley, get inside." He shot a warning look at

Christina. Right on cue, she began to sob, tears welling in her eyes. Brumley put a protective arm around her shoulders, and walked her straight into the center of the action, hugging her to him while she wept into his chest. "The princess was attacked," he kept repeating. "Her bodyguards saved her. She is overwrought. I must take her to her room."

Finally, a man with bulging muscles and no neck bellowed for silence. He said something in Dutch. Jansens answered him. After a moment, he nodded and waved Brumley through. Christina sagged against him. Not too much, Gabe thought. Just enough drama, but not too much. As though she'd heard him, she pulled herself upright, tears streaking her cheeks, and put on a brave face. Ronnie's countrymen responded immediately, becoming solicitous as they encouraged Brumley to take their princess into the house.

Nicely done.

Neither she nor Brumley had needed to be told their cover would be blown if the police realized their crown princess suddenly forgot how to speak both French and Dutch. They would want to interview her later; but later, he would be able to control the environment. Now, however, he found himself hauled to his feet and searched. He forced himself to keep his hands loose and nonthreatening, even when they found his Glock and began shouting at him again.

"We are the princess's executive protection team," he said at least a dozen times. "Bodyguards. We're her bodyguards."

As he'd known it would, the chaos eventually resolved itself. The police bagged the duct tape, blindfold, knife, and map as evidence. When they tried to return Deputy Police Commissioner

Jansens's sniper rifle, Gabe pitched such a stink they finally took that as evidence as well, probably just to shut him up. Gabe didn't know why Jansens bugged him. Sure, he was pissed the minister had apparently ignored Brumley's request for secrecy and then hadn't notified him of a police presence. Something else nagged at the edge of his mind, though.

"We were attacked back there, behind the trees," Gabe said for the third time. "The man you have in custody is one of the attackers. Our sniper killed one, and your Federal cop killed the other one."

"Why?" This time, a pinch-faced woman in uniform, wearing a boat-shaped hat on top of a severe ponytail, jotted notes.

"I won't know that until I talk to him." Gabe jabbed a thumb at the third assailant, squirming in the back seat of a police cruiser.

The policewoman didn't look up. "Chief Van den Nieuwenhuyzen will question the suspect."

"Then I need to talk to Chief Van New . . . your chief."

The policewoman raised her head. "Where is Princess Véronique now?"

"Up at the house. Her fiancé, Lord Brumley, wanted her out of the public spotlight. Wanted her safe. That's what we all want, isn't it?"

Again, the woman ignored his question. "I will need to get her statement."

"Once we're done here, I'll be happy to escort you up." His teammates had all been taken to separate locations and questioned individually. It was starting to get on his nerves.

"We are finished for now," the woman said. "If we have any follow-on questions, you will be contacted."

Gabe stood. "Who has our weapons?"

"It is irrelevant. All weapons involved in the shooting will be held until the investigation is over."

Gabe thought about arguing, but it wouldn't get him anywhere, and might antagonize the local cops. "Fine."

Soon enough, his teammates were also cleared and gathered around him.

"Tag, go get checked out," he ordered, flicking his head toward the ambulance that wailed its way onto the drive. The siren cut out and it drifted to a halt. Half a dozen rattled guests watched the paramedics climb out.

"I'm fine," Tag said.

Gabe shot him a look. Tag nodded as though he'd spoken. He turned and walked over to the paramedics.

Chief Van den Nieuwenhuyzen joined him. "You've made quite a mess here, Mr. Morgan."

"Not us," he said at once. "Alex, Gavin, Mace, head on up and make sure the princess is secure." His men departed.

"So you say," the chief said. Despite his words, no condemnation lurked in his eyes. "We'll know more after we interview your captive."

"I'd appreciate a copy of that report."

The chief inclined his head. "You'll have it. And now, I must interview Princess Véronique." He gestured for Gabe to precede him.

Gabe led the way inside and up the stairs to the outer balcony. "The interview will need to be in English. We need to know what she saw, too."

"I will provide you a copy of the report."

He halted on the stairs, forcing the cop to stop as well. "English, or it doesn't happen."

Displeasure darkened the chief's face. "I do not need your permission to interview Princess Véronique. You are in my jurisdiction. I could just as easily have you arrested."

True enough. Gabe hesitated. Everything would go sideways if the chief realized Christina wasn't Ronnie. Still, he didn't have much choice. He climbed the rest of the way.

Mace stood at the top of the stairs. Gavin had planted himself outside Christina's door, which stood open. Gabe entered in front of the chief.

Deni sat next to Christina, with Brumley on her other side. Alex stood behind the sofa, ready to wrestle Brumley to the ground if necessary. Good man.

"Your Royal Highness," the chief said, bobbing his head respectfully. "I am Chief Van Den Nieuwenhuyzen. Your bodyguard has requested I interview you in English. I am disinclined to grant this request, as it seems odd to me, but he was quite insistent." He drew out a notebook that had clearly seen better days, and seated himself in the nearest chair.

"Now, if you would take me through the events this evening, please."

Christina explained the events calmly, sitting with her knees together and her hands clasped. Brumley's palm rested on her knee. "And one of them grabbed me and put a gun to my head. I was terrified. He said he intended to kill me. I had no reason to think he might be bluffing. It was then that Federal Deputy Commissioner Aart Jansens shot him."

The chief sucked his bottom lip. Reflectively, Gabe thought, not suspiciously. "Did you have a prior arrangement with Deputy Commissioner Jansens?"

"No. We did not know he was there. The first clue we had was when he shot the man who held a gun to my head." Christina's voice trembled. Was she still acting? He hadn't gotten the chance to reassure himself that she was okay. Brumley slipped an arm around her shoulders, and Gabe realized he was grinding his teeth as he glared at the man.

"Princess, do you have any idea why these attempts are being made on your life? We know, of course, about the attempt in Brussels."

Christina shook her head. "I haven't the faintest clue." Her head moved toward Gabe and she swallowed. "Indeed, it is a mystery to me." Her French accent deepened. "I cannot fathom what I have done to so anger anyone that they would wish me dead."

The Chief rose. "All right. If we get any information from our prisoner, I'll call your man." He nodded toward Gabe.

"I would be grateful."

Deni escorted the police chief to the door, speaking to him quietly and then closing the door behind him. When she came back, her brows were pulled down.

"He is concerned about a third attack. He knows nothing of our experience on the road to Grasvlakten, and I didn't enlighten him. However, he wants to assign some uniformed police officers to help you."

"No." Gabe's reaction was immediate and absolute. "They would just be in the way."

Christina shifted in the armchair. "This is getting too public. I thought . . . well, I thought it would be over quickly, frankly. I figured there'd be one more attempt, and we'd catch the bad guys, and Ronnie could get on with her life."

"We caught one of them," Mace pointed out.

"Yeah, but will he talk? Will he tell us who and why?" Christina chewed a fingernail. "I thought it was one man. A crazy. I mean, the God-told-me-to-kill-you kind of crazy. Now with three of them, that changes the game."

She wasn't wrong. "I need to call Trevor," Gabe said. "I want to know where he is on vetting that list." He threw an annoyed look at Brumley. The man caught the look and had the gall to smile at him blandly. Gabe's fists clenched.

THE POLICE WERE GONE. Deni had gone back outside to lend a hand calming the rattled guests. The Delta Force operators stood at various points around the room. Christina slouched back in her seat. Tag hadn't returned yet from the paramedics' examination, so it was the seven of them. She exhaled, hard.

"That wasn't fun." She'd stopped shaking once she and Julian reached the sanctuary of her room, but the chief's questions rekindled the shock of the attack. There was something familiar about the way they'd swarmed her. Her thoughts flashed back to her time in Washington, D.C., when she'd been followed by the men in the blacked-out van. She still didn't understand what those men expected to achieve. Some part of her still believed it was a training exercise; that if they'd succeeded in getting her into the van, they would have laughed and high-fived each other. She made a mental note to call Jay and check in.

She should remind them about the van, for thoroughness' sake.

She opened her mouth. Tag entered the room, pulling a cold pack off his chest and tossing it onto the nearest flat surface.

"What's the word?" Gabe said at once.

Tag spread his arms wide. "Bruised my sternum. No penetration."

A tension she hadn't even known was in the room relaxed. His teammates, for all their stoicism, had been worried.

Gavin barked out a laugh. "No penetration, speak for yourself. I got my eye on this cute little maid downstairs."

"She's not going to be looking at you with me in the room," Mace said, flexing his biceps, a smug look on his face.

Christina chuckled, pulling the comb from her hair and unwinding the rolls. Hair had pulled free of the sophisticated chignon during the attack, but she'd left it in disarray as a show for the police. Now she raked her nails through it, trying to tame the mess. "Someone find me a cute butler, then."

Gavin made a show of unbuttoning his suit coat, spreading it one side at a time to showcase his abs. "How about a chauffeur? Mature men know what they're doing, unlike these young punks."

"Punk this." Alex flipped him the bird and settled back against the wall. "If the chauffeur looks like you, fuhgetabout it."

"How about that actress with the big doe eyes?" Mace laced both hands under his chin and made a show of batting his eyes. "I'd take a bullet to the chest to penetrate that."

"Gentlemen." Julian broke up the laughter. "This is hardly appropriate. There's a lady present."

The joking ceased. What had been easy camaraderie shifted into something awkward. Christina sighed. Julian meant well, of course. But the more she blended with the team, the easier time they would all have together.

"All right. To business," Gabe said. "We all know the details of the shot fired in Brussels. This was different."

Tag nodded, face settling into its usual glower. "They aimed for us, not Christina. Their goal was to snatch her, not kill her. The strip of cloth for a blindfold, the duct tape for her hands or mouth."

"Maybe they changed tactics, considering their sniper sucked?" said Mace.

"Did anyone get a look at the map?" Julian asked.

"Yeah," Gabe said. "Before the cops put it in an evidence baggie. It was a map of Concordia. Nothing circled, no arrows pointing anywhere, no addresses. That would have been too easy." He sounded disgruntled. Christina could relate.

"What do we do now?" Julian asked.

"We do nothing," Gabe said at once. "You go home."

Julian's eyes narrowed. "You barely made it through this evening without my help," he pointed out, none too gently. "If I hadn't taken Christina into the villa, the gendarmes would have been asking her questions she couldn't answer. Unless I'm wrong, and you can speak French and Dutch fluently?"

"Not a word of either. I'm grateful," Christina hastened to assure him. "You were a huge help. Thank you for going along."

His smile was warm. Gabe glared. Christina didn't care. She knew she'd made the right call by telling Julian the truth. He could be trusted; she could feel it.

Gabe dialed a number and put his phone on speaker.

"Carswell."

"It's Gabe. We've had an incident. Is Ronnie safe?"

There was a pause on the line. "Yes," came his clipped British accent. "We've had no trouble here. What's happened?"

"Three men came at us outside the Nabourg house. We dropped two and the third is in custody. So far, we don't know who or why."

"Any injuries?"

"Tag took a round to his vest, but he's good to go."

"Glad to hear it."

"Anything new on Ronnie's list?"

"Since our update four hours ago? No, mate," Trevor said.

Gabe kneaded the back of his neck, his gaze landing on Christina and then skittering away. She knew she wasn't going to like the next words out of his mouth.

"What about the fiancé?" Gabe's voice held no expression.

Christina shot him an annoyed look. Did he have to be such a jerk? She turned to Julian. "He's just trying to be thorough. He didn't mean anything by it."

"Of course he did." Julian's tone was less genial. "But I accept it. My first priority is to keep Ronnie safe. If that means letting Trev rifle through my life, then so be it."

"Trevor's your cousin, right?" asked Christina.

"Second cousin, on my mother's side. We've never been particularly close, but we know one another well enough."

Gabe glowered. "Trevor, tell Julian he needs to go back to London."

"He's there?" Trevor was startled. "Julian, my good man, what are you doing in Grasvlakten?"

"Visiting my fiancée," said Julian. "Or so I thought. Did you know we talk every day?"

"I knew, of course," Trevor admitted. "I advised her to keep up the pretense of keeping to Christina's schedule, so you wouldn't worry. I wanted to prevent exactly what apparently happened."

Julian looked unhappy. "Do you mean to say that I was the

target? That I flew here and your assailants followed me, and that's why we were attacked?"

Trevor was silent.

"Trev?"

"Very probably not, but I can't know with absolute certainty," Trevor admitted. "We're assuming the target is Ronnie, because no one accosted you either before or after. I can tell the rest of you, though, without reservation, that he's in the clear."

Gabe frowned. Christina sighed. Why had Gabe chosen Julian to dislike? He could help them. It would be nice to think that it might be jealousy, but that was beyond silly. Gabe liked control. Perhaps he felt that things were getting out of hand, and that guarding Deni and Julian both would burden his team too much.

"I'd still like to help," Julian said firmly. "I can lend legitimacy in many ways. In the language department, certainly. Everyone is happy to speak English when I'm with Ronnie. You've had difficulties, I'm certain, with Christina not speaking the language."

"We've had a couple of close calls, but we've managed," Christina said.

"It's settled, then. I'll remain with you until these men are caught, as long as Ronnie stays safe with Trevor."

"No," Gabe said. "You're a handicap. Our focus needs to be on Christina. No distractions."

Julian leaned against the back of the sofa. "Short of shooting me, old chap, how do you propose to keep me away?"

The tension level inside the room skyrocketed. The two men locked stares. Gabe shifted his weight to the balls of his feet.

"Gabe." She made her voice sharp, and as authoritative as she could. "Trevor cleared him. You heard that, same as the rest of us."

"I'm team leader here," he reminded her calmly. As though

she'd forget it. His implacable tone made her shiver. "I'm nothing like that fool in Iraq."

"If there's one thing I learned in Baghdad . . ."

On the open phone line, Trevor cleared his throat. "Gabe, I'm not sure what she's told you about that mission, or what you've heard. There's more to the story . . ."

"No." Gabe cut him off. "That's the end of it. Thank you, Lord Brumley, but it's time for you to go home."

Julian cocked a curious look at him. "If Christina wants me to stay, I stay. *That's* the end of it, chum."

Gabe turned to Christina, pinning her with a look she understood all too clearly. Unwilling to be the cause of strife within the team, she took a deep breath. "Julian, it would probably be better if you went back to London. Stay the night here, though. It's very late."

He gave her a rueful smile. "That's it, then. I'll have a footman bring my bags up."

Wait . . . what? He was going to stay with her? Well, hadn't she just invited him to? She almost laughed out loud. It was perfect. It would get Gabe off of her couch and out of her room.

DESPITE GABE'S GLOWERS, Julian had his bags brought to Christina's room. Into her fucking bedroom. The maid unpacked his suits and slacks, and hung them next to Christina's in the closet. It came as no surprise that he and Ronnie were sleeping together. Who waited for marriage anymore? He certainly wasn't saving himself for anything.

It didn't take Christina very long to notice that his duffel and sleeping bag were still tucked behind the couch.

"Seriously?" She rolled her eyes. "Really, Gabe, you're being—"

"Is Brumley an operator?" he asked. Too bluntly. Too rudely, but he didn't care. "Can he protect you if someone breaks in here in the middle of the night? Can he defend against a knife attack?" He didn't wait for her response. "No, he can't. My job is to keep you alive until we figure this mess out. And now, apparently, my job includes keeping his ass alive, too." He jerked a thumb at Brumley, who was at the other end of the room peering out the window. He didn't turn or react, but Gabe knew he'd overheard. He'd meant the other man to hear.

"Gabe, for God's sake. It's one night."

"Fine. Whatever." With bad grace, he stomped out of the room and went next door, where his teammates were cleaning weapons, sharpening steel, and yapping their big mouths. All conversation stopped as he entered the room. The ribbing started immediately.

"What happened, Romeo? Did you get kicked out of Juliet's bed?" asked Mace.

"Fuck you. I was sleeping on the couch, not in her bed."

Tag laughed in his face. "We know that's not where you wanted to be, though, you dog."

"Fuck you."

Gavin made a cutting motion near his crotch. "Decapitated," he said, grinning.

"Fuck . . ."

" . . . You. I know." Gavin punched him in the arm, which actually stung a little. Even at fifty, the man was preternaturally strong. "Tell me you didn't have some idea of saving Christina and having her fall all over you in gratitude?"

"I'm not going to dignify that," Gabe retorted. "I'm a professional, and so is she."

Alex chimed in, a little tentatively. "Gabe, so far she's done a hell of a job. Sometimes I forget she's not one of us. When we're out in public and she's doing her thing, she's great."

Gabe rubbed the back of his neck, where tension seemed to have taken up permanent residence. "I know. She's a natural at this. I just don't want rash decisions to put any of you in jeopardy."

That was met with bewildered looks.

"We've all done executive protection," Tag said. "When we're guarding a principal, they don't know what the hell they're doing. And we cope. Christina's at least had training. Hand to hand. Weapons. Not like that senator's kid from Georgetown we guarded a couple years ago."

"That ditzy airhead," Mace said, with a healthy amount of disgust. "She couldn't put two syllables together that didn't add up to 'fuck me, Mace.'"

"Too bad about that, dickhead," Gavin said.

"Fuck that. I like a woman with a brain in her head."

Tag stood. "Gabe, what's going on? She's been an advantage from the start. Did something happen?"

"Have you forgotten tonight already? Teammates don't challenge the team leader's decisions in the heat of crisis. She jeopardized the mission, spilling it all to a potential threat."

The room went dead silent.

"What?"

"She made a gut-call. Any one of us would have done the same," Gavin said. "We're trained to think beyond orders. Let's be honest, man. You reacted emotionally instead of acting logically."

Alex, slouched back against the wall, folded his arms across his chest. "Like you didn't like the fiancé being there. Like you were jealous."

He threw a death glare at the kid. Alex had the sense to deflate.

His teammates were looking at him oddly. Mace was the first to say it.

"Jesus, Gabe. Do you have a thing for her?"

He swung away, irritated. "Of course not. We have a job to do, is all."

Mace and Tag exchanged a look.

"What?" he demanded.

Suddenly, they were all innocent faces and wide eyes. He had no trouble reading their minds.

"Fuck you all."

They laughed.

Gavin punched Gabe in the arm again, harder, and in the same spot. "You're an idiot."

Ow.

Maybe he was. He wondered what Christina and Julian were doing. Were they really going to sleep together in that bed, in the nasty yellow room? Well, yeah. If he insisted on staying on the sofa, they would have no choice.

He stomped next door and banged it open without knocking. Christina and Brumley were sitting side by side on the couch, heads close together as they talked. Christina had her head thrown back as she laughed. Gabe's heart nearly stopped at the beauty of the sound.

They both looked up in surprise. Christina rose to her feet. "Gabe, what's wrong?"

"Nothing," he bit out. He hefted his duffel onto a shoulder, feeling his biceps expand as he twisted the heavy bag and scooped his sleeping bag into the other hand. Without another word, he stalked out.

In a thoroughly pissed-off mood, he returned to the team

room and dropped his gear. He stripped off his tux. The attack left it covered in dirt and some leaves. He draped it over the back of a chair. With any luck, he wouldn't need it again.

"I'm going for a run," he announced. Maybe that would calm him.

"I'll go with you," Tag said.

"Me, too." Gavin changed into shorts and a T-shirt.

"Under no circumstances is she to leave this house," he said, pointing a finger at first Alex, then Mace. They nodded assent.

The police were gone. A few guests still milled around, both in the ballroom and outside, chattering about the evening's excitement. Gabe bypassed them and hit the road hard. After two miles, the tension in his neck started to relax. At four, his blood calmed.

Gabe pushed himself faster. He'd screwed up earlier, disparaging Christina's decision. They'd started to understand each other, even trust each other. And then he'd cut her down in front of the entire team.

He owed her an apology. She'd been right to trust Brumley. Instead of shouting at her, he needed to listen to her. Plain old green jealousy had reared its ugly head when he'd seen them dancing so closely together. He'd wanted to be the one holding her. And the strength of that wanting scared the hell out of him.

His men seemed to know this wasn't the time to talk. They kept pace, letting him gather his thoughts. At six miles, he turned them around and started back. When they hit the last mile, he stretched his legs, and it became a race between the three of them. However childish, the impulse to win was so strongly ingrained in them that it never occurred to any of them to lose. Gabe and Tag crossed into the driveway neck and neck, with Gavin a step behind. Slowing to a trot to cool down, they circled the villa. By now, it was deserted and quiet.

Quelling the impulse to seek her out and apologize at once, he paced the hallway while the others showered. Mace, on guard duty outside Christina's door, finally shook his head.

"You're not gettin' in there tonight, buddy."

Gabe finally stopped and leaned against the wall. "I know. I'll fix it."

"If you can." Mace gave him no slack. He didn't deserve any. "I thought—we all thought—you were just sniffin' 'round her skirts. But Christ, Gabe. Are you in love with her?"

Gabe stiffened and began pacing again. "No. Hell, no. I don't do love."

"Not since Leanne. She fucked you over good, no denying it. That was four years ago, though. When are you going to get back up on the horse?"

"Never." But Christina's beautiful face swam through his mind. "And for fuck's sake not with another fucking CIA agent."

Tag stuck his head out the open door. "Your turn, man."

He scrubbed his sweat-slicked skin as though he could slough off every mistake he'd made since he first met her. He'd been too harsh, too cutting. And his men had it right. She'd performed admirably, up to and including her decision to trust fucking Brumley with the truth.

The others had already chosen sleeping spots in the bed and on the couch and floor. He moved his things into an unoccupied corner, cursing under his breath the whole time.

# Chapter Seventeen

CHRISTINA SPOKE FIRST. "I'm sorry for the deception."

Julian spread his hands apart. "It's Ronnie's deception as much as yours."

"Are you . . . please don't be upset with her. Even Trevor agreed it was best to keep you apart until we get this figured out. If you'd known . . ."

"I would have insisted you tell me where she was staying so I could join her," Julian finished for her. "Yes, I realize that now. Until this is sorted, I agree to stay away from Ronnie." He surveyed her, peering closely. "It's an amazing resemblance. I knew as soon as I touched your arm, but in the dim lightning, even I might have been fooled for a few seconds."

"My arm?" Christina twisted her head and grabbed the T-shirt's sleeve, pulling it up to peer at her scar. "I should have been wearing long sleeves, but Ronnie's dress was custom made for her. So how did you and Ronnie meet?"

"At a symposium two years ago. She is very passionate about

her causes. Children's welfare, adequate care for war veterans, things like that. We were arguing before the European Union's Environmental Policy Council about oil exploration in Concordia. On opposite sides, no less, and I found her arguments so persuasive that I asked her out that very day."

"She changed your mind?" Christina wondered what that would feel like.

"Not in this case. She believes it's necessary for Concordia's economic growth. I voted against her proposal. But her passion intrigued me." His face softened. "We've been on the same side ever since, though. She's truly one of the kindest-hearted women I've ever met."

Christina felt a slow bump of envy. Ronnie and Julian found something together that she could never hope to have. "From everything I've seen, I agree. I guess I'm not exactly what you'd call gentle."

Julian cocked his head at her, much as Trevor used to do. They did resemble one another, though one was fair and the other dark-haired. Julian had the same short curly hair, which probably had the same soft consistency as Trevor's, and the strong jawline. He'd been a good friend when she needed one.

The SpecOps community was a small one. Everyone who'd been at Prince Nasser Hospital in Azakistan's capital city seven months ago knew she'd shown up wearing Trevor's clothes. Never mind that her own had been filthy by the time Trevor paid her fine and sprung her from jail, where she'd ended up because a conservative imam didn't like her not wearing a hijab. Never mind that his apartment stood miles closer than hers. Everyone'd taken one look at her and assumed.

The political counselor, Shelby Gibson, had gone white as a sheet when she'd seen Christina. She'd assumed, too. And then broke things off with Trevor.

"I disagree," Julian said now. "I see a strong woman in front of me, yes, but an intelligent and empathetic one as well. You're concerned about Ronnie's feelings, that's clear enough. It's her reputation you're wearing, after all."

Christina hadn't thought of it in those terms. Butterflies started in her stomach.

"Relax," Julian said, surprised. "I didn't mean to worry you. It was inevitable that I would know you weren't my fiancée." He shot her an unrepentant grin. "After all, I've counted the freckles on her back."

Christina relaxed even as her cheeks reddened. "I see."

"Which brings me to a rather delicate subject." Julian cleared his throat. "Our sleeping arrangements. Will you be comfortable with me on the sofa instead of one of your bodyguards?"

"Yeah, I'm fine with it. We're safe for tonight. We were attacked on the way here. Two in as many days. I'm confident they won't be able to pull together a third so fast."

He frowned, clearly unhappy. "I'd rather I were the target."

"I know. Trevor's investigating everyone either of you knows. We'll have something concrete soon."

He sighed, hands clasped loosely between his knees. "I can never express my gratitude for the risk you're taking."

"Uh, all in a day's work?"

"No. Above and beyond. I'll see you get a medal for this."

She didn't know how to respond to that. Her goal was simply not to get fired.

Deni knocked as she and Gabe came through the door. It astounded Christina that after everything that had happened that evening, she still looked as polished and proper as a queen. "I wished to ensure you took no ill effects from tonight's drama," she said. "I could not come any sooner. All the guests were detained and questioned. Many were upset at this, and required some feather-soothing."

"Their feathers got ruffled?" Christina rose from the sofa and put the width of the room between herself and Gabe. His eyes were laser-sharp, his face an expressionless mask. His gaze followed her as she retreated.

"*Oui.* Gunfire is not customary at formal galas." Though her voice and face remained bland, mirth lurked in her eyes.

"Oh, my God, Deni, did you just make a joke?"

A small smile tugged at her mouth. "Perhaps. Between the excitement of the drive here and tonight's drama, I find myself feeling peculiarly alive."

Christina could relate. "I get that. It's normal. Surviving danger wakes up your senses." She couldn't help a glance across the room. And then wished she hadn't, because the heat in Gabe's eyes nearly scalded her. Oh, yeah. His senses were awakened, all right. But he'd missed out on his chance with her. Whatever game he'd been playing last night, she wanted no part of it.

His eyes narrowed. She glared right back at him.

To Julian's surprise and Deni's amusement, Gabe stamped across the room and clamped a hand around Christina's upper arm. Without ceremony, he dragged her into the bedroom, kicking the door closed with his boot. He swung her around, slammed her up against his chest, and proceeded to kiss the living shit out of her.

This was no gentle seduction; this was full-out war. He thrust his tongue past the seam of her lips, demanding entrance. Her body reacted of its own accord, curling into him and opening her mouth beneath his onslaught. Gabe excited her. She wanted him. Craved him. Running her hands up his shoulders, she angled her head to fuse their mouths together. His tongue dueled with hers, stroking urgently. His taste addicted her; hot and carnal, giving and receiving pleasure.

She wrapped a leg around his, her body roaring to life. His hands dropped to cup her rear, lifting her against him. Her hand tangled in his long hair. Taking two steps, he planted her against the wall and himself between her legs. He caressed the length of her thighs and up her ribs, then covered her breasts, kneading gently, still kissing her. Her nipples pebbled, and he growled into her mouth in satisfaction as his thumbs stroked across them. Little mewls burst from her at the incredible sensation. She rubbed herself against him, desperate to feel his skin against hers. When he finally broke the kiss, they were both panting feverishly. He glowered down at her, but his wrath had fizzled, and he looked somehow confused and lost.

"I was so worried about you," he admitted, voice low and rough.

"Gabe, I'm so sorry I disobeyed you tonight. I know you're team lea . . ."

He placed a finger across her lips and closed his eyes. "You made the right call. I was wrong."

Surprise rounded her eyes. He was apologizing? To her? "Gabe . . ."

"Don't worry. The showers run cold here," he whispered. He let her slide to the floor and turned away. "I oughta know."

# Chapter Eighteen

By TEN O'CLOCK the next morning, Christina still hadn't put in an appearance. Gabe eyeballed the door more often than the food going down his gullet. Was she okay? She'd had quite a scare last night during the skirmish. He half heard his teammates discussing last night's attack compared to the ambush on the road to Grasvlakten. Damn it. He should be brainstorming with them, not worrying about Christina. She'd handled herself well the night before, both during and after the attack.

"The road ambush took coordination. Premeditation." Gavin cut a piece of sausage and chewed it. "Last night felt rushed to me. Impulsive."

"Multiple attackers versus one shooter changes the game entirely. What upped the ante for them?" Tag said. "Us?"

"Or maybe a deadline." Frustration roiled through Gabe. They seemed no closer to answers. Meanwhile, their enemy remained one step ahead of them.

Brumley entered, smiling, with Christina a step behind. Gabe scrutinized her. Were those bags under eyes? Had she not slept well?

Was it his fault? He shouldn't have given in to the temptation to kiss her.

It wasn't until Mace snapped his fingers in front of his eyes that he realized someone was talking to him.

"We need to regroup," Tag said, obviously not for the first time. "We should stay here while we figure out our next move."

"Why here?" Gabe asked, forcing himself to focus. He valued his teammates' opinions. "My thought is to get the hell out of here as fast as possible. There's too much property and not enough overwatch for us to have positive control."

"We should be able to control enough to lay a trap," Mace said. "I can't position myself on that damned roof well enough, though. It pisses me off that I didn't know there was another shooter up there. If he'd been the assassin instead of a cop, Christina would be dead by now."

"Christina what?" And there she was, standing by the table, smiling down at Mace. "My ears were burning."

Mace stood, holding a chair for her. She smiled her thanks. Julian brought two plates from the sideboard buffet, and slid one of them in front of her. A maid was next to them in an instant, serving her coffee and orange juice.

Mace sat down again. "We're trying to figure out our next move."

"Stay here," she said at once. "If we go back to the palace, no one will be able to get to me. But if we stay here, we can corral the bad guys where we want them. Anywhere else we go, we won't know the terrain and layout."

That was SpecOps thinking, and gutsy. He felt a swell of pride and respect. Despite the attacks, she remained calm and professional. His impulse to take Christina away from here had less to do with his actual mission, and more to do with his need to protect her. "What about the roof problem?"

"Two shooters? Or put Gavin somewhere where he can see both the access to the garage and access to the roof."

Gavin fingered his earlobe thoughtfully. "I can do that, actually. Southeast corner of the driveway will give me a straight shot to both. Only issue is if someone tries to gain access by the back way."

Mace slurped orange juice. "That must be what happened, I think. It's a damned maze up there, but I can move around to cover different fields of fire. I can lift and shift pretty fast."

Brumley tasted his coffee, with his pinky out, no less. Gabe's lip curled. He'd never demean himself to be part of such a ridiculous lifestyle. He glanced at Christina. Her pinky, too, was arched as she sipped, looking every inch an upper-crust woman. Or princess.

He looked over to find Mace laughing at him and making no secret of it as he said, "Well, we were very comfortable last night in the corridor."

Christina looked up, startled. "What?"

Gabe laid it out for her. "Since no one was on hand to protect you in your suite, we took turns sitting in the hallway outside your door." He wasn't being fair and he knew it. The only one displaced was him.

Christina's shoulders hunched, making him feel more of a shit. But before he could tell her they were pulling rotating guard shifts outside her door anyway, the viscountess made an entrance, followed by Deni and what looked like a footman in some sort of livery. Lady Nabourg fussed over Christina for a few minutes, then seated herself at the head of the table, ceasing all conversation. Deni ensconced herself next to the viscountess, across from Brumley. She and their hostess chatted amiably.

Christina tapped a boiled egg with a tiny spoon, adding just a sprinkle of salt.

Gabe peeled his egg with his fingers. "Lord Brumley, do you need a ride to the airport? Deni can call you a taxi."

Brumley gave him a pleasant look. "I've ordered a car service. It will be here in an hour."

Apparently, politicians didn't take taxis.

Gabe was no politician.

"Lady Nabourg, your home is as lovely as you," Brumley said smoothly.

"How kind of you to say so," she replied. "Your unexpected visit perked up my niece. She seemed rather withdrawn until your arrival."

Gabe swallowed too much coffee and felt it burn its way down his throat, the pain a welcome relief. He needed the caffeine. Even when he wasn't on guard duty, he hadn't been able to sleep. His brain had been on a loop. His mother, Leanne, Christina, the CIA. Over and over, until he wanted to howl. Yeah, he'd been burned. He'd trusted where he shouldn't have. But at some point during the night, he'd come to realize that what he'd felt for Leanne paled to nothing beside his feelings for Christina. Christina, who was feisty and cool under pressure. Who stood up to him and told him when she thought he was wrong. Who had courage in spades.

Who had promised never to lie to him.

He wasn't exactly sure what to do about these newfound feelings. He certainly wasn't ready to run out and buy a ring. Still, maybe when this was all over, they could go somewhere. Just the two of them. See where things led.

AFTER BRUMLEY DEPARTED, he pulled Tag and Mace outside with him. They quartered the landscape, searching in the daylight for any clues to last night's attack. Nothing. The local police had trampled the area. Pulling out his cell phone and the chief's card, he dialed and identified himself.

"Ah, yes. Mr. Morgan. What can I do for you?"

"I'd like to get an update. What have you found out about the attackers?"

The chief's voice grew amused. "Since last night? Not a thing. We have yet to identify the two dead men, and the live prisoner has said nothing. I know you Americans tend to be impatient, but even we cannot solve a case overnight."

"Did the Federal cop tell you who assigned him to Princess Véronique?"

"I have yet to speak with him. He's due in my office later this afternoon."

Gabe sighed. "Are you going to autopsy the dead men?"

"To what end? We know the cause of death. They were shot."

Gabe ran a hand along the back of his neck. "Can you at least pull the slugs?"

"Slugs?"

"Bullets."

"Ah, yes. Naturally, we will run a ballistics test. We do know how to investigate a wrongful death, Mr. Morgan."

Gabe held on to his patience. "It wasn't a wrongful death. It was self-defense, pure and simple. They were trying to grab Princess Véronique. Anything the prisoner can tell us would be more than the squat we know now."

"Squat? Crouching?"

"Nothing. It means we know nothing at the moment. I need another favor, if you can spare the manpower. We were attacked on our way to Grasvlakten. The state limousine has bullet holes in the front quarter panel. Would you send someone to dig out those slugs—bullets—and run ballistics against them as well? It might lead us to who's responsible."

"I am sorry to hear about the attack. Why didn't you report it?"

Gabe clenched his fingers around his cell phone until they turned white. "I should have," he admitted. "Our protection plan for the princess relied on total secrecy, because we didn't—and still don't—know who is involved or why. It's crystal clear, though, that someone knows our movements anyway. I should have reached out to you. I'm sorry."

The chief sighed down the phone line. "The case has our undivided attention. You must understand how beloved the crown princess is. Still, you must give me time to mount a proper investigation. As soon as I know something, you will know. Will this be sufficient?"

"Yeah. Thanks."

THAT DAY AND the next tested Christina's patience. Neighbors and friends visited in an endless stream to check on the Nabourgs and their distinguished visitor, and to gossip about what had transpired. They were full of theories, even the ones who hadn't been there that night, or had been inside and not known anything was amiss until the police corralled them all.

Trevor checked in with them several times, going over Ronnie's list and telling them whom he'd cleared and who was still a suspect. The Delta Force team combed every inch of the house and grounds, laying out emergency egresses and discussing various places a trap could be laid.

At lunchtime, Christina found herself in front of her computer, dialing Heather.

"Hi," the other woman said, her cheerful face filling the screen. Ever since she and Jace had gotten engaged, her happiness shone from her. It made Christina a little wistful.

"Hey," she said. "Just a quick call to update you."

"On the mission? Gabe calls in every evening to brief Jace."

"Um, yeah, well . . ."

Heather relaxed into her chair. "Tell me."

Christina sighed. Where to start? "We were attacked last night."

"I know. Are you okay?"

"Yeah. Your boys kept Julian and me safe."

"Who? Oh, yeah. The fiancé." Heather tapped the arm of her chair thoughtfully. "How are you getting along with the team? My boys, as you call them."

She grimaced. "Great! With everyone except my team leader."

Heather chuckled. "Remember what I said three weeks ago? Are you sure you're not butting heads because of some unresolved . . . issues?"

Christina made a rude sound.

"Well, all I can tell you is that he's made no complaints to Jace. If he's unhappy with your performance, he hasn't said anything."

That surprised her. "He likes having a hundred percent control over things. I'm an unknown entity with a shitty reputation."

Heather's shrug was noncommittal. "Opinions vary about that. But I'm more interested in your personal interaction. Is the electricity still there?"

She rested her chin on her hands. "I'm being honest here. Yes, on my end. I . . . well, I don't know what he wants. I don't think he knows, either. And I sure as hell don't know what I want. I mean, there's this spark between us, yeah. But what does it mean?"

"Everything. Nothing."

"Well, that's useful." She frowned at the computer screen. "I'm being serious here. Gabe makes me remember I'm a damned good operative, despite Baghdad. He pushes me, but he's always got my back."

Heather grinned. "Take it for a test run after this mission is over. See where it goes."

Tempting, but . . . "That's probably not a good idea."

Heather leaned forward, staring at her with knowing eyes. "You're afraid of falling in love with him and getting your heart stomped on."

She let her head fall back, staring up at the ceiling, not ready to admit anything. "He's an outstanding team leader. He listens to everyone's input. He's decisive and fearless. Even though he knows my background, he . . . ."

"Yeah, yeah. Is he a good kisser?"

"What?" Christina jerked back, then sighed. "He's amazing," she admitted softly. "He barely touches me and I go up in flames. But that's not the same as I—" She couldn't even say the word. Could barely think it. She didn't know Gabe well enough to be in love with him. Half the time, he was biting her head off. When he wasn't trying to shove his tongue down her throat.

Out of sorts after her blunt conversation with Heather, she decided a warm shower might relax her. About to lock the door, she hesitated. She wouldn't have to worry about Gabe barging in, as he was wont to do. Why didn't she just lock the door?

Because she hoped he'd barge in.

She adjusted the water and stepped under the spray, feeling sorry for herself. The water pounded down onto her shoulders as she felt an emptiness in her heart.

Someone pounded on the bathroom door. "Christina!"

It was Gabe. "Go away," she shouted. "I'm in the shower."

"I know you're in the shower. Get out here. We have news."

He'd used his command voice. Alarmed, she turned off the faucet and stepped from the shower enclosure. News was good, right? It had to be important for him to interrupt her. She threw on a pair of cutoff jeans, couldn't find her bra, and finally just yanked a T-shirt over her head. Her hair lay damp and curly on her neck as she rushed into the main room.

"What's happened?" she asked. The entire team, including Deni, had assembled in the main living area.

Gabe glanced at her when she came through the door, then looked again, staring hard. He swallowed several times.

"Gabe?"

He shook himself like a dog shedding water, but still had that peculiarly intense look in his eyes as he told her the news.

"The police chief got back to me," he said. "They ran ballistic tests on the rifle the cop, Jansens, was carrying. Obviously, the round in one of the tangos—the attackers—matched Mace's rifle, and Jansens's the other one. But you'll never guess what other ballistics result popped up."

"You gonna make her guess?" Mace asked. "Play twenty questions?"

She threw an appreciative grin at the team sniper. "Someone fill me in."

"The rifling on the bullet that killed the second tango matched the rifling on the bullet they dug out of the wall of Le Monnaie Opera House."

For a moment, the words made no sense. When it finally clicked, her eyes rounded. "Jansens was the shooter in Brussels? But . . . why?"

Gabe frowned, fists on his hips. "He's on the take? He shot at them in Brussels, then found out we were coming to Grasvlakten and came here to finish the job?"

It was on every one of their faces. She finally said the words. "And missed? Killed one of his own teammates instead of Ronnie or Julian?"

Mace made a clicking sound with his teeth. "No way. I was about to lift and shift locations when those men came out of the trees. He had a better angle than I did, but it was a damnably tough shot. He had night vision goggles, but everyone was moving fast. And he only fired once. If he'd missed his target, he would have fired again. And, his sniper rifle is a good one. A professional one. An amateur couldn't have made that shot."

Christina flopped into an unoccupied chair, mind racing. "An amateur who flubbed an easy shot in Brussels. A professional who hits a target cleanly here, but shoots one of his own instead of me?"

"Two people?" Alex offered. "One rifle, two shooters?"

"Maybe," Gabe said slowly, drawing out the word. "And maybe he hit exactly what he was aiming at both times."

Yeah, the thought rattled through her mind, too.

Deni stood and began to pace. "That would mean, correct me if I am mistaken, that it was this man, this police commissioner, who shot at Princess Véronique in Brussels? And deliberately missed?" A hand rose, as if in supplication. "But why?"

There were a lot of bewildered looks and head shaking all around.

Christina said, "If Jansens deliberately missed in Brussels, and hit his target here, that means he wasn't trying to kill Ronnie. Or Julian. He was protecting one or both here, but trying to frighten them in Brussels?" She shook her head. It made no sense.

"Fuck." Gabe made a noise that was halfway between a groan and a laugh, but held not one whit of humor. He pulled his phone from his pocket, held up a finger as he punched in the numbers one-handed, and put the call on speaker. "This is Gabe Morgan. You need to question Aart Jansens. Ask him about the conference on Geothermal Exploration in Vienna next month. Ask him point-blank if the attack has something to do with keeping Ronnie—Princess Véronique—away from the summit. Ask your prisoner if Jansens hired him."

Chief Van Den Nieuwenhuyzen's voice came briskly onto the line. "What would be the purpose of keeping her away?"

Gabe rubbed the back of his neck. "She's speaking, and she's got influence. She's the driving force supporting oil drilling in Concordia."

Christina sat forward. "So, by that logic, if Jansens was trying to get me to stay away from the summit, why kill his own man? They were trying to kidnap me, but maybe he changed his mind at the last minute? Or he felt it would be more convincing if he came away the hero, but still frightened me enough to go to ground?"

"Who benefits the most if the princess misses the summit?" Gabe asked, but it was clear he already knew the answer. "Groups opposing new drilling."

"Bonnet," Christina said. "Émile Bonnet."

The police chief didn't miss a beat. "I will question Lord Bonnet. I will telephone you when I know something." He hung up.

"Fuck that," Gabe said. "I'm going down there."

"Me, too." Christina darted into the bathroom, found her bra, and tugged it on while the others chimed in. When she emerged again, Gabe skimmed a look over her breasts with a pained expression.

She giggled.

# Chapter Nineteen

IN THE END, Gabe, Gavin, and Deni made the trip. It hadn't been easy convincing his little hothead that she needed to remain behind.

"I'll change," she said. Her stretchy top and cutoffs emphasized her slender curves, but they were Christina's clothes, not Véronique's.

"It's not prudent," he said gently. He'd nearly swallowed his tongue when she'd come out wearing that tight top without a bra. Ho-ly Jesus! He'd gotten hard so fast, the tightness inside his jeans nearly ripped his balls off. "We need to limit your interactions with the locals, remember? There's too much potential for disaster if you go into that police station."

"Because I'll screw up?" she said bitterly.

"No." He wished they could have this conversation in private, but the entire team looked on. "Not at all. You've done a first-rate job every step of the way."

Her mouth dropped open and she stared at him.

"Look, I owe you an apology," he continued doggedly. "A public one. I said the other day that you showed poor judgment in trusting Brum . . . Julian. I had no right to say that. You've acted professionally from the start. You've been a good asset to my tea . . . you're part of my team. I value your input."

She stood frozen, her body tense, and her eyes so wide he could see into her soul.

"I need you to wait here because you don't speak Dutch, okay? They'll fuss over you if you go. Their princess, in their little town? It's a big deal."

Slowly, her mouth closed. Her shoulders relaxed. He knew he'd won.

"All right. I'll stay here in the room," she said. "Don't keep me in suspense, though. Call me when you know something."

"I will," he promised. "Deni, if you would keep Christina company?"

"I can lend some authority to the proceedings," Deni said. "Let me help."

Gabe hesitated, then nodded. "All right. Let's go."

The Grasvlakten police headquarters squatted in the center of a row of one- and two-story buildings crammed together on one side of the street. A metal plaque screwed to the side of the brown brick building identified it in Dutch, French, and English. The three of them trooped past the desk sergeant and up the narrow steps to the second floor, earning them startled looks from the few officers at their desks. The town was small enough that the police station boasted only two jail cells and one interview room. Unlike their counterparts in the States, there was no observation room with video and sound. Chief Van den Nieuwenhuyzen reluctantly allowed the three of them into the interview room.

"You will remain silent, of course," the chief said. "I will ask the questions. You will observe."

The modest room seemed to double as a storage area, considering the number of accordion file boxes stacked around.

"We are digitizing our records," the chief explained. "It is a slow process."

Aart Jansens stopped pacing the floor as they filed in. A spate of French followed.

"We will conduct this interview in English, out of respect for our guests," the chief said evenly.

Jansens glowered. "If I must. Why am I here? You should be giving me a medal, not dragging me in here like a common criminal."

"I invited you, rather than arresting you," the chief said. "Out of respect. Nevertheless, I have questions."

He seated himself on one side of the pitted, scarred metal table, and gestured for Jansens to sit on the other side. The others stood.

Aart Jansens relaxed into a faded blue plastic chair. "I told you what happened the other night."

"Tell me again."

Jansens looked like he wanted to argue, but instead leaned forward and set his clasped hands on the table. "I knew Princess Véronique would be at Viscount and Viscountess Nabourg's anniversary ball. The private secretary's office announced she wouldn't attend, but I was told this was misinformation, planted to throw off any potential attacks. If I could find this out, so could others, if they knew who to ask."

"Who told you?" The chief pulled his worn-out notebook from a pocket and opened it to a fresh page.

"A *commissaris* in the ministry."

He was lying; Gabe could feel it. The chief narrowed his eyes. Gabe felt better that he seemed to know it as well.

"We ran ballistics against your rifle," the chief said bluntly. "We know you shot at Princess Véronique and Lord Brumley in Brussels. We know you shot at them again here in Grasvlakten."

Jansens didn't blink. "I would never harm Her Royal Highness."

Gabe stepped forward. "You have a damned funny way of showing it."

The chief pinned him with a warning look. He forced himself to deflate.

"You deny your involvement?" Chief Van den Nieuwenhuyzen didn't seem surprised. "And yet you were caught on the scene with a sniper rifle."

"Protecting Her Royal Highness. I told you." Jansens crossed his arms and lifted his chin toward Gabe. "He botched it. I'm the only reason she survived."

"That's bullshit. You tried twice. You failed twice."

The chief gave him a long look, then flicked his eyes meaningfully toward the door. Gabe backed off, figuratively and literally.

"How do you explain your involvement in Brussels?" the chief asked.

Jansens lifted a shoulder and let it drop. "Someone must have used my rifle and then returned it. There must be a cop involved."

There is a cop involved, Gabe wanted to say. But he clamped his mouth shut.

Chief Van den Nieuwenhuyzen evidently thought the same thing. "So you're asserting that one Special Units officer tried to kill Princess Véronique, and another—you—then tried to save her?" Skepticism rang in his voice.

"I did not try. I succeeded."

Deni clasped her hands together. "Do you know who I am?"

Jansens hesitated, but then nodded. "You are Dame Van Praet, personal secretary to Her Royal Highness."

"In Brussels, you fired at the crown princess and her fiancé, and missed deliberately," she said, steel in her voice. "Why?"

"I didn't shoot at them."

This interrogation would go a lot faster if he were allowed to punch the man in the face a few times, Gabe thought.

"You hit the wall next to the princess's head," Deni said. "You hit what you aimed for. Correct?"

Jansens gave her a long look. "Why would someone shoot to miss?"

The chief slapped a hand on the metal table, causing a loud clang. "That is the question we are here to answer. You will cooperate, or you will go to jail. You choose which."

A knock on the door interrupted him. The chief shoved back his chair and stalked to the door, yanking it open and glaring at whoever was on the other side. Gabe could feel the man's patience eroding. Good. Maybe they could get some answers now.

A brief murmured conversation culminated with the chief grabbing a file folder, locking the door, and whirling on Jansens. He slammed the folder on the table.

"Now, Commissaris Jansens. How do you explain that the same handguns used to attack the princess on the road to Grasvlakten were also used in the attack at the Nabourg villa?"

Jansens's head came up fast and his arms dropped. "Another attack? That's not possible."

Gabe forced himself to slouch against the wall. The man's surprise felt genuine. What the hell was going on here?

"But it happened. You say it is not possible because you were responsible for the other attacks. And I will prove it, and arrest you."

Aart Jansens looked like he wanted to argue, but in the end sat back, hands in his lap.

"Here is what I think," the chief said. "You lied about the minister of internal affairs sending you. So who told you where Princess Véronique would be?"

Clamping his mouth shut, Jansens glared around the room.

Without warning, Chief Van den Nieuwenhuyzen lunged around the table, wrapping his hands in his prisoner's collar, and hauled him upright. He shook Jansens. "Who told you?"

"Let go of me, you diseased idiot." Jansens tried to pry the chief's hands off his collar.

"When you start telling the truth. How did you know Princess Véronique would be in Grasvlakten?"

Jansens hesitated. "A friend in the private secretary's office."

"Now we're getting to the truth." Chief Van den Nieuwenhuyzen released his hold and glanced at Gabe. "So you were right about internal security breaches. It's good you didn't trust anyone close to the princess."

Deni stiffened. "I must insist you tell me which member of my staff gave you this information."

Surprisingly, Jansens gave her a name. "Truthfully, he wasn't one hundred percent certain Princess Véronique would make the trip to Grasvlakten. I'm glad I was there to save her."

Deni looked down her nose at him. "As am I, if you did not also hire those men to frighten my princess. What was the objective of shooting at her in Brussels, and again, as you intended, at the estate? To keep her from attending the Vienna Summit on Geothermal Exploration?"

Jansens didn't answer.

"It's no use denying these allegations," the chief said. "The evidence is too overwhelming. All I want to know is why."

Gabe also wanted to know who. "Did Émile Bonnet hire you?"

His expression didn't change, but something flickered in the depth of Jansens's eyes. "I don't know who that is."

"Of course you do." The chief returned to his seat and jotted something in his notebook. "Lord Bonnet, then. I will be interviewing him next."

Jansens leaned forward abruptly. "There's no need to involve him. I admit it. I fired the shot in Brussels."

Gabe blinked. The sudden turnaround surprised him.

"I acted alone," Jansens continued. "But I meant Her Royal Highness no harm."

"No?" the chief scoffed. "How not?"

Jansens wiped his palms on his pants. "I'm a patriot. I would never have injured Princess Véronique. Concordia has my complete loyalty."

"Concordia might have your loyalty, but who holds your paycheck?" Gabe asked. Calmly.

"I am a patriot," Jansens said again. "My allegiance is to Concordia's best interests and future well-being. I defended her. I saved her."

The chief nodded. "It seems so. But why Brussels? And why were you on the roof at the villa?"

Jansens grew quiet.

"Who decides what is in Concordia's best interest?" the chief asked. "Is it in Concordia's interests to prevent Princess Véronique from speaking at the Vienna conference?"

Jansens blanched.

"I'll take that as a yes. And Émile Bonnet hired you to frighten her?"

"No," he blurted. "No one paid me."

Gabe's lip curled. "No way this was your idea. Bonnet wanted the princess out of the picture, and paid you to get it done."

Jansens threw up his hands. "All right, yes. Lord Bonnet asked me to help. I didn't get paid. I agree with him; oil exploration in Concordia isn't the right approach for our economy. Oil exploration is invasive. It will destroy natural resources in the mountains. For our future generations, the damage to the land must outweigh a temporary influx of capital. Princess Véronique is wrong. Without her presence, Lord Bonnet felt he could turn the vote."

Now they were getting somewhere. They had the why; now they needed the rest of it.

"The group who attacked us the other night," Gabe said. "Who were they? Yours?"

"Not mine," Jansens said at once. "I didn't recognize them. But when one of them put a gun to my princess's head, I acted."

The room grew quiet. Finally, the chief shifted in his seat.

"Do you think Bonnet hired a second group? A contingency, in case you failed?"

Jansens looked suddenly small and gray. "It's possible."

"Chief, has your other prisoner said anything useful?" Gabe asked.

The chief stood. "He's said nothing at all."

THE NEXT MORNING, Federal Police escorted Émile Bonnet to the Ministry of Internal Affairs. The minister himself questioned the earl, who confessed his role in the effort to prevent Véronique from supporting oil drilling in Vienna. His arrest burst across

Concordian news services, reverberations rolling through the country like a tidal wave.

The minister then informed Trevor, politely, that the special operators' services were no longer required in his country. Their crown princess was safe. They were welcome to depart at their earliest convenience.

"He's kicking us out?" Gabe sounded outraged. "What about the second team? Have they confirmed Bonnet sent it?"

"No," Trevor said over the phone. "He won't discuss it with me. Won't confirm or deny anything Bonnet might have said. I think he's anxious his ruse isn't discovered. The faster he can get Christina out of the country, the less likely it is that someone will suspect something."

"So we're done here." Christina could hardly believe it.

"Yeah." Gabe searched her eyes, but she had no clue what he was thinking. "I guess the minister thinks we've eliminated a second threat. Two are dead and one's in custody. I wish we could confirm Bonnet sent them, though. This feels incomplete to me."

The team gathered back in her suite for an after-action review. Gabe sat next to her, including her in the discussion. At least for the next hour, she still counted as a member of his team. They dissected the sequence of events, what succeeded and what hadn't. The operators spoke bluntly about where things went wrong, and how they could do better next time. The mutual respect was absolute.

At last, they were done.

Gabe slapped his hands together and rubbed them. "All right, boys and girls. Let's get this place put back together. Pack your gear. We'll leave the state car. The Nabourgs are lending us one of their sedans, and the butler, Rietveld, is going to make sure the limo gets back to Parvenière."

The rest of them rose and headed next door to pack. It wouldn't take them long; Delta Force operators could pick up and move at a moment's notice.

Gabe hesitated, looking down at her. She could feel the weight of his gaze. Tilting her head back, she looked up at him. He wore an odd expression, one she couldn't interpret. Finally, he bent his head and brushed his lips across hers.

"You did a great job," he whispered.

She felt her eyes widen and her mouth part.

"Thanks," she managed. What did his expression mean? Was he sad their time together was over? She sure was. Working next to him had been exhilarating.

She stared longingly after him as he disappeared out the door. It was over. She would go back to the Washington beltway, and he would go . . . elsewhere.

# Chapter Twenty

GABE FOUND HIMSELF hovering outside Christina's room, vacillating between going in and waiting for her in the car with the rest of his team.

His team.

As of now, she no longer counted as one of them. He would miss working beside her. Her energy, her intelligence, and her courage would move on to another assignment.

They'd said their formal goodbyes. He could hear Deni and several maids in the bedroom packing Christina's clothes.

The plan had them linking up with Ronnie at the safe house and transporting her back to the palace. Trevor and his team would head back to Stirling Lines outside Hereford. Christina and Gabe's team would simply disappear onto a commercial flight back to Washington, D.C.

He hated the plan.

He knew in his gut that this drama hadn't fully played out yet. There was nothing he could do about Princess Véronique, but he wasn't ready to let Christina out of his sight.

He paced into the room, pausing when Christina appeared in the bedroom doorway. She stopped abruptly, confusion and surprise on her face.

"Hi," she said awkwardly. "I thought you'd be outside."

Gabe cleared his throat. "The team is. I, ah, I wanted to make sure I said goodbye."

Her eyes crinkled in amusement. "Again?"

"I liked having you on my team."

A pink tongue stroked across her bottom lip. Her cheeks flushed an adorable shade of pink. "Wow. That's . . . good of you to say."

Gabe shifted from foot to foot, uncomfortable. "Well. See ya."

She laughed. "Man, you suck at goodbyes. Deni is going to take one of the Nabourgs' cars back to the palace. That's what she'd do anyway, if Ronnie had been here. I've made my farewells to our hosts. So, I'm ready." She started across the room toward the door.

Which put her within grabbing distance.

Instead, he stepped in front of her. "Christina," he whispered.

Her breath caught. She looked at him, eyes shimmering. "Yes?"

"Come away with me," he said in a rush. He'd meant to lead up to it gently, reverently, telling her how much he wanted her, desired her, respected her. Wanted to crawl between the sheets with her, yes, of course. But he also wanted to listen as she whispered her secrets in the dark of night. Comfort her. Find out what thrilled her, and do it beside her. Take her skydiving and snorkeling. Walk on a beach holding hands. It terrified him. He pushed the words out anyway. "Let's go somewhere. Just the two of us."

"What?" She didn't sound outraged, which was a good sign. She hadn't laughed, either.

"You and me." He took a step closer. "It made me nuts, seeing you with Brumley. All I could think about was getting you away from him. And then when we were attacked, when I saw that bastard put a gun to your head . . ." He stopped, finding his throat clogged with emotion.

"Gabe . . ."

"You know there's something between us." He pushed the words out past the constriction. "You know it as well as I do. Let's, I don't know, explore it."

A slow smile lit her eyes. He stopped breathing, she was so beautiful. "Have sex, you mean."

He found abruptly that's not what he meant. He'd made a big mistake last time when he'd tried to seduce her. "Sex, yes, if that's what you want. But really I want us to get to know one another. Come away with me for a few days. A week. Two."

She sidled closer. Her breasts almost, but not quite, touched his chest. He forced himself to keep still. "Where would we go?" Her voice had dropped several octaves. Sweet, heavy, seductive. He forgot what he'd been about to say, simply stared at her helplessly.

"Gabe?" He heard the anxious note in her voice, and forced himself to think. What had they been talking about?

"I don't know. London? Paris? I can take a couple of weeks off. I'll clear it with Jace. Wherever you want to go. Hawaii?"

She leaned forward, her lips a hair's breadth from his. "Okay."

"Okay?" Relief swept through him.

"Yes." That tiny pink tongue swept out, licking once across his lips before disappearing back into her mouth. He groaned. Before he could sweep her into his arms, though, Deni appeared in the bedroom doorway, followed by the maids. She spoke to them rapidly in Dutch. They trooped out.

Deni hovered by the door. "If you wish to leave, now is a good time. The footmen are coming to take the luggage to the car."

Christina broke from Gabe and trotted over to Deni. She threw her arms around the other woman, hugging hard. After a startled moment, Deni hugged back.

"I couldn't have done this without you," Christina whispered. "Thank you so much for everything you did, both for Ronnie and for me."

The older woman smiled gently. "My pleasure. You are very much like my princess. You are both warmhearted, gracious young women. It's been my honor to work with you."

Christina sniffled as they left the suite. Gabe put a hand at the small of her back. She edged closer to him and he grinned, warmth suffusing him.

The ride back to Parvenière and the safe house couldn't have been more different from the trip out. The team joked and joshed. Gabe pressed his shoulder to hers several times, gratified when she returned the small pressure. Oh, yeah. This was going to work.

Suddenly unable to keep from touching her, he slid his fingers into her warm palm. She closed her fingers around his, not looking at him. He was so attuned to her that it took every bit of self-restraint not to haul her onto his lap. That would embarrass her, though, and he wasn't going to screw this up.

She moistened her lips. He watched them, mesmerized. Her mouth curved up very slightly at the corners. He swallowed a groan.

"The temperature's rising fast," Mace said in disgust. "You two need to get a room before you combust."

They looked at one another guiltily, then burst out laughing. It broke the tension long enough to finish the drive.

They pulled up into a nondescript driveway in front of a non-descript townhouse, on a block where every house looked the same. This one was some sort of pale yellow. The ones to either side were blue and green. The group trooped up to the front door. It opened before they arrived and Ronnie hurtled out, almost toppling Christina as she threw her arms around her.

"My friend," the princess murmured. "You 'ave been so brave. Julian told me what happened. I worried so about you."

One look at her face, and it was obvious she was sincere. Christina laughed and returned the hug. "I'm just glad it's over."

Gabe looked from one to the other. He couldn't imagine now ever having trouble telling them apart. Yes, the physical resemblance was eerie, but he could never mistake Christina's lust for life for Ronnie's natural elegance.

Julian appeared at the door, and Ronnie gave him a radiant smile. "Let's go inside, shall we?" he said.

The townhome was small, and became cramped with the addition of Gabe's team. Gabe knew several of the SAS operators. There was a lot of backslapping and handshaking, as some of his men had worked with some of Trevor's at one time or another. The SAS men had packed up, and backpacks, duffels, and sleeping rolls cluttered the foyer.

"Glad that's done with," Conall Havanaugh said. "Can't take any more of Archie's snoring."

"Your ass, nancy-boy," Archie Bell replied promptly. "Your pardon, ladies."

Christina smothered a laugh. "Where can I change?"

"My room," Ronnie said at once. "These poor boys have been on their best behavior. They need time to decompress."

The room dimmed somehow when the two women went upstairs. Even as he caught up with Trevor's team, he kept one eye on the doorway. When she finally reappeared, she wore fitted jeans and cross-trainers. Her hair curled around her face like a living force.

"I don't envy you," she told Ronnie, who followed her in. "It's frigging hard work."

"I am accustomed to it. And my position lets me help out in small ways."

"Well, I think you're safe to go to the summit and kick ass." Christina smiled.

"Excellent."

"I really need to check in. Excuse me." She withdrew to a corner and took out her cell phone. Gabe drifted closer.

"Madison," Jay Spicer said, by way of greeting. Gabe heard the sound of his chair springs squeaking. "When the hell you getting your butt back here?"

"I need some time off."

"What, you think being in a shootout and almost being killed gets you a vay-cay?"

She smothered a smile. "Yes, actually. So can I have a couple weeks?"

The chair springs stopped. "Yeah. You bet. Come back when you're ready."

Julian went up the stairs, returning a few seconds later with a suitcase and Ronnie in tow. "We're headed out," he said.

Gabe and Christina joined the others downstairs. She gave Tag, Alex, Mace, and Gavin each a quick hug.

"This was fun. Let's do it again sometime."

Mace chuckled. "I'll work with you anytime, *chérie*."

Gavin peeked out the front window. "Car's here. Time to bounce."

The new, bullet-free state limousine would carry Ronnie, Julian, and the rest of the Delta Force team back to the Palais du Parvenière. His team as escort would complete the transition between the fake princess and the real one. Gabe stayed behind.

A quick call to Jace Reed, his commander, and he was free for two whole weeks, barring a live mission that would call him back.

Trevor and his team departed next. He hugged and kissed Christina on the cheek while Gabe glowered, reminded uncomfortably that the two had history.

He would make her forget all about Trevor Carswell. A week and she'd be begging to stay with him. Two weeks, and they'd be married.

He pulled up short. Where the hell had that thought come from? Delta Force operators did not settle down. Well, Jace had, but Heather was an extraordinary woman who worked tirelessly beside the team every single day. The incidence of divorce among the SpecOps community as a whole was absurdly high. The pressures of no-notice deployments and dangerous missions took their toll on families.

Besides, he just wanted a few weeks with her. He didn't want to marry her.

He scratched his chin, watching her say her goodbyes. Who the hell was he kidding? He wanted more than a few weeks. Much more.

But marriage?

By unspoken agreement, they remained at the safe house. Where they went from here would be up to Christina.

When everyone else had gone and the door had closed, they stood in the foyer, staring at one another.

"Are you hungry?" Christina finally asked. "The fridge might still be stocked."

Hell, yeah, he was hungry. Starving. But not for food. "Sure. Let's see what they've got."

Thanks to the voracious appetites of the SAS team, the refrigerator and cupboards had been picked bare. All they could find were cheese slices, green olives, and a bowl of strawberries dipped in whipped cream. Both eyed the whipped cream with speculation, met the others' eyes, and burst out laughing.

"Good to know we're on the same page," Gabe said.

"Taste one," she urged, selecting a strawberry and holding it to his lips. He bit into it, feeling the juice run down his chin. She scooped it onto a finger and licked it clean. Slowly, sensuously, the little witch. He felt himself grow hard.

He took the berry from her and brought the bowl over to the kitchen table, adjusting himself discreetly as he went. Hmm. The table looked to be the right height. He scooped more whipped cream onto the strawberry, a grin tugging at his mouth as he glanced over his shoulder, daring her to follow him.

"Have a bite," he said. She put some extra sway in her hips. His smile widened in appreciation.

She placed one hand on his shoulder as though for balance, reaching for the fruit with her mouth. "Looks yummy."

He moved it closer. Looking into his eyes, she flicked her tongue out and licked it. His groin twitched. She did it again, then swirled her tongue over the red skin. He imagined that same tongue, running over his body and down to his . . .

He jerked his fingers away, dropping the berry. "Christ, Christina. I'm so crazy hot for you."

The tease leaned toward him until her lips were a breath from his. "Good."

His hands rose of their own volition and cupped either side of her face. "Yes," he said huskily. "It is good." Closing the microscopic distance between them, he traced his tongue along the seam of her mouth, nipping at her lips until she parted for him. He slipped into her dark heat.

Dropping into a kitchen chair, he yanked her into his lap and kissed her, hot, openmouthed kisses full of a desperate hunger. "I've wanted you since the first second I met you," he admitted in a low voice. "Back in Azakistan. You strutted into our Tactical Operations Center like you owned the place, and I wanted to kiss you senseless right then and there."

"You didn't show it," she said. "You were hard on me." She ran her hands over his shoulders, which felt unbelievably good.

"I was hard *for* you." He slid his hands under the blouse she wore, caressing the soft skin of her abdomen. She leaned away from him, but only to swing her leg over so she was straddling his lap. His brain short-circuited. He clamped his hands onto her hips and ground up into her soft heat. She rotated her hips. The sensation almost blew the top of his head off.

"You keep doing that, and we'll be done before we start," he growled.

"I like it fast and hard," she said. Every muscle in his body seized at once.

"Good to know," he panted, surprised to find his vocal cords still worked.

He captured her mouth again, thrusting his tongue in to duel with hers. His skin felt hot, feverish. Only the cool slide of her touch could save him. Kissing his way down her neck, he paused to lick the artery pulsing frantically in her neck. He ran his hands up her arms and back down, loving the silky slip of her skin, determined to make this first time last. She had other ideas, though. She almost tore his T-shirt yanking it over his head, then stripped off her own top. This passionate woman knew what she wanted, and that knowledge made him hotter than he'd ever been in his life.

He stopped her from shrugging out of her bra. The wispy, lacy thing was a soft blue. He stroked his fingers across the fabric, feeling it catch very slightly on the callouses of his fingers. She made a noise and tried to push her breasts farther into his hands, but he pulled back. When she stilled, he resumed his exploration. At last, he gave in to her moaned demands and brushed the pads of his thumbs over her nipples, already peaked and flushed with arousal. She gasped and arched closer, so he did it again. Unable to stop himself, he bent his head to suckle one breast, his teeth worrying the bud. She cried out, a sharp sound that drew stark male satisfaction from him. He tasted her other nipple, drawing it deep into his mouth and sucked hard on it. She bucked against him.

"Like that. Oh, yeah. Again." She dug her hands into his hair, trying to force his mouth back to her breasts. He pulled away, blowing across her nipples, sensitizing them. She urged him closer, but he stayed where he was until, with a frustrated groan, she released his hair and gave him control.

Reaching around with both hands, he trapped her against his chest as he slid the little hooks free. The bra parted in tiny increments, baring her to his searing gaze a little at a time. She whimpered. Good.

When he finally dropped the delicate material from her breasts, he exhaled hard. "Magnificent. You're one incredibly sexy package."

She gave a full-body wriggle that jolted him half out of his chair. He completed the movement, picking her up and settling her onto the table. She leaned back on her elbows, gazing at him with dilated pupils, her face flushed. She rolled her hips, giving him access to the button on her jeans.

He popped it and tugged down her zipper. Her panties matched her bra. He stroked a finger across it. She jumped.

"I want to touch you," she whispered. "Like you're touching me."

"Later."

He curled his fingers into the waistband of her jeans and stripped her out of them, then slowly, so slowly, slid off her panties. When he could see all of her, he stopped and stared his fill, his eyes hot and predatory as they roamed her body. He rested his hands at the tops of her thighs, thumbs brushing the sensitive inner flesh. Back and forth, light little strokes designed to light her on fire.

"More," she gasped. "More."

"Not yet," he growled. He shucked off his shoes and pushed his pants down his hips. She lifted her legs and wrapped them around his waist, pulling him in. Her heat scorched him, and that was all she wrote. He grabbed for his wallet and the condom inside, ripped it open with his teeth, and flung away the wrapper. He sheathed himself in seconds.

Pushing her flat against the table, he pulled her to the edge of the wood, spread her legs with his hips, and pressed forward. She lifted her legs and again wrapped them around his waist, and this time, he slid home.

"Uhn," she gasped. "Yeah. Oh, God, you feel so good, Gabe."

He couldn't speak, couldn't see. Could only feel her incredible heat, her legs pulling him in tighter, deeper. She was passion and flame, searing him as he plunged into her over and over. She was right there with him, squirming and writhing under him. He lost control, pistoning frantically and praying she came before he did.

She arched beneath him, crying out his name over and over as she shuddered and shook. He followed her over the edge, face buried in her breasts as he drove himself impossibly deeply and froze. His muscles seized as he orgasmed, the sensations so intense his vision grayed.

# Chapter Twenty-One

CHRISTINA SPRAWLED, BONELESS, on top of the kitchen table. Gabe rested on top of her, his face pillowed on her breasts. All too soon, however, her back began to protest the awkward angle. She stirred, and Gabe lifted himself off her.

"Too heavy?" he asked, voice thick. He looked down at their bodies, where they were still joined, and gave that peculiarly male grin of satisfaction. "You are one hot piece of ass."

His tone had been gentle, teasing, and she found herself laughing as he gathered her into his arms and carried her out of the kitchen, down the hallway, and into a bedroom. He laid her on the bed and stretched out next to her, one finger idly caressing her from shoulder to hip. She rolled onto her side to face him.

"What am I going to do with you, Gabe?" she murmured.

"Keep me?" he said. His face immediately closed down, as though the words had startled him. She touched his shoulder reassuringly, and he caught her hand, turning it over to press a kiss into her palm.

"For a while." The thought of commitment unnerved him, it

seemed. Her, too. But he'd said the words, and she mulled over the implications in her mind. After a few minutes, Gabe swung his legs over the side of the bed. Christina stroked his back. He pulled away from her and left the room. Before she could worry, though, he reappeared with his pants, sliding his cell phone out of a pocket. He punched in some numbers.

"Hey, Tag. Just checking in. You guys make it okay? Yeah? Good. When do you go wheels up?" He listened and frowned. "How come? What . . . yeah. No, nada. Should I . . ." His grip on the phone tightened. "Thanks." He disconnected.

"Problem?"

Gabe glanced her way without quite meeting her eyes. Wow, he really had scared himself with his earlier comment. "Maybe. The guys are boarding now. Jace recalled them. I'm not . . . so far, I haven't been called. But you know that could change at any minute, right?"

"Of course." She kept her voice noncommittal. "But, you know, if we're in the middle of doing it, you have to make me come before you dash out the door."

A surprised laugh burst from him. "Deal." He sat next to her on the bed and pressed more numbers on the keypad. "Trev. Anything new on the guy we caught?" He listened and rolled his eyes, laughing a little. "Yeah. Let me know, okay?" He tossed the phone onto the bedside table.

"Nothing yet?"

"Well, they did leave less than an hour ago," he said. "I just want full closure."

"What's bothering you?"

Gabe twisted around and stretched out beside her again, this time playing with her hair. "You let it go curly again."

Christina batted at his hands halfheartedly. "What if I like looking like a princess?"

Gabe cocked a curious look at her. "Do you? 'Cause I'll love your hair either way."

Her stomach dropped into freefall. He'd used the L-word. Not toward her, it was true, only her hair. She didn't want to read anything into it. Better to ignore it. "Nah. Takes too much work. I'm happy to go back to being just me."

Gabe laughed again, shaking his head. "You couldn't ever be 'just'."

"Well, thank you," she said, pleased. "So, seriously, what's bugging you about this?"

Gabe scratched his chin. "Well, let's look at the facts. Aart Jansens, on order from Émile Bonnet, shoots to miss in Brussels, hoping to scare the princess into hiding, which she does. You take her place, and both Jansens and Bonnet follow you to Grasvlakten, where Jansens sets up for a second shot at you. Only a second team gets to you first, and in the firefight, Jansens comes down on our side and saves the day."

"He denies hiring the second team," Christina said. "And we don't know what Bonnet admitted, if anything."

"Yeah," he said, clearly unhappy. "If the third man, the prisoner, talks, we might not even be told what he says. I'm concerned Ronnie's still in danger."

"Gabe, there's nothing we can do about that. We're off the mission. We've been told to get out."

"I hate leaving things unfinished. Like you lying here. I think I'll just keep you here, chained to my bed."

Christina stretched, luxuriating like a cat. "I could be okay with that. As long as I can handcuff you, too."

"Then who would bring you food? And feed it to you. Slowly." Gabe bent his head and licked across the top of her breast. "I wonder if they have any honey in the pantry?"

Christina's laugh was breathy, and ended on a moan. "Or . . . or more whipped cream, but it's my turn . . . ungh."

Gabe leaned over her, gripped her wrists lightly, and stretched them high over her head. He transferred both wrists into one of his, and started a seductive onslaught that had her twisting. Their first time had been urgent and intense. This time, he set the pace.

"Seems I like it slow and sensual, too."

"You like my touch," he said. "I'm hot for yours, too."

He traced around her lips, allowing her to suck a finger into her mouth and scrape her teeth across the pad. The finger trailed over her lower lip and down, over her chin and to her collarbone. He explored her breasts, staying maddeningly away from her aching nipples, and when he stroked the soft skin under them, she groaned her frustration.

He stroked each rib in turn, causing her to flail as it tickled. When he stroked down to her hipbone, though, she bucked and gasped, trying to get his fingers where she really wanted them. He held her wrists firmly but gently.

As his fingers skimmed over the juncture at her thighs, she jumped at the electricity of his touch. "Please, Gabe," she pleaded mindlessly. "Please."

He released her wrists and replaced his fingers with his mouth. "I intend to. Please you." Starting at the top again, he kissed each eyelid closed, nipped at the corner of her mouth, and nuzzled her cheek. When she turned her head blindly, seeking his mouth, he pulled away, following the same path with his mouth that he'd just traveled with his fingers. He dipped his tongue into her navel, causing her stomach to contract. He nipped her hip, sliding his hands under her knees and pulling her around, draping her legs over his shoulders.

"Gabe, Jesus, God, please, there . . . now."

But he seemed determined to drive her out of her mind. He blew across her curls, and rubbed his cheek over the soft hair. Her hips rose involuntarily, seeking relief, but he moved his head back. "Lie still," he commanded. "Hands above your head."

Surprisingly, she found herself eager to obey. The edge of danger in his voice sliced through her nerve endings and raised goose bumps on her skin. Finally, *finally*, he spread her open with his big hands and dipped his head.

The first touch of his tongue had her gasping and arching. He tormented her with long, slow licks, interspersed with gentle nips at the insides of her thighs. He flicked the tip of his tongue across her tight nub, holding her in place easily as she jumped. When his teeth closed over it, she cried out.

"Gabe, please. God, please."

She was sobbing and writhing. He plunged his tongue inside her and stroked, then replaced his mouth with his finger. Her back bowed. He inserted a second finger and caressed her from the inside while his tongue laved her sensitive bud. She couldn't have stopped the orgasm if her life depended on it. Shrieking her release, she disobeyed his command and wrapped her fingers through his overlong hair, gripping a little too hard as she convulsed again and again.

Before the tremors had subsided, he prowled up her body, keeping her legs on his shoulders. Somehow he managed to grab another condom and roll it on. When he touched her sensitized opening, she gasped again. He pushed inside her in one long glide, dipping his head to capture her lips with his own. She met him kiss for kiss, their tongues dueling and dancing as he stroked in and out of her. He seemed in no hurry, and Christina threw her head back and just rode the sensation. In this position, he could penetrate her deeply. As he increased his tempo, it should have hurt, but the sensations were too overwhelming. She burned with pleasure, with sensation, with emotion. She rode the edge between pleasure and pain, rolling her hips to urge him on. He kept that maddeningly slow pace. She lowered her head to gaze at him. His eyes were tightly closed, the cords on his neck standing out as he focused on maintaining control.

She rolled her hips again, grabbing the sides of his face to pull him in close. "Now," she practically growled. "Now, Gabe."

He opened his eyes, looked deeply into hers, and began to thrust as fast as she could draw breath. No, scratch that. She couldn't catch her breath, just rolled along on the storm of his desire. She threw her head back.

"Look at me," he commanded. "I want to see you when you come."

That was enough to push her over the edge. The hot pulses of pleasure spasmed her body. He groaned and came with her, the cords on his neck standing out as he gazed into her very soul.

When they both floated back to earth, he rested his forehead against hers. "I think I'm addicted to you," he whispered, closing his eyes. He turned his head away and eased off her, collapsing onto the bed. Christina let her legs flop onto the comforter. She was so sated she could barely think. They lay together and maybe dozed.

When the air-conditioner began to chill them, Gabe slid out of bed and flipped the comforter over her. "I'm going to go look for food," he said. She watched him pad from the room, naked, and made a contented noise. She was asleep before he ever came back into the room.

# Chapter Twenty-Two

CHRISTINA SLIPPED ON her underwear and one of Gabe's T-shirts, and made coffee while she waited for him to return. A satisfied grin tugged at her mouth. As she had known he would be, he was an amazing lover. He'd lit her on fire until she'd been a raging inferno, then brought her to the heights of pleasure. She sat at the kitchen table and looked out the window. What did it all mean, though?

"Maybe nothing. Maybe everything." Laughing a little as she repeated Heather's words, she turned the cup around and around in her hands, not drinking the coffee as she searched her feelings.

She'd fallen in love with him.

She'd known since Grasvlakten; she just hadn't wanted to admit it to herself. His uncompromising protection, unexpected gentleness, and commitment to his mission and his teammates all appealed to her. He had learned to listen when she spoke, and to take her opinions seriously. And he'd admitted to being jealous when she'd danced with Julian. That had to mean something, right?

Gabe wanted her; he'd proven that in spades. He cared for her, too. She knew it, despite his shabby treatment after dinner that night at the villa. Had his feelings been so strong the only way he knew how to deal with them was to withdraw emotionally?

Was he looking for a fling, though, or something more?

The knock at the front door had her jumping to her feet. He'd been quick at the grocery store! Maybe he'd been that anxious to get back to her. She raced down the hallway, heart leaping.

With a hand on the knob, her training took over, and she peered out the side window, just in case. A dark shadow shifted just out of her periphery. Adrenaline slammed though her as she realized, belatedly, that Gabe had a key. He would not have knocked.

She didn't wait to find out who was at the door. Turning, she ran for the bedroom and her purse, where the baby Sig nestled. Just as she reached the room, a dull crash thumped from the kitchen. Whoever it was had gone around to the back door. Rather than kick it in, he had simply broken the glass pane, and was no doubt even now reaching through to unlock the dead bolt.

It could be a random robbery, but Christina didn't really believe that. Someone had found the safe house.

The small residence had two access points, front and back. With Trevor's team in the house, they could have covered both directions. She wracked her brains. Not knowing who or how many, would it be better to try to force her way out or shoot it out inside the house when the person came in?

The faint creak of the kitchen door made the decision for her. She thumbed the safety off the Sig Sauer and crept down the hallway, back sliding against the wall. She waited, heart pounding. The house remained silent.

A slam against the front door made her jump. They would

be able to force the door open, she had no doubt. This suburban home had been chosen for its anonymity, not its ruggedness. If she did nothing, she would be flanked on both sides.

Left with little choice, she threw herself around the corner into the kitchen. Two men wearing ski masks raised their weapons, one stepping back in surprise. She pulled the trigger in rapid succession. The man on the left collapsed. The other one rushed her, tackling her around the middle and bodily taking her to the floor. Her head smacked against the linoleum hard enough that she saw stars. He snatched the handgun from her and threw it in one smooth motion. It bounced and spun crazily across the tiles.

Undaunted, Christina smashed her palm into his nose. He rolled away from her, grunting and cursing. She went with him, digging into his pockets, looking for anything that would help Gabe find her. She would lose, ultimately. Three against one were bad odds even for a Delta Force operator; she would go down fighting, but go down she would. Her fingers curled around some paper, and she pulled it out and dropped it onto the floor even as she brought her knee up, missing his groin by a hair's breath as he turned his hips.

The Taser caught her high on her shoulders. She spasmed under fifty thousand volts of electricity, back bowing as her muscles short-circuited, pain streaking through her body. When it was over, she flopped onto her back, gasping, knowing she needed to get up, face her attackers, fight. Cursing the lethargy in her muscles, she made it to her hands and knees. She looked up into the face of the third man, who had stripped off his ski mask.

He grinned, and triggered the Taser again.

# Chapter Twenty-Three

GABE BROWSED THE aisles of the supermarket, looking for tidbits that might appeal to Christina. He was frustratingly unfamiliar with her tastes, although he could confirm a fondness for strawberries and whipped cream, as cliché as it was.

"*Kan ik u helpen iets te vinden?*" A young woman stood in front of him, wearing a red checked apron and an inviting smile.

Gabe shook his head. "Don't understand."

"Ah. I asked if I may help you find something?" Her look suggested she would help him find what*ever* he was looking for.

"No, thanks. I got it." He gave her a brief smile and turned away.

"Häagen-Dazs ice cream is on sale at the moment. The mint chip is especially tasty." Somehow she had crept closer. Gabe looked her over. Blonde and curvy, but too young for him. Besides, now all he could see was Christina as he'd left her, curly mahogany hair spread across the pillow and a minx's smile on her lips. He briefly thought about finding a specialty store and picking up some handcuffs and strawberry-scented massage oil, but that would take too long, and he was anxious to get back to her.

"I'm good. Thanks." This time, he turned and walked away. She did not follow.

He did browse to the proper section and picked up a box of condoms. They'd made short work of the two he carried. He wanted her exactly where she was—naked and in his bed. Maybe he should reconsider the handcuffs. If he did, though, he suspected she'd turn the tables on him fast, and have him tied to the headboard and at the mercy of her pleasurable torment. He paused to consider that, and discovered the thought turned him on. Straddling him. Moving on top of him as he strained upward . . .

His cell phone rang. He pulled it out eagerly, hoping it was Christina. No such luck.

"Trevor. What's up?"

"I've got bad news," Trevor said, and suddenly Gabe was all business.

"Tell me."

Trevor's voice was calm enough, but Gabe heard the thin edge. "The third guy folded. Once he realized he'd been left high and dry, he spilled his guts. He claims they had nothing to do with Émile Bonnet. He maintains he was as surprised as anyone when Jansens fired at them. He didn't even know Jansens wasn't with us."

Oh, shit.

"They were separate groups," he said flatly. He'd suspected as much.

Now they knew.

"Did he say who he worked for? Or why they attacked her?"

Trevor whistled through his teeth. "Here's the bad news, mate.

The three men were a mix of Iraqi and Ukrainian enforcers, working for a man by the name of Fedyenka Osinov. That name mean anything to you?"

"The smuggler from Baghdad. Christina killed his brother." He searched his memory. "Yuri."

"Yes. My team went in and yanked them out of there. It was a little too close for comfort."

"Is Christina in danger?" How could he sound so calm when he wanted to rip someone's head off?

"I'd have to say yes. Fedyenka Osinov is wily and dangerous, with a wide network of contacts. If he knows Christina killed his brother, he'd never stop until he extracts revenge."

Gabe dropped his shopping basket and ran for the door. The girl in the checked apron gave him a strange look as he rushed past. No doubt he looked nearly as deranged as he felt. Nothing mattered except getting to Christina and keeping her safe.

Christina had told him Fedyenka saw Christina shoot Yuri in the stomach. Now his men were here, in Concordia. These same men must have been behind Christina's mysterious panel van in Washington, D.C., and they must have followed her here, to Parvenière. Ronnie hadn't been the only target.

Had Ronnie ever been the target?

He broke every speed limit getting back to the safe house. He was out of the car and running up the walk even before he shoved the car into park. Nearing the front door, he slowed, crouching, sliding to one side of it and pulling his Glock.

Shit. It was ajar.

Carefully, he placed his hand flat on the door and pushed it open a few inches. The silence scared the crap out of him. If Christina were inside, she would be struggling, fighting, making noise.

The silence meant that she was either no longer inside, or . . . he could not make himself think it.

Without hesitation, for he knew the house would be empty, he went through and cleared each room. As he entered the kitchen, he observed everything at once—a coffee cup shattered on the floor. The bowl of plastic fruit from the counter sat upside-down on the linoleum, two apples and some grapes strewn nearby. And a body by the open back door.

He holstered his Glock. Christina was gone.

And there was blood on the floor.

# Chapter Twenty-Four

CHRISTINA CAME AWAKE abruptly, hacking and choking as water rushed into her nose and mouth. A blurry man set a bucket down next to her and retreated a few feet. She tried to raise her arms to wipe the water from her face, and discovered her hands were tied to the arms of a chair. So were her feet. She yanked and pulled.

Blinking her eyes rapidly to free them from water, she stopped tugging and looked up. Her gaze immediately found the man sitting in a chair across from her. The chair was identical to hers; a straight-backed teak dining room chair with a blue-and-green patterned cushion. Unlike hers, however, his had no arms. Why did she notice such trivialities? Why note his Burberry slacks and dress shoes, with a suit jacket hanging neatly nearby?

Because she didn't want to look at his loose, jaundiced skin. His heavy face, his double chin. His thick brows, or the bags under his eyes.

His eyes, black with hatred.

Adrenaline kick-started her heart and sent her stomach plummeting. Her gasping breaths sluiced more water into her lungs, and she coughed again. She tested the restraints on her arms. Anything to avoid looking at him.

Fedyenka Osinov.

He contemplated her, saying nothing, not a twitch of emotion on his face. Just the burning malice in his eyes. Somehow, that frightened her more than rage would have. They looked at each other for endless moments.

"Untie me."

Christina broke first, uttering the words as a command, as defiance. It amused him. His eyes crinkled at the corners, though his mouth did not even twitch.

Instead, he nodded to the man who'd thrown water on her. Stas Noskov. She remembered him from Baghdad. He was a forty-year-old brute of a man, with broad, heavy features and pulled-down brows. His hair, beating a fast retreat from his forehead, was buzzed close to his scalp. He'd been a boxer, but now he was fat over muscle, with piggish eyes and fists as big as hams.

Without changing expressions, he backhanded her across the face.

Pain exploded in her cheek, radiating up through her neck into her skull. Blood filled her mouth and ran down her face where his big iron ring cut her. She waited for the pain to ease, head hung. When she could, she spat the blood from her mouth. She tried to reach Fedyenka, but he was too far away. Someone laughed.

Turning her head, Christina saw an eerily familiar face. Anger burst through the terror, and she glared daggers at him, loathing stamped baldly onto her features. She'd been flanked, and had been Tased into near unconsciousness before he clapped a cloth over her mouth that smelled of sweet acetone, antiseptic, and sweat. He'd held it there while her vision blurred and her hearing faded.

Then she'd blacked out.

Now Shay Boyle grinned at her as though they were old friends meeting on the street for coffee. "Hey, Chris. How're things?"

"Did you sell out Interpol for money?" she asked. "Is it as simple as that? No ideology except cash, no allegiance to your country or any other?"

Shay shrugged. "Nothing's ever simple. You should know that, Chris."

She blanched. "Don't call me that."

"That's right," he said. "It's Christina, right? Christina Madison, of the CIA." He drew out the letters slowly, punctuating each letter. "Not Chris Barlow from Chicago."

He drew a knife from a sheath at his hip and began to toss it end over end. Flip, flip, flip. She knew that blade. It was eight inches from end to end, sleek and sharp and deadly. His habit of tossing and catching it by the hilt each time had annoyed her. Whether a nervous habit or from boredom, she'd never found out.

Fedyenka stirred and rose, displeased at being ignored. His sagging body had seen better years. He was a bear of a man and while most of his muscle had turned to fat years ago, his arms were still huge. He came to stand in front of her, forcing her to crane her neck back to look up at him.

"You killed my brother," he said, so low she had to strain to hear. Rage buzzed in his voice. Like Gabe, it dropped when he was angry.

Gabe. Poor Gabe. He was going to return from his trip to the grocery store and find her gone. He'd know she hadn't left of her own accord when he saw the mess. She'd ripped anything she could from Stas as they'd struggled, but she didn't know whether or not it would help Gabe.

"You killed Yuri," Fedyenka said again, almost monotone.

"He was a criminal," she said, trying to sound brave. "And you are a criminal, all of you. You belong in jail."

Shay laughed again. "There's nothing to connect me to any of this. I'm Interpol. After this, I go right back to Baghdad and pick up where I left off."

"You're shit. I'll know." If I'm alive, she thought. One look at Fedyenka's face, though, and she knew the truth. She wasn't leaving this room.

"You pretended to be fucking Princess Veronica pretty good," Fedyenka said, staring down at her. "If I hadn't already known what a lying bitch you are, I might have been fooled. 'Course, now you look like the cunt you are."

With her bare feet tied to the legs of the chair and the over-large shirt sliding off one shoulder, she felt vulnerable. And sick at heart.

She should have told Gabe she loved him.

"Véronique."

"What?" This time his voice was whip-thin, lashing her.

"Véronique. Her name. It's not Veronica."

Fedyenka leaned down and grabbed a fistful of Christina's hair at the crown of her head, yanking her head back brutally. "Do I look like I give a shit about her name?"

Christina blanched. Fury banked in his eyes, ready to spring forth like a serpent.

He released her hair with a shove and returned to his seat, breathing heavily.

She took her eyes off him long enough to glance around. The

structure probably had been a barn at one time. It stood roughly forty feet long and maybe thirty feet wide. Made of timber and brick, it had clearly seen better days. The wood warped and curled; the mortar crumbled around the bricks. Ivy climbing the outside poked tendrils through the windows. Stalls had been ripped out to make room for farm equipment, leaving marks along the floor, but only an old thresher remained.

When he'd gotten himself back under control, Fedyenka nodded and gestured to Shay, who went to the table. Christina looked at it for the first time. Her heart stuttered.

A large car battery sat in the center of the table, attached to some sort of control box with a manual dial. Long thin wires connected the box to a wand with a bronze tip and an insulated handle. Shay picked up the wand and held it out for her inspection.

"Do you know what this is?" he asked, smirking.

Fearful she did, fearful she understood why she'd been doused with water, she looked back at Fedyenka. He hadn't moved.

It was an electric cattle prod.

"My team will find me," she said, trying for brave.

"Don't count on it," Fedyenka said. "No one even knows I'm in Europe. I rented this farmhouse through my lawyers for cash, under one of my aliases."

Christina worked some moisture into her mouth. "Where . . . where are we?"

"In Concordia, still. In Brodeur, as it happens. Plenty of farm-land, plenty of places to hide."

Christina felt a pang of despair. How would Gabe find her? She didn't doubt he'd try, but he'd never find her. There would be no cavalry to rescue her this time.

"Now. What did you tell the CIA about me? My operation?"

Spurred by a sudden spurt of courage, she glared. "Everything. They know everything."

Fedyenka nodded to Stas Noskov, who flipped a switch on the machine on the table. A low hum filled the room. Shay swaggered over to her, holding the wand in front of her eyes and waving it to and fro. She tried to swallow, but her mouth felt like the Sahara.

"This is called a picana," Fedyenka said, crossing one ankle over his knee. "It's got advantages over Tasers and cattle prods. Wanna know what they are?"

Christina looked around the room for anything that could help her escape. Maybe if she appealed to Shay's greed? "I can double what he's paying you," she said a touch desperately.

Shay grinned at her. "Doubt it."

"My business is damned profitable, despite your fucking interference. You cost me a helluva lot of money, though, and I intend to take it out of your hide. Literally, you bitch."

Stas Noskov leered down at her, pulling the collar of the shirt out and peering in at her breasts. She spit at him. He slapped her, then grabbed the collar and ripped. It tore to her shoulder, baring skin from her neck to her biceps. Fedyenka nodded again, and Shay touched the tip of the wand just above her collarbone.

She screamed.

# Chapter Twenty-Five

GABE FOUGHT AGAINST unfamiliar feelings of helplessness and despair. He'd felt rage many times in his life, but never coupled with panic.

He dialed Mace. Straight to voice mail, which meant the team had already gone wheels up. The hand holding his cell phone shook. Had they hurt her when they took her? Were they hurting her now?

He combed through the house, looking for anything that would tell him where Fedyenka Osinov had taken Christina. He found a couple of brown buttons, a torn receipt, and a pair of broken sunglasses in the kitchen. Even in the midst of his anguish, he experienced a flash of pride. Christina had been trying, even as she fought for her freedom, to give him a clue.

The receipt was for a Q8 petrol station in a place called Brodeur, Concordia. It was faded, blurry. He squinted hard.

He pressed a speed-dial on his cell phone.

"As I live and breathe. Archangel. To what do I owe . . ."

"Stephanie, it's an emergency. Christina's been taken."

"Shit," Private Stephanie Tams said. "Colonel Granville . . ."

"Tell him later. Right now, I need my team back here yesterday." He didn't know how much time he had. Maybe none. "Get it cleared."

"Yes, sir." Through the phone line, Gabe heard Stephanie yell for someone. "Tell the colonel we're not done in Concordia. And get the team back to . . . where are you, sir?"

"The safe house we stashed the princess at."

"Got it. Wait one."

The silence on the phone grated on his already fraying nerves.

"Gabe." Just by her voice, he knew he wasn't going to like what she had to say. "Colonel Granville won't authorize the plane to turn around. They've got a live mission. Don't tell anyone I said so, but you're going to be recalled, too. I'm sorry, sir. You're on your own on this one."

Fuck and double fuck. He dropped his head into his hand.

But that wasn't going to help Christina. "I found a receipt for a gas station. Pull up a map of Concordia."

"Done. Where in Concordia?"

Gabe squinted at the receipt. "Place called Brodeur. Zoom in on a gas station at Rue Grande 41."

"Okay. Using Google Earth. Wait one."

It couldn't have been more than ten seconds, but it felt like a lifetime until Stephanie said, "Switching to street view. I found the gas station. What now, sir?"

"Okay. I need a map of the surrounding areas. I need isolated areas where he might be holding her. Farmhouses, abandoned castles, windmills. God, I don't know." The truth was, he couldn't think. His heart was frozen in his chest at the thought of what they might be doing to Christina at this very moment. They would kill her; he had no illusions about that. But Fedyenka Osinov would want revenge for the death of his brother.

Osinov.

"Get back to me, Steph." He disconnected and dialed Trevor.

"Carswell."

"Where are you?" He couldn't keep the tenseness out of his voice. "Fedyenka Osinov snatched Christina."

"Shite. How the hell did he know about the safe house?"

Gabe exhaled hard. "And the timing stinks. They wait until Ronnie's gone to attack? Somehow, some way, they knew Christina was impersonating the princess. They must have been waiting . . . dammit."

"Breathe, mate. I'm still in Parvenière. Where are you?"

"Still at the safe house, but I'm leaving for Brodeur."

"I'll meet you there. Ninety minutes." He paused. "Me, mate. I can't involve my team in an unauthorized mission."

"Haul ass." He'd take whatever help he could. "Thanks, man."

His next call was to the local police.

"Chief Van den Nieuwenhuyzen."

"I need Federal Police help," he said. "I need Aart Jansens. Are you still holding him?"

"*Ja.* I can talk to him for you. What do you need?"

"I need his sniper skills. I need a shooter."

Silence.

Gabe pressed on. "Also, I need him to help me find an isolated area in or around Brodeur. I need information about any houses or buildings that have been rented or leased recently, or have been owned for a long time but unoccupied until recently. Ones where the renter or new owner paid in cash, or went through a broker. Uh, I have to tell you something. About your crown princess." He briefly closed his eyes. He could go to jail for this. The operation had been classified from the start. But he didn't hesitate one iota as he filled the police chief in. "I have to find Christina soon. She doesn't have long."

"An interesting tale. And quite the conundrum for you, I suspect. You may rely on my discretion. However, what you ask might take some time," the chief said.

"Christina doesn't have time," Gabe practically roared down the phone line.

"I'll use every influence," the chief promised. "Jansens will cooperate for a reduced sentence."

Gabe threw himself behind the wheel and pointed the car toward Brodeur.

# Chapter Twenty-Six

"Wakey-wakey."

Pain exploded in her skull as Stas Noskov slapped her. She pried her eyes open. Shay and Stas had apparently switched places. Shay now controlled the rheostat dial. Stas stared at her breasts.

It was Shay who had spoken. Christina coughed. She must have bitten her tongue during the last round with the picana, because she was bleeding from her mouth. It was a struggle to lift her head.

"Let's start over," Fedyenka said. "What did you tell the CIA about my operation?"

He kept asking variations of the same question. He didn't care about the answers. This was about punishing her, exacting revenge for the death of his brother. When he grew tired of it, he would kill her.

"I told them what an asshole you were."

It didn't matter if she told him the truth or lied. His reaction was always the same.

He nodded to Shay, who turned the dial to the right a few clicks. Stas pressed the tip of the wand to her temple. She shrieked as fast as she could draw breath, one after another until her voice was hoarse. Even when he took the wand away, her head throbbed and pounded and threatened to explode.

"The picana is a peculiar tool," Fedyenka told her, as casually as if he'd said he'd like coffee with his lunch. "Did you know it was developed just for situations like this? Fucking imagine that. A product designed specifically for one human being to torture another."

"Fas . . . fascinating." Her eyes refused to stay focused. Her head dropped forward onto her chest and stayed there.

"The high voltage makes the shocks hurt more, but it's got a low current, so you're less likely to die while we're talking. Pretty damned cool, huh?"

"Why don't you just kill me and get it over with?"

The rage simmering behind his eyes abruptly burst forth. He nearly threw himself out of the chair and stalked to her, grabbing her hair and forcing her head back. "Not until you've suffered as much as I have," he screamed into her face, spittle landing on her skin. "Not until you're begging me to kill you. Or maybe I will kill you now."

He yanked a revolver from the back of his belt and pointed it at her. "Are you ready to die? Do you want to die?"

It was hard to push the words past the dread clogging her throat. "Go to hell."

Fedyenka raised the revolver over her head and pulled the trigger.

The roar of discharge so close to her head caused her entire body to flinch, the sound physically painful. She took in huge gulps of air, eyes squeezed shut, as agony lanced through her skull. "Son of a *bitch*."

"So you live awhile longer. A pity."

Fedyenka intended to terrorize her, torture her. It was working. Christina started hiccupping gulps of air, trying to suppress the sobs clawing their way up her throat.

"Who do you work for at Langley?"

"A man."

"Did you work for him when you lied your way into my business in Baghdad?"

"Yes."

"What is his name?"

"Boss."

Shay stopped flipping his knife and put the tip of the blade on her knee, over the top of her T-shirt. He pressed down slowly, letting her feel the blade penetrate through the cotton to her skin below. She grit her teeth. When he'd made a hole in the shirt, he canted the blade sideways and sliced through the material, baring her upper leg.

Finally, he slammed the knife back into the sheath at his hip. Christina was close enough to grab it, if only her hands were free.

"You're a coward," she hissed. Maybe she could get him to lose his temper and . . . and what? Cut her loose? Kill her? "Only a coward tortures a woman who's tied up and can't even defend herself. A real man wouldn't do that. Only a sick, twisted one."

"Was that insult meant for me, or for Fedyenka?" Shay chuckled. "Neither of us cares what you think, though."

But Fedyenka cared what she felt. He wanted her in agony before he ended her life.

"Where are we?" she asked. Keep them talking. Keep them away from the picana.

"Concordia. Didn't we tell you that already?" Shay frowned, annoyed.

"Why should it fucking hell matter to you? You're going to die here," Fedyenka growled.

"Call it morbid curiosity."

"We're at a farmhouse on the outskirts of Brodeur. Far from civilization." Shay shrugged. "No one to hear you scream, Chris."

Fedyenka threw him an annoyed look. "Shut your fucking hole."

"What difference does it make? She's not leaving here—"

*Alive.* It didn't need to be said.

"I was followed in D.C.," she said, trying to gulp back her terror. "I thought it was a training exercise, but it was you, wasn't it?"

"Yeah," Stas answered. "You don't got a clue, do you? You got no fucking idea what's going on."

"Why don't you enlighten me?"

Shay laughed. "It's all about you, Christina Madison of the CIA. It's always been all about you."

That brought her head up. "What are you talking about?"

Fedyenka rose and went to the table, where he picked up a metal pipe, maybe three feet long. He idly twirled it as he came over to her. "You're thinking too much about the past. I want you to think about now. What I'm going to do to you for killing my brother." He tapped the pipe against her knee. "What do you think I'm going to do with this? Or would you prefer the picana again? I'll let you choose."

She'd be damned if she'd choose her own pain. He'd just pick the other to torment her anyway. When she didn't answer, Shay tore a strip off a roll of duct tape, and pressed cruelly against her mouth as he stretched it taut. She glared her disgust. He grinned at her, dropped a kiss on top of the tape, and walked away. Fedyenka took his place.

He tapped the pipe against her knee again. "How would it affect your career as a cheating, whoring liar if I broke both your knees?" he asked. "They used to do that in Chinese POW camps, you know, during the Korean war. My father had both his knees broken by the camp commander. That fucking bastard was determined to break my father, but he never did. My father hobbled out of that camp using two sticks, and he spat in the commander's face as he left."

Give me a chance, Christina thought. I'll spit in your face, too.

# Chapter Twenty-Seven

GABE PACED THE parking lot like a caged tiger. The inactivity drove him insane.

He waited. Waited for Stephanie to send him the layout around Brodeur. Waited for Trevor to meet him with supplies. Waited for Aart Jansens to get back to him about recently rented properties around Brodeur.

And he prayed.

His phone rang. Even before the first sound died away, it was up at his ear. "Morgan."

"It's Jay Spicer," came the voice on the other end of the line. "I hear you lost my operative."

It threw him for a moment. "How did you . . . ?"

"Private Tams from your unit called me," Spicer said. "She brought me up to speed. It's a good thing she did, too. I remember reading a report about a week ago from my guys in Parvenière. They make it a point to have good relations with local police. So this guy calls the police, right? He says he's the farm manager for some remote farm outside of a tiny town in the middle of fucking Nowhere, Concordia, right? He says he rented the place sight unseen to a foreigner—that's what he said, apparently—talked funny, right? So he goes to give him the keys, and there's like eight guys there, and the main guy, speaks funny, tells him to get lost and not come around again. So this guy, this farm manager, he thinks this is odd, so he kind of drives by every now and again, and it's all quiet, but there are always guards outside, right, walking around with machine guns. That's what this guy says. Doubt he'd recognize a machine gun versus a machete, but whatever. So I'm thinking, where better to take someone . . ."

His phone beeped. "That's Stephanie," he said. "Anything else?"

"Nawp. That's the gist of it. Call me with an update. Madison's my operative, right?"

Gabe switched over to Stephanie Tams. "What'd you find out?" he asked. He didn't have time for hellos and goodbyes. Each moment wasted was one moment more that Christina might die.

"I'm sending you an aerial layout of the farmhouse Jay Spicer thinks Christina might be being held at. You know, don't you, that we might be off base here?"

He didn't want to hear that.

"It's the best I've got," he said, frustration leaking through his control. He thumbed open the JPEG Stephanie had emailed him. Aw, hell. It was farmland, all right. A single house and what looked like a couple of outbuildings in the middle of at least a mile of planted fields. The nearest tree line was at least half a mile away.

He called Trevor back. "Where are you?"

"Fifteen minutes. I stopped at a sporting goods store to pick up some stuff."

"Good. I'll send you the layout. It's bad. No cover, no concealment."

"We might have to wait until dark to go in."

"Not an option," Gabe clipped. "Every moment I waste here is one step closer . . ." He couldn't say it. Couldn't even think it. She had to be alive. She just had to be.

He'd broken all land speed records getting from Parvenière down the E46 toward Brodeur. The Q8 petrol station was nestled between an empty lot and a row of townhome apartments. He'd pulled as far into the back as he could and killed the engine.

Now what? It was suicide to go rushing to the farmhouse in broad daylight. He had his Glock and an extra magazine—thirty-one rounds—and his boot knives. Not enough. Not nearly enough.

A nondescript blue Audi pulled into a pump. A man emerged, capturing Gabe's attention immediately. Despite the warm day, he wore a light jacket concealing a holster under his arm. His short hair had a prominent window's peak, his features broad and Slavic. Gabe hunched down a little in his seat, keeping his face turned away and watching in his mirrors as the man went inside, coming back out about ten minutes later with a bag of burgers, a six-pack of beer, and cigarettes. He pulled out and started through the tiny town, driving past the old stone church and out onto the two-lane local throughway. Gabe let him get far ahead before he pulled out and followed.

He hung well back, keeping several cars between himself and the man he was tailing. He punched up the farmhouse's address in Google Maps with one hand. Sure enough, the man was heading toward the farmhouse. He made no attempt to backtrack or hide his destination, nor did he seem to notice his tail. When he turned down a long access road, Gabe drove past, keeping pace with other cars heading out of town.

About fifty yards ahead, he found a place to turn around.

Again, he didn't slow at the drive, although he did risk a quick look. Two guards outside. What had the property manager said? There were eight of them. Not impossible odds for a Delta Force operator, but still pretty bad.

He returned to the petrol station because he had nothing better to do, filled his gas tank, and bought food from the burger stand at the end of the convenience store. He chewed, tasting nothing. Just waiting. He hated waiting at the best of times.

Now it was intolerable.

# Chapter Twenty-Eight

HER STRENGTH WANED with every passing minute. Her world narrowed to this place and this man, to her fear and the throbbing pain. She let her head hang, because it hurt to hold it upright.

It displeased him.

He rose abruptly from his chair and was in front of her in two strides, jerking her chin up with cruel fingers. "You will look at me, so you know who is in charge here."

"Go to hell." She couldn't think of anything better to say. Her nerves and neurons were scrambled, and it hurt to talk.

One of the guards brought in a bag and a six-pack. "Food."

Stas and Shay tore into the burgers at once. Fedyenka turned her face this way and that. She had no clue what he looked for. Finally, he moved to the table and unwrapped a hamburger. He took it to the door and leaned against it while he chewed, turning his face to the breeze.

"Hey," she called. "I'm hungry."

Shay snickered. He popped a beer, chugging down half of it before stopping to belch. "How 'bout a beer instead?"

Stas crammed fries into his mouth. "No beer."

"Moron. I wasn't serious."

Christina brought the image of Gabe to the forefront of her mind. She had to hold on. For him. He wouldn't stop looking for her. Therefore, she couldn't give up.

"Why wait a year?" she asked Shay. "You obviously knew where I lived in D.C. Why wait until now for this?"

Fedyenka came back, spinning the cylinder on his revolver. "He couldn't find you. Damned international police can't find one stupid bitch. But he finally tracked you down."

Shay lit a cigarette. "I have contacts everywhere. I knew where she was the whole time."

Fedyenka looked at him in disbelief. "You fucking took my money to look for her when you knew where she was?" He raised the revolver, thought better of it, and lowered it again.

Shay grinned, scratching through his short beard. "Aren't you glad I did? If you'd've already killed her, she couldn't have come to Concordia to take Princess Ver-on-i-ca's place."

"What if we lost her? What if she went to Vienna anyway?"

The Interpol agent laughed. "I told you, I have contacts everywhere. One of the Household Guards knew me. It was dead simple to put a tracker on the royal limo as soon as I knew Chris was on her way. I told him it was for her protection. I knew where she was every step of the way. So when you told me to bring her to you, I sent my men to grab her on the road to Grasvlakten."

"Where you failed," Fedyenka growled.

Shay scowled, flinging his cigarette down and grinding it with his boot heel. "I underestimated her bodyguards."

"You failed me again at Grasvlakten. I had to go get her myself."

Christina gave her head a quick shake. Surely, she'd heard

wrong? "What . . . what do you mean? You said before . . . this was all about me?"

Shay swaggered over to her. "Does that surprise you, princess?"

Her head was whirling, but from residuals of electric shocks or this new information, she didn't know. "I don't understand."

Fedyenka laughed. The sound grated along her nerve endings. "Story of your life. Princess. Har-har-har."

Shay shot him an annoyed look. "I knew where you were and I knew what you looked like," he said, with the exaggerated patience of someone talking to a dim child. "When Fedyenka here told me to get rid of Princess Ver-on-i-ca, I knew the perfect way to do it. I contacted Émile Bonnet. He's hot to protect his retirement. See, there's these rare sheared minks. Very expensive. He has men who trap them and sell them to Fedyenka. I told him the entire supply would dry up if he didn't get the princess out of the way. So Bonnet contacted a guy he knows to fake a shooting. Just enough to drive the princess out of the castle and into a safe house."

"But how did you know about the safe house?"

"I have contacts . . ."

"Everywhere. I know." Christina rolled her eyes. "But how did you find it?"

Shay chortled. "Dead easy. I'm law enforcement, remember? A cop. I told Interpol in Parvenière that I had a high-profile case— classified, of course—that might require a safe house. He gave me the run-down on the three the government keeps. Addresses and everything. And then told me one was in use. Imbecile. Then I just waited for your bodyguards to catch Bonnet's fake assassin. Véronique goes back to her life. And I take her out for real. Boo-hoo. So sad. But she doesn't show up at the Vienna summit, and Fedyenka gets his sheared minks."

"And I went to the safe house," Christina said, realization dawning. "You followed me there?"

"Nope. We were already there. Watched you go in and her come out. When your boyfriend left, we snatched you. Dead simple."

The way he emphasized *dead* caused a shiver to make its way down her spine. *Keep him talking*, she chanted to herself. *Give Gabe time to find me.*

"What if . . . what if he hadn't left? Or we'd gone together?"

"He'd be dead," Shay said matter-of-factly. "Two birds with one stone. Fedyenka gets both his mink supply and you. A win-win."

Fedyenka added, "Really rare mink. Women pay a fortune for them. Men, too. Problem is, their primary breeding grounds are smack dab in the middle of where they want to drill for oil. I'd lose too much money if my supply dried up. Bonnet told me the princess would never change her mind. Worse, she's pushing to get the damned things regulated and monitored to make sure nothing happens to them because of the oil drilling. Do you know what regulation means in my business? Lost revenue."

"This was only ever about money," she said. "You disgust me."

Rage crawled across Fedyenka's face. "You're a mouthy bitch. You need to learn respect. And it's not just about money. It's about my fucking brother!"

Shay wandered outside, lighting a cigarette.

Christina could think of only one way to stop the torment. She raked him with a look of contempt.

"Yuri was weak," she said. "But better than you. You're weak and stupid. You can't hold on to the business now, can you? Yuri was the brains, tiny as they were."

And then she did it.

"He was easy to kill. I'm glad I did it."

Fedyenka's face purpled and veins popped out in his face and neck. He dropped the revolver as his big hands rose, clamped around her throat, and squeezed. Christina closed her eyes, waiting for the blessed darkness to take her, though her body twisted and fought for air. Just as spots began to dance behind her eyes and she felt herself begin to fade, the pressure around her neck disappeared. Her eyes snapped open and she gasped as life-giving oxygen rushed back into her lungs.

"No," Fedyenka said. "I won't make it easy for you. I'll kill you when I'm ready, not when you want to die."

He picked up the revolver and set it on the table, returning with the metal rod. He hefted it a few times, then ran the metal edge across her cheek. "You need a lesson, though. Respect."

Before she could register his intent, he swung the pipe and smashed it into her knee with all his strength. She screamed, and passed out.

# Chapter Twenty-Nine

FULL DARK HAD settled in by the time Trevor pulled up beside him. He motioned, and Gabe started the car and followed him up the street and into a brick alley. They parked the cars next to one another. Trevor popped the trunk. Gabe wasted no time burrowing through the two duffel bags inside.

Binoculars, two pairs. Cheap walkie-talkies, but they would do. Lots of .40 caliber ammo and, best of all, three shotguns. "My blokes send their apologies," Trevor said.

"It's better than what I have." Gabe wasn't going to look a gift horse in the mouth.

There were also two sets of Army-surplus camouflage pants, shirts, and kevlar helmets. "My choices were somewhat limited," Trevor said apologetically. "Crops are growing, but it's too early in the season for them to be high enough for us to crawl through. Some are green soybeans, some are wheat. The gold kind."

"There's a stand of trees separating this property from the next," Gabe said, showing Trevor the aerial map. "We can start there."

They changed into the camouflage clothing and loaded up on ammunition, then got into Trevor's car. He followed Gabe's directions, parking at the end of a driveway about a quarter of a mile from their target. The two of them slipped into the trees to make their way to the farmhouse. Once they reached the edge of the tree line, they settled in to watch.

"It's up to us." A lead lump settled into Gabe's gut and remained there.

Trevor put a hand on his arm. "We'll get her out."

While they waited, Gabe and Trevor mapped out the land, moving from tree to tree until they knew every inch of the property. Forest surrounded the farm on three sides, but the closest sat more than fifty yards from the house.

The farmhouse itself was two stories, old brown brick with three separate roofs and two chimneys. The center roof jutted out from the other two sections. The front door was on one side of it. A sun room had been added to the left side of the house.

The area around the house was paved with flagstones. The flagstones turned to gravel leading away from the right side of the house, which turned to a paved road when the long gravel drive dead-ended. There were trees where the gravel driveway turned onto the paved road, but the area surrounding it was grass; no way to get to it unseen, and nowhere to go after they got there. Gabe dismissed it.

An outbuilding squatted halfway between the main house and the road. It might have been a barn at some point. Maybe storage for farm equipment, since a rusted-out tractor sat off to the side, attached to some sort of device lined with disks that he thought must have been for ploughing at some point. The entryway seemed to consist of two wooden doors at one end that looked to him like the door on a horse stall. One sat propped open.

The whole thing looked rickety, with plenty of gaps. Piles of man-height bricks rested along one side; maybe someone at some point had thought about fixing it up. Even the red roof was missing tiles.

Even if they were able to make it to the main house, there was no way for them to get to the outbuilding unseen.

"There," Gabe said. "That's where they'll have her."

"Not the house? Why?"

"Gut check," he said. "The house rambles around, but the outbuilding is compact. Besides, if it's for equipment, there might be hooks . . . chains, or . . ." He couldn't continue.

Trevor put a hand on his shoulder and squeezed. "That kind of thinking won't help now, mate. Let's stay positive, okay?"

Gabe nodded, but the lead in his gut grew heavier.

Five men guarded the grounds; three patrolled randomly, while the other two took up positions where one could watch both the gravel driveway and the front of the house, while the other stood between two trees and watched the back. At least one guard always patrolled the side closest to the tree line, off to the left of the house.

His phone vibrated. He pulled back into the forest before answering. The number wasn't familiar, but he recognized the Concordian country code. "Morgan."

"It's Aart Jansens," came a deep voice. "I hear you want my services."

"If you're willing. You're still a cop. This might be a little outside your jurisdiction. A lot outside."

Jansens snorted a small laugh. "I am on administrative desk detail until my case is reviewed. Assassination of a royal is treason. I'll be lucky if I only lose my job, and not my head."

"Do you still have your sniper rifle?"

"No. It was confiscated at the Nabourg residence when I was arrested."

Gabe had forgotten that. Dammit.

"I have a personal rifle, however. It's very nearly as high quality, with the modifications I've made. Where are you?"

Gabe told him. "Uh, did Chief Van . . . did the chief fill you in?"

"Yes, and also swore me to secrecy," Jansens said. "Let me gather some equipment, and I will meet you. An hour and a half."

"Thanks, man. I can't tell you how grat . . ."

"Let us save the thanks until after we have saved your princess, *ja*? Am I right in thinking she is your princess, your love?"

Gabe didn't even hesitate. "Yes."

"Then I will help you save her."

Trevor joined him.

"We'll have a sniper in ninety minutes. Meanwhile, what kind of man is Fedyenka Osinov?"

"A brute," Trevor said. "Intelligent, but vengeful if he feels he's been ill-treated. He'll smile at you and stab you from behind in the next breath."

Yeah, that's what he'd been afraid he'd hear.

"And he blames Christina?"

"Undoubtedly."

"So what happened in Baghdad? From your perspective."

"Christina did nothing wrong. You have to know that up front."

Gabe nodded. "I know. She's too damned good to have fucked up that badly."

Trevor raised the binoculars to his eyes and swept the area. "The whole operation was coordinated by your American Customs Agency. It targeted criminal networks behind the illegal exports of parrots into Western Europe and the Americas. The largest network belonged to the Osinovs. Once Christina's team made contact with them, the Interpol police officer coordinated with Iraqi police for the takedown. Christina arrived at the holding pens to finish the deal, but someone had tipped the brothers off, and they knew the police were coming. There was a firefight. Christina was shot.

"Her team abandoned her, for all intents and purposes. They packed up and moved to their extraction point. She made it finally, but too late. The Osinovs knew where to find her. The US team was pinned down. If their pilot hadn't spooked and run, her teammates would have boarded the plane and left her behind."

Anger stirred inside him. She could have been killed because of their incompetence. "But you rescued her? Them?"

Trevor grunted an affirmative. "My team happened to be returning from a training mission. When the call came in for help, we responded. We pulled her team from the hot zone and got them to safety."

"How do you know all this? You handled the extraction, that's all."

"Because my team was involved, the Special Air Service launched an investigation, in partnership with your CIA." He lowered his binoculars and gave Gabe his full attention. "Someone betrayed them. We cleared everyone on her team except the Interpol officer, and that only because Interpol wouldn't cooperate with us. Instead, they launched their own investigation."

"And . . . ?" The rumors swept through the SpecOps community in the Middle East. Christina had been branded incompetent and untrustworthy.

Trevor sighed. "The story, the part that anyone knew about, had already circulated. Her reputation was in tatters. Jay Spicer and I both suspect, but cannot prove, that the Interpol officer tipped off the Osinovs. We couldn't unearth anything to incriminate him; his reputation is stellar. He's a highly decorated police officer. There was nothing we could do."

Gabe growled. "Except let an innocent woman take the fall."

Trevor's mouth ticked apologetically. "Jay took her with him to Azakistan, to give her as much cover as he could. He's a fair man."

"And you got involved with her?" He had to force the words out.

Trevor looked him straight in the eye. "No. We've never been more than friends. Those were just more ugly rumors. You, on the other hand, are in love with her. Does she feel the same?"

Gabe shifted his weigh, uncomfortable. He wasn't used to discussing his emotions with anyone. "I, uh, I don't know."

He contemplated that question during the interminable wait for Jansens to arrive. He would woo her properly. They would date, and she would fall in love with him. How they would manage it with him at Fort Bragg and her in Washington, D.C., he didn't know. But he had to try.

But only if they saved her now.

His phone vibrated. He read the text message. "Finally! It's Jansens. I'm going up to the gas station to meet him." He hated to leave even for an instance. What if the men up and left while he was gone?

"I'll go," Trevor said, clearly understanding. "I'll bring him back here, along with some food."

"Not hungry. Water would be good, though."

While he waited, and waited, and waited, he could not stop his mind from conjuring awful images of what Osinov might be doing to Christina at this very moment. Standing by had never been so painful. Every instinct he had said to rush headlong into the farming outbuilding, shoot everyone who wasn't Christina, and bring her out. Trevor was right, though. It was suicide.

As he continued to monitor through the binoculars, he noted that the roving guards steered clear of the outbuilding, and the stationary guards stood well away from it. Did that mean Christina and Osinov weren't there? Was it squeamishness? Sound didn't carry from this distance. He swallowed his frustration. Osinov knew what he was doing when he selected this place.

An eternity later, he drew back to where the cars were parked, striding up to Trevor's rental almost before they could get out.

"Jansens. Thanks for coming."

The police officer nodded once, sharply. "I owe you this help," he said. "If not for me, you would have known about this second group sooner."

Gabe had to be fair. "And maybe without you, Christina might have been killed right then and there."

The cop grunted. "No matter. Now we fix it, *ja*?"

Gabe nodded grimly. "Yeah."

# Chapter Thirty

GABE WAITED WHILE his new teammate worked his way into position. They had a plan, such as it was. No one could come up with a better idea given the scenario, and the clock was ticking. Between the three of them, they had one sniper rifle, three shotguns, and plenty of ammunition. Trevor had a Browning Hi-Power semiautomatic pistol and a black commando knife. Gabe had his Glock, his boot knives, and a thin length of wire; not the least armed he'd ever been in his life as a SpecOps warrior, but near enough.

"They could be in the house after all," Trevor said. "No one seems to be paying much attention to the barn."

Gabe ran a hand down his face and scratched the stubble on his chin. "A feint?" he suggested. "You said Fedyenka's wily. Is he smart enough for that?"

"Yes."

"So could be we waste time storming the house, and he has time to get to the SUV and run. With Christina, or after killing her." His voice failed him, and he had to clear it several times. "No matter what, he's dead."

"Yes," Trevor said again.

"Gut says they're in the barn, not the house."

Trevor nodded. "Right, then."

He and Trevor waited in the tree line to the west of the house. The guard near the SUV chain-smoked, lighting a new cigarette from the old before grinding the butt into the gravel. A roving guard wandered down the driveway. Another patrolled in front of them. He walked past, not noticing the two warriors, invisible in the shadows.

Aart had the most difficult position to get to, having to travel nearly a mile through heavy forest, circumnavigating the property until he was north and east of the farmhouse. From his position, he could see both the stationary guard at the northwest corner of the house, and the guard patrolling the tree line running north to south on the west side of the property. It seemed to take forever, but in less than an hour a staticky voice came through the walkie-talkie. "In position," Aart said. "I have clear line of sight."

Finally!

"Go," Gabe said.

He erupted from the trees like a demon from hell, swarming the guard before he had even half turned, garrote in hand. He threw the loop over the guard's head with his left hand, drawing the wire taut. Closing his right hand around the loop, he slapped his hand against the back of the guard's neck and straightened his arm, twisting the wire. A knee strike to his lower back and the guard arched back, chin dipping, his own body weight helping to throttle him. The man's yell died gurgling in his throat. In eight seconds he was unconscious; in thirty-five, windpipe crushed, he was dead.

A sound vaguely like the snap of a pneumatic nail gun reached him.

"Target one down," Aart said. Another snap. A moment later, "Target two down."

"Target three down," Gabe said. He caught the shotgun Trevor tossed him with one hand, and they raced across the grass.

Now came the hard part. The other two guards would not be taken unawares; they were out in the open, and so were Gabe and Trevor. They ran, bent over and zigzagging, trying for the old red tractor.

Their first inkling that they'd been spotted was the ripping *ktchak-tchak-tchak* of automatic gunfire. Both men dove the last few feet to reach the tractor, putting their backs against the huge tires. Gabe risked a quick peek around the front of the tractor and jerked back. Bullets tinged off the metal where he'd been. Before his target could fire again, Gabe racked the shotgun, popped up and squeezed the trigger. The shotgun belched, deep and powerful, and the slug shot toward his target.

He missed. The man retreated behind the SUV parked in front of the house. The fifth man had hunkered down at the right side of the house. Trevor and Gabe were pinned down.

They needed to get past the house to the barn, but the two remaining guards stood solidly between them and their objective. Running across the open ground would be suicide. Staying here would allow Fedyenka Osinov time to escape, either with or without Christina. Gabe's stomach knotted.

Trevor glanced at him. "I'll draw him out."

He nodded. Trevor lifted himself up and fired three blasts with the shotgun. Even before he'd ducked back down, Gabe peered around the front of the tractor and steadied the sights.

The blast caught the man square in the chest. He staggered backward and fell.

A round pinged off the metal so close to his head he felt the heat of it. He pulled back. Too close.

For a moment, it was eerily silent. Then the barn door lurched open. A third body appeared, hiding behind it. A fourth crouched by a window.

The gunman behind the SUV yelled toward the barn in Ukrainian. One of the newcomers answered.

"You're outnumbered," the other—a redhead, incongruously enough—shouted. "Throw down your weapons and come out, and I promise you won't be harmed."

Trevor snorted a laugh. "Yeah, mate. Keep saying that. We'll believe it."

Gabe knew Aart Jansens would be moving to his secondary location. Would it be fast enough? He didn't think so. It was a stalemate.

He smelled the smoke before he saw the flames start to lick up the sides of the structure. His heart stuttered in his chest. Osinov had set the barn on fire. Was he out of his fucking mind?

He appeared in the opening, a beefy arm wrapped around Christina's neck, hiding behind her like the candy-ass coward he was. Christina's face was swollen, her lip split and dried blood on one side of her face. Her hands were bound in front of her with duct tape. She kept her weight on one leg, shifting her bare feet gingerly as Osinov yanked her around. Her T-shirt had been torn almost to the end of the sleeve and again at the hem, and she wore no pants. Rage lit a fire deep inside him.

"Steady on, mate." Trevor glanced at Gabe, gripping the shotgun firmly. "I have a clear shot to the man by the car."

The man had stepped forward, as though to help his boss, leaving him in the clear. It would enrage Osinov, but it would even things up a bit. He gave a sharp nod.

The blast spun the man around. He hit his head on the driver's side mirror as he fell, ripping it from the SUV's body. Osinov screamed obscenities, pressing his handgun to Christina's temple. "I'll fucking kill her! I'll do it in a heartbeat. Back off!"

The crackle and roar of the fire nearly drowned out his voice. Behind him, flame and smoke twisted up the sides of the barn and across the top of the doorway. A thunderous scraping and impact sounded from inside. Something large had fallen in.

The redhead and the big brute exchanged worried looks. The brute tried easing out the door, laying down a spray of gunfire to clear his way. His machine gun clicked back and stopped. Uttering a feral growl, he threw the empty weapon to the ground, running on thick legs toward the SUV. Trevor's shot took him full in the face. He jerked backward and crashed to the ground.

"I'll throw her in," screamed Osinov. He yanked Christina around and shoved her closer to the fire. "I'll burn her. She'll die screaming. Is that what you want?"

Shit. *Shit*. He gestured sharply, twisting his head toward Trevor. "No more."

"Copy that." Trevor lowered his shotgun.

"I'm taking her to the car. You fire another round, and I shoot her in the head." Osinov pulled Christina back in front of him, pushing her ahead of him, supporting her weight as her leg collapsed under her.

"Gabe," she called. "Shoot this motherfucker."

His gun barrel ground into her temple. "She'll die first. I swear I'll blow her brains all over the ground." He took one step, then another. The redhead followed him out, ducking away from the barn just as a portion of the roof collapsed. Black smoke and ash billowed around them.

Gabe watched for the slightest opportunity, his entire body tense, but he couldn't think of a single plan that didn't result in Christina's death. Despairing, he allowed Osinov to drag her to the SUV. The man climbed in first through the passenger door, then half lifted, half dragged her in. Not bothering to shut the door, he gunned the engine, slewing in every direction on the gravel before the tires gained traction. Gabe leaped to his feet, racing at top speed after the SUV, barely raising a hand to shield himself from the spray of gravel.

The unmistakable bang and rolling echo of a sniper rifle and the shattering of the driver's side glass came simultaneously. Jansens was close. A second shot blew out a rear tire. The SUV slid sideways and crunched sickeningly into an ash tree. Gabe forced himself faster.

A body rammed him from the side. He rolled to his feet, already crouched defensively as he spun to face the redhead. Who drew eight inches of steel from a sheath at his hip, spinning it in his hand until the blade rested along his forearm. Gabe yanked one of his knives from his boot and mirrored the motion.

Throwing knives weren't ideal for a knife fight, but it was shit better than nothing. His at least had leather-wrapped handles.

"You must be the piece of shit Interpol traitor."

The man grinned, his hands moving slowly back and forth as he studied Gabe. "Shay Boyle, at your service. Howya?"

Gabe cast a look toward the SUV. No one moved. Trevor shouted something at him, lost as Boyle lunged at him. Gabe spun aside, bringing both hands up to slam against his arm at shoulder and wrist. He slid his left palm into Boyle's armpit and shot his right hand with the knife toward the man's gut.

Boyle brought both arms down, trapping the blade with his elbows, and countered with a backhanded slash. Gabe leaped back, but immediately closed again, arcing the knife up and over, aiming for Boyle's neck. Boyle ducked away and turned. Gabe let his momentum carry him past, then whirled just in time to block Boyle as the blade darted up.

The fight was brutal, the men and knives whirling faster and faster as each tried to bury his blade into the others' flesh. Carbon clashed with steel. Boyle's next cut caught Gabe near the eye. Blood dripped down his face, partially obscuring his vision. He stumbled back.

Boyle pressed his advantage with an overhead thrust to the neck. Gabe barely moved away in time, throwing an arm up to block the attack. He felt the deep bite of steel into his forearm. Boyle punched him several times in the ribs; short, vicious jabs. He grunted, forcing himself not to fold over.

He dropped his left hand, knowing the next thrust would come up and in. Checking the knife, he closed his hand over Boyle's wrist and managing a shallow slash across his chest. Boyle clamped on to him, pulling him into a clinch and head-butting him.

Dazed, Gabe dropped his body weight, trying to throw his opponent off balance. Boyle rode him down, trying to take him to the ground. Instead, he stepped back with one leg, digging his thumbs into Boyle's hipbones to gain some room, then brought his knee up sharply into the man's groin. Then again, and a third time, hard enough to lift the man off his feet.

Instead of collapsing, Boyle hooked a leg behind Gabe's and pushed. Gabe hit the gravel with Boyle on top of him. His blade clattered to the rocks next to his head. Gabe grabbed the man's wrist, locking his arm out to prevent the blade from piercing his neck. Muscles corded in both men's arms as they fought for control.

The walkie-talkie at his hip squawked. "Roll right."

Gabe never hesitated. He pulled his feet in close to his ass, then arched up onto his left shoulder, pushing Boyle to the left. Even before the weight left him, Gabe rolled right, over and over until he heard the single gunshot.

Boyle flopped face-down onto the gravel, blood pooling from the hole in his chest.

Gabe struggled to his feet, scooped up his knife, and pressed a hand over the cut on his forearm. He nodded his thanks to Trevor, stumbling toward the SUV.

Osinov stood outside the driver's side door, cradling an arm against his chest, bleeding from his nose and head. He pointed his handgun inside the car, straight at Christina's head.

"You'll still die," Gabe hissed.

"But so will she. Can you live with her blood on your hands?"

The passenger side door started to open. The mangled metal scraped and stuck. Osinov turned his head to look inside.

Gabe flipped the knife in his hand and snapped his arm straight. Blood fountained as the blade buried itself to the hilt in Osinov's throat.

# Chapter Thirty-One

THE WAIL OF sirens heralded the arrival of the police and several ambulances. In minutes, uniforms swarmed the area, slapping handcuffs on the living and marking the dead, rolling out crime scene tape, and treating the injured.

The Urgent Medical Aid Service eased Christina out of the SUV, settling her onto a yellow-and-black gurney and strapping her down as Gabe watched anxiously, hampered by the handcuffs pulling his wrists behind him and the paramedic trying to clean his wound. He shook the man off, hopping off the ambulance and shouldering past him.

A policewoman stepped in front of him, placing a hand on his chest. "Sit back down, sir," she said.

He took a half step back. "I have to see her."

As she had the last three times he'd tried this, she shook her head. "Until we figure out what the hell happened here, no one goes anywhere."

"No one will tell me how she is," he said, his voice catching. "I just need to know she's okay."

Something that might have been sympathy flickered in her eyes. "Sit down, and I'll ask," the woman said. She watched, steely-eyed, until Gabe plopped back onto the ambulance. He barely noticed when the paramedic cleaned and wrapped his arm.

They hadn't yet put him in the back of a police car, but it wouldn't be long before they did. Aart Jansens was talking to them now, hands flashing as he recounted events.

The medics wheeled Christina to a second ambulance.

"Let me go with her. I promise I'll cooperate," he pleaded as the policewoman came back.

"I'm sorry," she said. "We need to interview you."

"How is she?"

Her expression became shuttered. "The paramedics aren't certain of the extent of her injuries."

His gut howled to fight his way to her side. "What the hell does that mean?" he snarled. The last thing he wanted was for her to wake, alone and frightened, in a strange hospital.

She gave him an expressionless stare. "Is he done?" she asked the medic.

"He needs stitches, but he's stable."

She took him by the bicep. He let her take him to a grassy area, where Trevor sat. He settled himself awkwardly to the ground.

"Let's see if Jansens can get us out of these cuffs," Trevor said. "Worst case, we land in jail overnight until our respective countries can get us sorted."

He grunted. He watched as Shay, Fedyenka, and the others were zipped into body bags.

"Odds are she just bumped her head," Trevor said. "The airbags deployed, did you see?"

He couldn't even bring himself to nod. Worry gnawed in his gut.

Finally, after about a year of forevers, a middle-aged man in a buttoned-down shirt with the sleeves rolled to his elbows hunkered down in front of them. He wore a trilby on his head and a detective inspector's badge on his belt. The policewoman translated as he spoke.

"Well, now," he said. "Would one of you like to tell me just what in the hell happened here today?"

# Chapter Thirty-Two

CHRISTINA BECAME AWARE of the pain first. Every part of her ached and throbbed. Reluctant to open her eyes, to face reality, she contemplated drifting back into a nice drug-induced dream.

Rustling sounds nearby pried her eyes open. The grayish-white walls of the tiny hospital room swam into focus. Her neighbor, an elderly woman who had fallen and broken her arm, struggled to open a bag of potato chips. Gabe bent over to help her, smiling in a way that had the woman beaming and chatting, seeming not to realize that Gabe couldn't understand a word. He squeezed her shoulder and turned away. For a moment, he simply stared out the small, dirty window. She couldn't hazard a guess what was going through his mind, but she'd never seen him look so serious.

"Hi," she croaked.

He whirled, striding to her bed in an instant. Fatigue rimmed his eyes, but his mouth curled up at both corners when he saw her conscious. He picked up a cup of water, stuck a straw into it, and held it up to her lips. "Welcome back."

"Was I gone?" She sipped cautiously, then sucked the water down hard as she realized how parched she was. When she hit bottom, Gabe refilled it. She took it from him.

"I'm going to go get the doctor."

She held out a hand. "Wait. How long was I out?"

He came back and took her hand. "Not long. Do you remember the ambulance?"

She started to nod, felt her muscles seize, and forced herself still. "Sort of. They gave me morphine, I think. Then a doctor examined me here, and took X-rays? Everything's hazy."

He squeezed her hand. "I don't know anything. I just got here. We . . . had some things to work out."

She closed her eyes, tempted to drift back to sleep. She needed to know what was going on, though, and that meant breathing through the pain of her battered body. Her head ached. When she put a hand to it, she found it wrapped in gauze. Memories of Fedyenka's torture, the fight, and the subsequent car wreck beat back the drug-induced haze. Where was Gabe?

He returned shortly, followed by a doctor, nurse, and a small woman who spoke English. As the doctor spoke, she translated. "They want to do an exploratory knee arthroscopy to see how bad the damage is. The anesthesiologist will be in at seven tomorrow morning. He'll put you to sleep, and when you wake up, they'll know more."

She must have muttered some assent, because the doctor jotted some notes on her chart, spoke with the nurse, and left again. The nurse took her vitals while Gabe hovered.

"How do you feel?" Gabe asked.

She shrugged. Not well, she could have said. But she was alive, and he was alive, and that was pretty fantastic. "I'm all right."

"That you are." He came over to perch gingerly on the side of her bed. "I thought you might appreciate an update."

Christina tried to force herself to focus. It was harder than it should have been. "Do I have a concussion?"

"I think so. Your head's got a big lump on it. They won't tell me anything." Frustration burned in his tone. "Are you dizzy? Nauseous?"

She moved her head back and forth across the pillow. No way was she telling him how much she hurt. "I just need some rest."

"Close your eyes. I'll be here."

She struggled to sit up, hissing as her muscles seized. Gabe slipped an arm around her shoulders to help. "No, tell me what's going on."

He left his arm where it was, and she slumped against him gratefully. Blood smeared his face from a cut near his eye, which had been closed with butterfly bandages. His shirt sleeve was ripped and bloody, but a dressing wrapped his forearm. "What happened?

"Shay Boyle. We fought when Osinov crashed the car."

"Did you kill him?"

"Yeah."

She tightened her fingers in his. "Good."

A hand stroked across her hair. "You weren't moving. I was afraid . . ." He stopped, cleared his throat.

"I banged my head against the door frame, I think." She closed her eyes, fatigue hammering at the edges of her consciousness. "What happened after Fedyenka died?"

Gabe snuggled her closer to his chest. "The cavalry arrived. They arrested everyone. The usual amounts of chaos when local police get involved."

She screwed up her face, trying to bring blurry images into focus. "Did I imagine seeing our fake assassin there? Aart Jansens?"

Gabe's lips lifted at the corners. "A good guy to have at your back, it turns out. Misguided, and he'll lose his job, but his help today will keep him out of jail. The police chief here promised no charges would be filed against him."

"Well . . . good."

An attendant came in to shoo Gabe out. He squeezed her hand and moved back. "Sleep, now. Listen . . ."

"Will you be here when I get back?"

He hesitated. "Yeah."

But when she woke in the morning, he was gone.

# Chapter Thirty-Three

*Six weeks later—Silver Spring, Maryland*

CHRISTINA TOUCHED HER toe to the floor, wincing as pain shot up her leg to her knee. The knee brace, a complicated contraption of metal and buckles, kept her knee immobile while she worked on strengthening her quadriceps.

"Again," Sally said. The physical therapist held tight to Christina's hand, bracing her as she touched her toe again. "Weight bearing will come in stages. Keep in mind you've lost a lot of muscle strength. Don't be worried if you can't put much weight on it yet. It's too soon."

The orthopedic surgeon told her she'd suffered a comminuted fracture of the patella. Fedyenka had shattered her knee into three pieces. The surgeon had pinned and wired her knee back together, but no one could assure her that she would make a full recovery. She could still be active, the surgeon assured her. Assuming her knee recovered sufficiently, she could still walk and run. But the knee would always be weak, and he'd warned her to avoid squatting or deep-knee bends. He'd gone so far as to tell her to avoid climbing ladders and steep staircases. When she'd told him she worked in an active job, he'd given her a pitying look and told her not to get her hopes up.

Her parents had flown in to visit her in the hospital, and her mother had stayed to care for her. After the first few weeks, though, it was easier just to manage on her own. The extra effort helped her not to think about Gabe, who had disappeared from the hospital without a word right after she'd been admitted.

"Touch, touch, touch . . . and lift," Sally said. They'd been working together for nearly an hour, and Christina was sweat-soaked and exhausted. She adjusted the crutches.

"Enough."

"Okay," Sally said. "Time to ice your knee. How's your pain level today?"

Excruciating. "I'm okay."

A movement near the door caught in her periphery, and she turned her head out of habit. Her breath caught.

Gabe.

He was filthy. Mud streaked his combat uniform, and traces of camouflage paint smeared his ears and neck. Sweat matted his hair, and he smelled . . . really bad.

But he looked fantastic to her.

He scrutinized her for several long moments. She knew what he saw. She balanced on crutches, her leg from thigh to calf encased in a metal-and-plastic contraption that immobilized her knee. She was flushed and sweating.

Sally touched her sleeve. "Let's get you on the table, and I'll bring some ice."

Christina settled her rear onto the edge of the table, then scooted back. She swung her good leg onto the table; and, when she went to swing the brace, Gabe was there, supporting and lifting it carefully. He grabbed her crutches and put them off to one side.

"What are you doing here?" she asked.

Instead of answering, Gabe placed a bundle in her arms, then nudged a forefinger under her chin and turned her head toward him, lowered his face to hers, and kissed her. This was no sweet hello. This was a full-out, tonsil-touching, I-want-to-screw-you-now kiss.

When he finally pulled back, both were breathing heavily.

"Well, o-kay," she said. "Hello to you, too."

He gave her a lopsided grin. She looked down at the bundle he'd placed in her arms, and started to laugh.

It was her leather jacket. The one with the zippers.

"I figured you could use some bad-ass."

"I hope you didn't scare Frank the Fink too badly."

Sally cleared her throat. Christina blushed while the physical therapist secured an ice pack around her knee. She set a timer and left them alone.

Gabe finally spoke. "We just got back."

Christina smiled, gesturing up and down his body and wrinkling her nose. "So I gather. Didn't even stop to shower, huh?"

He slowly shook his head from side to side, his gaze never leaving hers. "No. I didn't know if anyone told you we deployed."

No one in Gabe's unit had told her a thing, but Jay Spicer assured her that no-notice deployments were common. She'd wanted to believe that's what had happened, but doubts had gnawed at her through these long weeks alone. She didn't know if she'd ever see him again.

"I thought . . . I hoped," she said. "I mean, we never made any promises . . ."

Gabe took her hand in his, twining their fingers together. "Don't doubt my love ever, from now on. I'd've never left your side if Uncle Sam hadn't called me."

Some tight, frightened part of her inside relaxed and opened. "Can . . . can you stay a while?" she asked.

Gabe smiled tenderly at her. "I can if you tell me you love me back."

Her breath whooshed out. She loved his sense of honor, his dedication, his courage. Even his stubbornness. But all she managed was a soft, "I do love you, Gabe."

He kissed her then. Sweet, tender kisses, kisses that promised happiness and a happily-ever-after. Kisses that promised dark, carnal nights in sweaty, twisted sheets. Christina loved them all.

When he pulled back, heat and desire mixed with love in his eyes. He cleared his throat and pulled a rolling stool close to her treatment table. "I have two weeks of leave. I know that's not much, but it's all I could get."

She beamed. "It's more than I hoped for."

He finally looked down at himself. "Sorry for the funk."

The fact that he'd come rushing to her side as soon as his mission was over warmed her from the inside out. "I can deal," she assured him.

He grinned a cute, sloppy grin. "I knew you could. So." He cleared his throat, looking down at her knee. "What's the prognosis? How soon will you be back to one hundred percent?"

Her smile faltered. It was painful to think about. "Well, maybe two or three months."

He grew serious. "But?"

"My kneecap was shattered when Fedyenka hit me with a pipe. I will probably be able to run eventually, but the knee will never be a hundred percent again."

As she explained it to him, she couldn't help the tears that filled her eyes. He pulled her into his arms, cradling her and rocking her as she finally gave in and cried like a baby.

When her tears slowed and stopped, he found her a tissue so she could blow her nose. "So what does that mean for your long-term health? For your career?"

Christina sniffed and sighed. "Long term, I'll probably get arthritis in my knee. I can't play football anymore, though." She tried for a smile.

Gabe grimaced. "Fieldwork?"

"I'm done," she confessed. "The CIA won't clear me for fieldwork. Jay offered me a desk job, though."

"Desk job." Horror colored Gabe's voice. Christina could relate, but she'd had weeks to accustom herself to the idea.

"It's a good job," she said. "I'd be a staff operations officer. It sounds interesting."

Gabe blew out a breath. "Are you . . . okay with that?" he asked tentatively.

She thought about it. She'd been doing nothing but thinking about it for weeks. Until now, though, it had been with a certain amount of self-pity. "I am, actually. I'm not saying it won't be rough for a while, till I get used to the new normal, you know? But it's interesting work, and I can still travel. Just as a civilian." Her voice wobbled a little at the end.

"We'll get you whatever help you need," Gabe promised fiercely. "You can do anything you want if the desk starts to chafe. Anything you need, okay?

"Well . . . can I have you?" she asked in a small voice.

Gabe exhaled a laugh. "Babe, you already have me. Heart and soul."

Hope bloomed in her heart. Everything would work out.

"What do you think about the idea of coming back to North Carolina with me?" he asked softly.

She thought about it, frowning unhappily. "If I want to stay with the CIA—and I do, at least for now—I have to live in Washington."

"Okay. We'll figure it out."

"I would never ask you to quit Delta Force. I know it's your life."

"You're my life."

She touched his face. "You know what I mean. I won't let you resign."

He caught up her hand and brought it to his lips. "Good to know. Okay, so I won't quit the Unit. Not until I'm old and gray and have no choice." His eyes became anxious. "But it's a hard life. I train all the time. I fly at a moment's notice, and I might not even be able to call you to tell you. Like this deployment. You wouldn't know where I was, or how long I'd be gone. But I'd like to . . . we can try the long-distance thing."

She squeezed his fingers. "Lots of couples work in different cities. We'll just have to get together as often as possible. For lots of great sex."

He laughed, as she had hoped he would, but sobered much too quickly. "You're all I've thought about for the past six weeks.

I don't want just sex. I want you, lock, stock, and barrel. Christina . . . I want you to marry me."

She gulped in a lot of air and had to cough to clear her lungs. He couldn't have surprised her more if he'd started doing back-flips. But there was only one answer.

"Yes." Her voice was so faint he had to lean forward to hear her. "Yes," she said, more strongly. "Yes."

He beamed, pressing soft kisses onto her fingers one by one. "Thank God," he said. "I don't know what I'd've done if you said no."

"I'm finished for the day," she said. "Want to come home with me and take a shower?"

He pulled a face. "Do I smell that bad? I stopped smelling myself weeks ago."

Christina smiled. "Well, I was actually thinking . . . I could wash your back for you."

The flash of heat in his eyes was all the answer she needed.

"I don't want just sex. I want you. Lock, stock, and barrel. Christina . . . I want you to marry me."

She gulped in a lot of air and had to cough to clear her lungs. He couldn't have surprised her more if he'd started doing back flips. But there was only one answer.

"Yes." Her voice was so faint he had to lean forward to hear her.

"Yes," she said, more strongly. "Yes."

He beamed, pressing soft kisses onto her fingers one by one. "Thank God," he said. "I don't know what I'd've done if you said no."

"I'm finished for the day," she said. "Want to come home with me and take a shower?"

He pulled a face. "Do I smell that bad? I stopped smelling it myself weeks ago."

Christina smiled. "Well, I was actually thinking . . . I could wash your back for you."

The flash of heat in his eyes was all the answer she needed.